MW01205822

Ferret

Ferret

C.C. Wyatt

Me Myself Publishing

Copyright © 2015 C.C. Wyatt

All rights reserved. Except for use in reviews, no part of this book may be reproduced, scanned, utilized or transmitted in part in any way, without written consent.

Me Myself Publishing, USA
P.O. Box 9201
Chandler Heights, AZ 85127
info@memyselfpublishing.com

Hardcover edition by Me Myself Publishing, 2016

This book is a work of fiction. Any references to characters, events, or locales portrayed in this book are either coincidental or products of the author's imagination.

Ferret: a novel/C.C. Wyatt–New Hardcover Edition

{1. Florida–Fiction. 2. Bermuda–Fiction. 3. Television Programs–Fiction. 4. Dreams-Fiction. Characters-Fiction.} I. Title.

Summary: When sixteen-year-old Pia returns to the Florida beach house, she sets out to uncover the mystery surrounding the night she went missing, after meeting a troubled boy who may be key to solving the mystery.

ISBN 978-0-9967785-4-1 (hardcover)

Printed in the United States of America

To Alexus and Angel

CONTENTS

Ferret

First came the birds, flowers and trees.
You know the drill.
Now I dedicate this to you, my dear.

Preface

Not in my wildest dream would I have imagined a nightmare whisking me away in the middle of the night, only to return me with no memory of the time we spent together. I could never forget that night–how and why it happened to me. So when the opportunity of finding out came knocking at my door, I couldn't just let it slip away. And so once again, not in my wildest dream would I have imagined a moment as chilling as this.

The sun beamed down on the illusive island and ran through every pulse in our bodies as we ran against time, so desperate to see the side of change that awaited us, in a faraway place called home. I couldn't help myself; I had to put it to the test–fate, that is. Now we were grasping, running for our lives, and our only hope of escaping was an injured plane and a prayer.

Before long, the island's beauty would only be a memory etched in my brain. Its demise crept mercilessly beneath the burning sun. Before long, it would be what seemed...an ice age?

But how could that be?

Only in dreams, that's how.

Dream or no dream, surely we could die or be forever lost in this nightmare.

Chapter One

No Turning Back

In theory, there's only one day that comes and goes in precise intervals, that's unaware of itself and its unique charm. We rise accordingly and go about our daily routine, and near time for it to make its exit, we settle down in the same position as we started. And when the day rolls around again, we repeat. Almost mechanically. As if we were spellbound by the cycle of day and not know it. As if, when change comes along and snaps its fingers, the spell's broken. And it's a rude awakening...sometimes.

This day especially was like that. And it didn't matter that it had been four years and three months, two weeks and a day in the making, and should go down in history as Pia's day of dread, though I had the guts to face it somehow, one precarious step after another, as I embarked on a trip moments away from takeoff. No. What mattered was the unpredictable path I was on and how it would end about a week from now.

With my backpack hanging off my shoulder and a mild breeze playing in my hair, I led the way to the plane. I couldn't believe that I was actually going through with this. But not only that, I had a weird feeling I just couldn't shake. But when you find yourself returning to a dark part of your past—to a place you thought you would never see again because your last experience there resembled episodes of the Twilight Zone, this place much like home to you too—then how should you feel?

I drew in a deep breath, and then stole a few moments to make a wish. A mere request, because I believed with all my heart that anything was possible—and because I had the experience to back it up. So I closed my eyes and wished this moment away forever; wished away the nightmare and all memory of it forever times two. Then *one*, *two*...I counted to five for good measure. And then I heard it! Something magical! A whisper. And right then I knew. Knew that my "wish come true" would have been exactly that had the little voice only said, "*Your wish is my command.*"

But it disappointed me instead. *Is that what you really want...never know what happened during the most critical hours of your life?*

Of course granting my wish would have served me just fine, I thought with pooched lips. But I knew all too well. Knew that deep down I would give just about anything to know what really happened that night at the Florida beach house, where I mysteriously vanished in my sleep. And if it took going back to find out, ultimately proving my theory of what happened, then so be it. After four long years of not knowing anything, it would mean the world to me. Not to mention that it would probably be the greatest solved mystery of all times.

I arrived at the plane looking back at my parents coming up behind me. I settled the backpack on the ground, attempting to stretch precious moments I had left, by any means possible, before boarding the plane. I looked up as one flew over me, closed my eyes, and let my mind wander up to the universe. Suddenly I was amazed that we were all right here, right where we were supposed to be...*at a point of no return.* Or was I just plain crazy about all this? Some people, however, wouldn't have a problem thinking so.

Suddenly, I felt a nudge on my back. In an instant I turned, thinking someone had snuck up on me but...no one was there. I frowned. *That was creepy.* I lifted my backpack and contemplated that some more. *I could've sworn...it couldn't have been the wind hitting me like that in just that spot.*

"Pia is everything okay?" Dad asked as he and Mom approached.

"Yeah, sure," I replied, still in wonder. *Maybe it was the hands of the universe...had to be, urging me to get moving.* So I boarded the plane convinced that that was it.

Mom and Dad filed in behind me. And in moments the twin-engine plane roared to life.

"All set?" Dad's vibrant tenor reigned over the humming engines. Wearing dark shades and a ready-to-go smile, he looked back at me, as did Mom, her hazel eyes gleaming. Through them I pretended to read her mind. *Pia, if you're not ready, it's not too late to cancel this trip.*

I imagined her reading mine. *But Mom, it's spring break, and we're all set to go. And what about the pilot's convention? The house? Dad could sell it for real next time. It'll be okay, you'll see.*

Mom was the reason Dad hadn't sold the house already. She was right, though: the house had deep, sentimental value, had been part of the family for far too long to get rid of. Dad had lost sight of that and probably would've regretted selling it. And how could either of us blame the house? It hadn't whisked me away in the middle of the night, stolen sixteen hours of my memory, and set my mind to see creepy things. It hadn't...changed my life forever.

We just needed to go back...to heal and...and because destiny was calling and because...just because.

I gazed out the window. *Was I really out of my mind?* Suddenly my fingers were tap-dancing on my lap. I stared at them for a moment then curled them into a tight fist. If I was a real nutcase, I supposed I would soon find out.

The plane taxied into position for takeoff. Upon clearance, it became a straight line of roaring thunder up the runway. Up, up the plane climbed over Houston. My eyes shut tight, hands gripping the armrests as anxiety grew like fever through my body.

No turning back.

We were on our way.

No turning back.

Chapter Two

The Beach House

Finally, after all this time, I was back at the beach house in Pompano Beach. Dad pulled into the driveway, turned off the engine, and we sat quietly looking at the house. I had a grave feeling, though shallow, that I hoped would subside sooner than later.

As cute as ever, the house looked the same. It looked as though it'd gotten a fresh coat of yellow paint. The awnings were unweathered. The landscaping, though moderate, was so neatly trimmed we must have just missed the groundskeeper.

"Well, shall we?" Dad broke the silence then cracked open the door. He got out, opened the hatch. "Come on, girls."

Mom and I smiled a weary smile at each other before getting out. By then Dad had grabbed bags and gone in ahead of us. What was left we collected then closed the hatch. Then we started up the walkway.

As I crossed the threshold, a waft of suffocating humidity wobbled me, and I gasped. I continued on, stepping into the dark part of my past, slow and easy, as queasiness deep in my bones merged with escalating pulses. Then I paused, turned my head over my shoulder. Panic hurtled my heart against my chest. I then instantly blinked away the startling image of someone sitting on the sofa. A tan shawl over the couch, that's all it was. I took several deep breaths to calm myself.

Dad had disappeared somewhere in the shadows of the house. I could hear him now, doing something in the master bedroom. The air conditioner kicked on, exactly what this place needed.

"I have to say, I kinda missed this place," Mom said, looking the place over. She put aside her luggage. "Suppose it could use some sunshine."

At once, life began streaming through the windows as she went from room to room, opening drapes and blinds. I kept up with her movement as far as the kitchen, scanning as much of the house as my static position would allow. The kitchen divided the two bedrooms, and a half wall, about four feet high, separated the living room from the kitchen.

Only my head moved, as I looked the place over. The house didn't feel the same; it wasn't the same. The eeriness of that night permeated the walls and the suffocating warmth trapped in those walls. And I stood there, waiting for my feet to think, to move, knowing that they would decide to do just that. They had come this far.

I drew in more of the swollen air. Off from the kitchen to the right was my room. My feet made steps that way, sneaky steps, to a room that no longer felt like my own, rather a place of the unknown. A heavy dose of fright flushed through me and lingered somewhat. It's all me now, slowly entering the room. I eased the luggage alongside the bed and dropped the backpack in an old accent chair. I moved to the window and strung the blinds open. The room was aglow now, and I wasted no time scouring every corner of it—the bathroom, the closet, even under the bed—knowing all along my looking here and there was pointless because after all, I was dealing with a nondescript, a ghostly coward, and a conniving one at that.

I got off my knees and noticed how neat the room was. Pillows were plumped, the bedding smoothed over. It didn't appear as dusty as I would have thought. Everything else appeared the same too, untouched. The books in the headboard that I never got around to reading remained. Over the chair, still in the same place, hung a collage of photos and drawings I had created when I was much younger.

Not that I was expecting to see things out of place; as far as I knew, we were or had been the only ones who spent time here anymore, not since Grandfather passed away ages ago. The house then was passed down to Dad; he was the only one left with an emotional attachment to it. Uncle John had moved to Bermuda with Grandmother long before Grandfather's passing. Uncle John would use the house occasionally, but not for a long time now.

No...not anyone had been spending time here. "*Not a thing*," I mumbled, scanning the room again. I was at least 99 percent certain of that. But that 1 percent, that itsy-bitsy doubt, was as sketchy and as creepy as my world had been the past four years.

I stood staring at the bed now. *How did I leave this*

bed that night? One theory, sleepwalking, but it was quickly shot down. No one could see how I went undetected for hours. Neither could I. For a good sixteen hours, it was as if I had disappeared off the face of the earth. Until finally, there I was, like an airheaded doll roaming the beach with no clue where I was or who I was, or what happened...somewhat distraught by it all. The horrible images I'd been seeing ever since that night, I believed held encrypted clues about what happened.

If only I could remember.

I left the room then. Thirsty, I went straight to the refrigerator. Ice cold bottled water was on the door. I snatched one up, cracked it open, and took long delicious sips.

My parents came out of their bedroom, Dad with keys dangling and Mom with her purse dangling from her shoulder. I supposed they were about to leave to take care of the business they'd discussed on the way here.

"We're going to see George before he closes up," Mom confirmed. "Come on, we can stop and get something to eat afterward, then go to the supermarket for a few things."

"Do I really have to go? I'd rather hang out around here."

Mom glowered at me. "Sometimes I wonder if you bumped your head, causing brain damage or something." Translation: *This is your first day back, and you're not afraid of being here by yourself?*

Why I wasn't afraid was inexplicable. To have your life change overnight with no clue as to how or why it happened, then for some odd reason, practically insist on going back to the place it happened—well, that sounds like a person out of their freaking mind to me. That's what I had been telling myself anyway.

"I'm just tired of being crammed up. On the plane, in the car, and now you want to drag me to some office," I said earnestly, picturing stretching my legs out on the beach. *No harm in that,* I thought. I went on, "The office is—what?—just a few blocks away, not far...and you won't be long, right? Besides, I'll just be sitting around while you talk business. I'll be okay...really."

Mom looked over at Dad's burly frame. It was hard reading his thoughts, or maybe not.

"C'mon, Dad," I said. Almond-shaped lids framed my dad's smoky gray eyes though dark shades covered them. So I couldn't read his eyes.

"Just do what your mother says." He turned away and headed for the door.

"Isaac?" Mom called after him.

I couldn't believe he was leaving it all up to Mom to decide if I could be trusted. For so long I had been limited to the things I could do and couldn't do and when I could do it. Just this past year things got better. But still it felt like them breathing down my neck every waking hour of every day. I needed more breathing room and a little more trust. But first, they had to remove the leash from my neck.

Of course, they had legitimate concerns stemming from that infamous night four years ago. Their concerns were doubts (about me), which made the healing process for them...unyielding. If only I had proof of being kidnapped. If only I could remember something, so I could prove it to myself. Not that I had any doubts.

"Isaac?" Mom demanded before he got away.

"Just going next door to let the Jenkins know we're here," he answered.

Mom nodded and then approached me, smoothing a hand over my hair. "Look, honey–"

"Mom." I pulled away, refusing to let her butter me up with the caring-Mom bit. "I'll be fine."

"Yeah, well, that may be." She paused. "I, um...have decided not to go to the convention."

"What! Are you serious? You look forward to the conferences just as much as Dad. Why? Nah...don't bother." I didn't wait for an answer; it was clear why.

"Mom, I know it's rough. But for what it's worth, I'm not the same person I was four years ago. I mean I am, but I'm older now. Can't you admit that I've been the model kid?"

She frowned. "What exactly are you saying?"

"What I'm trying to say is that your little girl is growing up–I'm graduating next year for Pete's sake. At some point, you have to let go. You have to trust me...right here...right now. Because *here* is where you and Dad lost confidence in me to begin with, thinking here is where I made the worst judgment call of my life."

She looked down at the floor. "You sound so grown up. But you're known to wander off."

"But Mom, that was–"

"I know. It was different from when you wandered off at the amusement park or when you left the house in the middle of the night to join neighborhood kids to see a lunar eclipse. But I'm still your mother." She made a stern nod then pointed a finger. "And it's my right to worry, to protect you. All the more reason why I should pass on going to the convention this time around." She shifted weight to the other foot, crossed her arms.

"Okay. Stay. Babysit me. So does that mean I have to go with you now? Can't I just go...kick my feet in the sand?" I grabbed her hand. "Come on...See for yourself that you have nothing to worry about, Mom. The beach is swarming with people."

She let out a stiff sigh and resisted my hold. "I really don't have time for this...but okay, lead the way."

Gladly I did just that, surprised this was going easier than I would have thought. Maybe Mom was out of her mind. Maybe we were out of our minds together. For now, it didn't matter. I slid open the sliding glass door that opened to a screened-in porch overlooking a luscious green yard with an ancient willow tree. Bushes and rocks divided our property from beach property. We crossed the lawn to the far corner and descended wooden steps leading to the beach. It took only a few steps to prove my point.

"See, nothing to worry about," I said, smiling.

"Yeah. It's such a pleasant day for the beach," Mom said collecting the view, as a gentle ocean breeze tossed strands of our hair around. "I can't get over you not being afraid. You know, we found you just up the way. And still, there's that question loaded with great mystery: what happened that night? Can't you understand my wanting to protect you? The person that kidnapped you could be out there somewhere."

My eyes widened. "But, Mom—" I began, but she held up a hand stopping me.

I couldn't believe my ears. From the beginning, my parents couldn't fathom someone swiping me right under their noses. Neither of them had gone to bed that night; it was impossible for someone to get in and leave without notice. It was easier to believe anything but kidnapping. Only I believed, of which proved her point: why wasn't I afraid?

"All right," she said, lightly shaking her head. "I feel like a momma bird letting her baby fly out of the nest for the first time. I can't believe I'm going to do this. But okay, but so help me—"

"Mom. Don't worry. You'll see. I won't disappoint you."

She folded her arms, twisted her lips, and then led the way back. "And I don't want you straying too far. You hear me?"

"I won't get lost, Mom, promise."

Back in the house, Mom took a quick glance in the pantry and refrigerator, removed a pen and notepad from her purse. "I'm gone," she said, jotting some things down. "We shouldn't be long. Make sure you have your phone on you."

"I will. I always do." I hugged her around her thin waist, feeling proud of having gained her trust.

Moments later, the storm door closed behind her. Shortly after, I tracked her footsteps as far as the porch. They were pulling off now. "Bring Cheerios back," I called out.

I relaxed my head against the balustrade, dragged in the fresh air, and sighed. I looked up and down the shaded street. A few people were out and about. Up the street, just past the light, were high-rises of luxury apartments of at least ten stories. I thought about how close Dad had come to selling the house, how Mom's spirit wouldn't let him. Then I realized how much I really liked it here—the house in this exact spot, the many types of trees, the footpath out back leading to the beach, the feeling of anticipating fun, the kind of fun I used to have and missed—all while the desire deep in my core intensified.

Chapter Three

Freaky Encounter

My walk drew me to the boardwalk. Why people called it The Boardwalk was beyond me. It's just a long stretch of smooth pavement with various restaurants, quaint resorts, specialty shops, and ice cream and pastry stands. Benches and patio tables, some with umbrellas, were conveniently scattered along the way. About midway set an outdoor amphitheater where entertainment went on year-round.

I was close enough now to see a peculiar hut with straw roofing. This strange addition to the boardwalk wasn't there the last time I was here. Outside hanging upright against the hut was a scarecrow in a checkered shirt, black pants, and tacky red hat, an odd attention-grabber that inspired a grin. Was it there to scare birds? If so, I wondered if it was working. Or maybe it was for sale. However, the multicolored T-shirts hanging outside reeled me in. I stopped just to check the prices and was back on the move in a hot minute.

Maybe I'll pick one up on my way back, I thought as

my mood to shop took a backseat to hunger.

I got out my cellphone. I had to let Mom know I was grabbing something to eat. The phone rang...no answer. Voice mail picked up, so I left a message.

Up a ways, I stopped at a familiar café. A guy, twenty-something, came from the back to the counter. He was medium height, with cropped wavy hair, and kind of cute. He took my order: bacon double cheeseburger, French-fried sweet potatoes, and iced tea. I noticed him staring on the sly.

"Are you from around here?" he asked. "You look familiar."

"I guess you can say that. I've been here a few times. We have a beach house up a ways." I pointed that way.

His brows knitted together; he wore a thinking face now. "Uhh, yeah. I thought I recognized you. I don't recall your name though. You been okay?"

"Excuse me, have we met?"

"Uh, nah, not exactly. I, um, just remember you. That's all." He pressed his lips into a thin smile. And in a bashful manner, I lowered my head slightly.

I had a hunch what was behind his handsome smile. My mug shots (as I called them) had been plastered all over the place: on poles, in stores, on TV—probably the Internet—everywhere, for the eleven-year-old girl who went missing. My parents had wasted no time the next morning getting my picture out.

What little I remembered I reflected on: me, distraught, wandering around, no clue of who I was. The elderly couple, telling each other—and me—that I was the missing girl everyone was looking for. It wasn't until I reunited with my parents that I remembered who I was.

Things started happening fast after that. The specimen examinations, the intense, dragged-out questioning. They all seemed like heartless monsters, the detectives who didn't believe me, their minds fixed on me having a spare key that I used to let myself out of the house, as opposed to me being kidnapped. Nothing...I knew nothing of a key, nothing at all; I had no memory of anything but going to bed that night. Later I went under hypnosis. Nothing helped, of course. By then I'd started seeing creepy things, visions—that was all in my head they claimed. But I knew better than that.

Yeah, without a doubt, this guy recognized me from the pictures. It had only been four years since the incident, and I hadn't changed. Well, not that much. Besides, my case was like those from *Unsolved Mysteries.* So I couldn't blame anyone for wondering...including this cute one.

"Oh...okay." I crossed my arms, nodding. "Well, I'm taking a seat out on the terrace," I said, backing off, trying to avoid talk about the dark days of my past. A sweet melody went off in a messenger bag hanging off my shoulder: a text message. I reached in my purse for the phone.

"Sure, I'll bring your order out to you," he said, I nodded, and that was that.

Wrought iron confined the terrace, and a bulbous overhead awning shaded the area from the sun's glare completely. I pulled out a metal chair and seated myself facing the ocean. The text message was from my friend Tonya, checking to see if we'd made it okay. My thumbs went to work texting her back. The message was sending just as Mom was calling. I answered and assured her that

I was all right.

After leaving the café, I walked farther up the boardwalk, looking for something special to jump out at me. Time flew by, and I knew I had better head back before I got another call from Mom, wondering where I was. So I added a little tailwind to my browsing gait as I headed back, so far empty-handed. It was starting to look like I would end up with a T-shirt from the hut. And I knew exactly the one I wanted.

I claimed it immediately when I arrived. I browsed some more before finalizing the purchase. A pair of beaded earrings and matching necklace I adored. In the mirror, they looked perfect on.

As I continued browsing, a stiff breeze tickled my nose. I turned away quickly to sneeze, then looked off and spotted a group of boys putting on a show on skateboards, singing a cappella. With a ticking clock rushing me, they were very much a distraction.

But all of a sudden, I felt light-headed. I lowered my head with closed eyes, allowing time for the feeling to pass. Except it didn't, it got worse. Voices sharpened, gradually sounding like bees humming all around me, then came the floating-away sensation, anchored by a sinking one in the pit of my gut. I knew exactly what was happening. The symptoms were all too familiar. I had been living with them for far too long. And for the sake of feeling or seeing myself move, I ran a hand over barely opened eyes.

Another one of those creepy visions. I just knew it. I was having the symptoms, so something had to be there. Usually there was. I wanted to look—no, I didn't. Yes, I did.

I stopped fighting the urge already, and my eyes flashed open. What I saw was a skateboard sailing in my direction, its owner in midair, falling. His falling eyes fixated on mine, his mouth wide open. I couldn't hear him, though, only the soft humming sound playing around me.

Our eyes remained spellbound as his long, drawn-out fall came to an end. My body began lowering as my right arm went up to minimize the blow of the skateboard. Except now, I felt nothing, no motion, no sensation, as if I really wasn't in my body controlling its movement. Yet in this awkward state that seemed to last forever, our eyes still locked as one.

And when he hit the concrete, at once my eyes shut.

The feeling subsided. The humming was nearly gone, and the voices were clearer. Though it felt like an eternity, in a matter of seconds I could feel my body again.

The stocky man with a distinguished accent from the hut was at my side now.

"Oh my, the board got ya good," he said, looking at my forearm. "How are you feeling? You okay?"

I didn't feel my aching arm until he mentioned it. I looked, saw the bruised bump, and instinctively added pressure. "I'll be fine," I replied. He suggested that I sit for a moment. I thanked him and stayed put. My attention wandered over to the boy.

His friends hovered over him now, astounded by the incident that landed him hard on his behind. Their faces wore aching smiles as they helped him up. Other people slowed to observe but kept moving seeing nothing serious was going on.

Back on his feet, he brushed off his loose-fitting clothes and checked his body for cuts and bruises. Our eyes met again, but something about his glance made me feel nervous.

He carried on in conversation with his friends, each of them periodically looking my way. Then he was walking toward me, gently rubbing the arm he'd fallen on.

As he approached, he leaned over me, his hands on his knees. "Hey, I'm Cameron. You okay?"

I nodded. "What about you?"

"Yeah, a hard fall but I'm okay." He angled in closer, spoke in a lower tone. "Say, um...that was really something...that...whatever it was. We were in some kind of zone. You saw that, right?"

"What do you mean?" I asked.

His eyes narrowed, forehead pleated. "That thing between us. While I was falling."

I shook my head nervously, feeling violated with him staring into my eyes as if he had the power to drag anything out of me—his thoughts, for instance. Was he serious or on drugs or what? I didn't see anything, that's for sure.

"You saw it, right?" he continued. "You had to. Why else were you looking at me like that? Like...like—"

"Like what? What? What exactly...are you talking about?" I stuttered. "You fell off the skateboard—it's what I saw, all I was looking at."

"So you're saying you didn't do...um—?"

"*What*? Just come out and say it," I demanded, fear trembling my lips now. Was he accusing me of causing his fall? Was he pissed off because we made eye contact? Or was he that bad at coming on to girls?

"You mean to tell me..." He grabbed my arm.

Scratch all the above; he was just stone crazy.

"Hey!" I shouted, yanking loose.

"Hey you! Get off her." The attendant was back in half-rage to my rescue. "Why you all up on her like that? On another insanity trip, huh?" The attendant shoved him. "Huh? Get out of here and take this with you." The attendant forced the skateboard into Cameron, then shoved him again. "Get out of here causing trouble—now!"

Cameron backed off some and waved off his buddies who had taken steps forward as if they were going to get involved.

The attendant continued, "See the mess you caused, eh? You see, eh?" He was pointing to clothes and other stuff still scattered on the ground.

"Come on, man. We don't have time for this," one griped. The other boys nodded in agreement.

"Hold up," Cameron encouraged.

We now had an audience wearing a "what's going on" expression. But that didn't bother Cameron as far as I could tell. He was back over me, speaking directly to the attendant.

"I'm really sorry, sir—really I am. But—" Something was troubling him that was clear. He turned to me, began to say, "You really—?"

"*Really* what? Didn't stick my foot out to trip you?" At this point, enough was enough.

He seemed surprised by my reaction and backed off a bit. "So you didn't...?" He paused, then recanted. "Nah...maybe I'm going too far with this. Maybe I'm just cuckoo." He made a face.

"*You think*?" I said, thinking this wasn't a joking matter.

During a brief silence, there it was again, that confused, flushed look about him. What was going on with him?

"What's your problem now?" the attendant demanded of Cameron.

"Nothing, nothing," Cameron said, not budging an inch. "I was wrong, and I apologize for coming down on you like that." He rolled his eyes at me, then back at the old man. I couldn't tell if he meant it.

"You got that right," the old man growled. "You need to get a grip on yourself. You can't go around treating people like that for no reason."

Cameron nodded, wiped a hand over his damp forehead. "Here." Surprisingly, he offered his hand. "Let me help you up. Suppose I should have done this first."

"First? Help me up first *then* harass me?"

"No, no...I didn't mean it like that."

Both of them helped me up, asking for assurance that I was okay. I nodded and thanked them.

"Well, I better be going," Cameron said. Still, there was that strangeness about him. And those eyes, the way they looked at me as if seeing something no one else could see. Something was really off with him, deeply so. I was seriously starting to think the shock of the fall affected his brain.

Cameron's friends patted him on the back, exchanged a few words, and they all hopped back on their boards and began showing off their tricks as they headed back in the direction they had come. The manner in which they carried on was nonchalant, I thought, given the tension left lingering in the air.

"You better watch out for that one. He's not altogether up here," the older man said, pointing to his head. "He's got a dead heart." He pounded his chest like an ape. "And he's nothing but trouble. The kind of trouble he's been in...a girl like you don't need to be getting mixed up in his troubles. You seem like a sweet girl so listen to me. Stay away from him."

"Mmm." I nodded. "But what...what kind of trouble he's been in?" I scoured his eyes for more.

"I won't get into that. I warned you, so just listen." He offered nothing more for me to go on.

"Insanity trip" were the words he threw in Cameron's face. I thought about that as I nodded to his warning. And I had no reason to disbelieve him. Already I had gotten a dose of what he was talking about.

Even as Cameron distanced himself, he couldn't stop staring at me. There was something else about him: a transformation in his sense of self. He now appeared cool, confident, and back in total control of that skateboard. In fact, he was too cool. And that final hypnotic stare, before he disappeared around the corner, was long and hard and–

I didn't know but had a strange feeling I hadn't seen the last of him.

Chapter Four

Girls Reunion

I gazed across the sea at a colorful twilight. The breeze off the ocean ruffled the airy white dress I wore. Cautiously, I turned. There stood Cameron, statue-like, amid a peculiar forestry backdrop. We held an intense gander, but I got an impulse to turn back to the sea. I quickly turned back and saw that he was closer now. Oddly, so was this strange backdrop. The same impulse whipped my head back to the sea. I couldn't understand why. Nothing was there. But fear began mounting, thumping in my ears, expanding all around me, compelling me to turn back to Cameron. This time he was too close. So was the backdrop, though now it had fanning edges, resembling that of a kaleidoscope, and I realized the backdrop was part of him, like wings. Suddenly I looked down and saw my feet buried in the sand. Horrified, I flung out my palm. *Stop!* Then in a blink he–everything–disappeared. Turning yet again to the ocean, I saw that a thick white cloud had appeared, thinning rather quickly, revealing a black shadow–the island, I knew. A bright light shot straight up from its center and divided into finger rays. One fell over me like a glossy white sheet. And then....

Then my eyes flew open; I think my heart stopped. But that was nothing because I was in my bed right where I should be, thankful that it was only a dream...just another bad dream.

The smell of bacon roused me, but not enough to get me up, not just yet. I rolled on my back, stared up at the running ceiling fan, thinking. *I've had many dreams of that creepy island so that wasn't new. Have seen it for real–for real–with my eyes wide open though no one else could; this wasn't new either. Have all sorts of weird things going on with me, again, not new.*

But Cameron being in the same dream as the island or that I even dreamed about him at all–well, that was new and it bothered me. It sometimes happens, though, when you go to bed thinking about someone (or something), you dream about them. I had to get him out of my head, that's all, so I could stop dreaming about him.

I rolled over and swung my feet to the floor, got up, and then scuffed a little on into the kitchen.

"Good morning."

Mom smiled. "Good morning, dear. I was wondering when you'd show up. I looked in on you earlier." Probably all throughout the night, I imagined. It was our first night back, so Mom probably didn't get much sleep either. "You must've gotten to sleep late?" She looked up from a magazine as she sipped from a mug of hot coffee.

I put bacon and eggs on the plate. "You can say that. I had a hard time sleeping. Where's Dad?" I looked around for him.

"He's not here right now. What happened to your arm?"

"Oh," I exhaled. "I had a little accident with a runaway skateboard yesterday. Just a little bump, it's nothing."

I set my breakfast plate on the table, then opened the fridge for something to drink. As I was about to sit, there was a knock at the door.

"Come on in," Mom beckoned.

A girl came through the door in orange jogging shorts and top and with a beaming smile.

"Stephanie!" I rushed to greet my long-time-no-see friend with a huge hug. "It's so good to see you. How have you been? Gosh, it's been so long."

"Like forever," said Stephanie.

"Come on in and have some breakfast." Mom motioned her to sit as she prepared a plate. I grabbed her hand and led her. We all sat around the glass table.

"Are you here for the week?" I was so excited we were here, together again.

"Actually, we're living here now."

"What? Really?"

"Yep. Just me and Mom. We moved here this past Christmas."

"Just me and Mom" was a hint there was more to come. With wonder creasing our foreheads, Stephanie went on about her parents' divorce, how she missed home, friends in Columbus, Ohio, and that she looked forward to going back for the summer.

Mom removed herself from the table and retreated elsewhere after sympathizing with the sudden changes in Stephanie's life.

"So what are you up to today?"

"I'm not sure what my parents have planned," I said.

"Well, there's a show at the amphitheater later if you want to go."

"Yeah, that sounds like fun. I love the shows they have there. What kind of show? Is it tonight?"

"Uh huh. And it's reggae night," she said lively, and we laughed.

"Ooh, it's going to be so packed. Gosh, let me check with Mom." I rose from the seat. "What time are we talking?"

"Seven thirty for the show, but see if she'll let you go to the mall too with me. I'm going to get something to wear to the show."

I pressed an index finger to my smiling lips. "Mom," I called out just as she came out of the room. I figured she'd heard most of the conversation. "So, Mom, what do you say? Can I go to the mall with Stephanie and the show tonight? Please?" I switched my smile to an innocent one.

"Mmm. Are you driving now, Stephanie?"

Stephanie shrugged. "Well, a little. I have my permit. But we'd be taking the bus. We can catch it in front of the bank and get dropped off right at the mall."

Mom gave me the okay as long as I cleaned up the kitchen. And that was done in a jiffy after Stephanie left. Then I took time deciding on what to wear. In good time, I was fully dressed and ready to go. I decided on the multicolored T-shirt I bought yesterday and jean shorts.

"Nice shirt," Mom complimented. "I don't think I've seen that one."

"The boardwalk, yesterday," I said, extending my

arms in a sassy pose.

"I really love the colors."

I nodded. The colors were yellow, blue, and green. Mom and I often saw eye to eye when it came to colors and fashion.

"You have your card, right?"

"Yeah," I said.

"Then you know the rules: bargain shop. And don't spend over forty."

"Okay, Mom."

Her phone rang. "Let me know before you leave," she said before answering it.

I went into my room to retrieve my bag, draped it across my body, and then stepped outside. I scanned up and down the street. The sky was clear, the temperature was perfect, and I felt this was going to be the best day ever hanging out with Stephanie. We always had so much fun together. This day would be perfect, I thought.

When I looked up the street again, Stephanie was already walking toward me. As if we had planned to dress alike, she had changed into jeans and a colorful tank top. I beckoned and she picked up the pace. I went inside to let Mom know we were leaving. She walked me back out to get time to expect us back, and as we started up the street, she was telling us again to be careful.

The bus arrived on schedule, and we took seats in the rear, away from the few passengers sitting near the front. Stephanie pulled Macy's leaflet out of her purse and pointed out the outfit she wanted to get.

"This will go good with the silver sandals Mom just bought me and with this purse, don't you think?" She was carrying a shoulder bag of a rich metallic blend with beads in the front, which I thought would look good with just about anything and said as much.

Then she got the idea we should wear the same outfit. We've been friends for a long time and had occasionally dressed alike, but this time, I wasn't feeling it. I don't know, maybe it was because we were older and I had my own identity and unique way of expressing myself.

I remembered times people thought we were twins or sisters, even though our features weren't identical. We both were fair-skinned with dark hair though hers was a shade or two lighter. My hair was long and wavy, and hers, long and curly.

"What's on your mind?" she asked.

"Mmm...how long it's been since we were together. Do you remember the last time? It was the Fourth of July. Boy, the fireworks were spectacular." It was the last Fourth of July we spent here. The same year I went missing. Thanksgiving weekend to be exact.

"Yeah. That was when I slipped and fell in the fountain. You remember?"

"Oh, yeah, how can I forget." I giggled, and she slapped me on the hand, saying, "You would remember that." We carried on, recalling our friendship over the years and teasing each other about our most embarrassing moments until suddenly the bus came to a screeching halt, jolting us forward. Our hands went out to prevent us from slamming into the seats in front of us, and when the bus came to a complete halt, the force of it slammed us back down in our seats. The bus driver rammed the door open and bolted off.

"Shit, did he hit someone?" Stephanie asked in the midst of all the commotion of other passengers. Of course, I wondered the same thing. We rushed up, along with others, to the front of the bus. A couple around our age had gotten off the bus behind the driver to investigate the incident.

What in the hell happened? We looked through the huge windshield and saw an SUV cornering the left side of the bus. It appeared the driver had tried to jump in front of the bus and stalled. No other cars were involved.

"C'mon, let's get off." Stephanie sounded excited.

"What?" I didn't see any reason to get off.

"Okay, stay." To my surprise, she got off without me. I watched over the heads and shoulders of others.

The bus driver, heavyset, a blue cap covering his slick hair, profusely scolded the driver of the gray SUV, a man of similar height and build. They were both going at it though I saw no damage to the other vehicle. Maybe I was missing something. It didn't make sense. We should just be on our way.

The feud between the two ended, and the driver shouted, "Back on the bus." They all began filing back on—Stephanie first.

"What was that all about?" I asked.

Stephanie frowned. "Beats me...but that man driving that car—crazy..."

Just as we made it back to our seats, the bus driver got off again.

"What now?" I grunted.

Stephanie was back to the front of the bus in a flash. "It won't start. They're getting ready to push the piece of junk off the road," she hollered back. Grumbling about this whole ordeal with the SUV taking a big chunk out of our time, I went back up for a front-row seat right along with Stephanie. Three men were pushing the SUV as the owner steered. The light changed, so they stopped, but suddenly things were different—everything went completely silent. My eyes began shifting rapidly. I was too afraid to move a muscle, wondering what was going on. This couldn't be another one of my visions—not like this. I wanted to scream to break the silence but figured it wouldn't matter anyway because everything and everyone had stopped cold like statues, motionless, lifeless, and quiet as death.

Suddenly I was in a horrifying panic. I tried really to scream, but the scream was trapped inside me. It started to sink in that I, along with everything else, was locked cold in a mummy-state, suspended in time. Other than the power to shift my eyes, I couldn't move them, not even to blink. Left to right, right to left, I moved them, hoping to feel them, hoping to see things back to normal. What about breathing?

My God! How could I not be breathing!

But wait. My eyeballs rolled sharply to my right...discerning movement. What I saw coming to view and ventilating through the lifeless congested street was this male figure. His height, about six feet; weight, evenly distributed; and his density, zero. I could see right through him. *He...was a ghost. Aaahhh!* Once more I tried to reach the top of my lungs and crack through the silence. Still, not a sound escaped. I was powerless. My only power was to stay glued to his movement until finally it faded into thin air. Then miraculously, as if hands on the clock awakened from death, everything and everyone was alive and moving again.

Stephanie's cellphone rang, and she answered right

away. Baffled, I scanned the bustling scene, paying attention to those closest to me, looking for signs, any sign, that I hadn't been the only one to witness the incredible incident. There weren't any, though. The light changed, and the men continued moving the SUV. Did anyone out there, somewhere, see what happened? I continued to wonder. *No, just you, kiddo,* I could almost hear a mocking whisper. And it seemed true because all was back to normal as if time never missed a beat.

I gazed over to where the ghost disappeared. "That was really something," the words escaped without permission.

"Hey, hold up." Stephanie broke from her phone conversation, eyeing me. "What was?" Her eyes narrowed.

I realized I was gawking, so I shut my eyes and gently shook my head. "Nothing, nothing." My eyes reopened with a smile. "I was just thinking about something and spoke out loud." I faked being perky. "Get back to your conversation, don't mind me," I practically ordered.

She gave me a distorted look, got up, and grabbed my hand. "Come on." She led us back to our seats as she continued talking on the phone, some urgent girl talk. The few people on the bus chatted, looking out the window, minding their own business as we passed.

Waiting to get moving again, I rested my head against the window, thinking. Was it the jolt? I had never had a vision like that before–if that's what it was. Never one without the warning signs out of the blue. Never. Could the jolt have caused something like that? I'd been jerked around before, from slamming on brakes and other situations. But...what else could it be? As I tried to find a reason, I realized it had been days since my last vision, actually weeks.

It had to have been the jolt. I had to blame the incident on something and get it out of my mind...for now anyway.

Finally, we reached the mall, and our first stop was Macy's where Stephanie found the outfit she was looking for. She wasted no time trying it on, primping before the mirror. She really did the outfit justice; it looked so much better on. Some things I liked, but neither of us was ready to decide. After all, we had plenty of ground to cover, so we had the store clerk hold the items for a while. We left and, as Mom suggested, shopped for bargains, one store after another, trying on different outfits, having fun. Came break time, we wound up in the food court with a shared plate of Chinese food.

"Hey...how did you hurt yourself?" Stephanie sounded as though she'd been meaning to ask the whole time. A chunk of orange chicken went into her mouth afterward.

"Yesterday on the boardwalk," I said, trying to chew, "some guy's skateboard."

"Dang. You have to watch out for those skateboarders. They can be lethal."

"Obviously," I replied. "So how do you like your new school?"

"More than I thought I would. I miss Columbus, but the kids here are nice. Would you believe I'm on the volleyball team?" The last words danced out. Then she did that funny twist with her lips.

"Ooh...I know that look."

“What look?”

“You know that girl-I-got-something-to-tell-you look. You have a he-friend.” I glared.

“A he-friend? Now that’s a new one.”

“Because I just made it up. Is he on the team, too?”

“He’s the team leader, not my ‘he-friend’...”

Stephanie went on as my mind jumped back to the scene on the bus. *What was that? Never before had I had an experience like that. Did Stephanie know about the disappearance? No, of course not. She would’ve said something by now. But how could she not know, or have heard something? Mmm, maybe I should tell her. Everything. Especially about what happened on the bus. But what if she started seeing me as a freak, like the other ones I thought were my friends?*

For a while I’d felt totally cut off from the world with this freaky condition doctors called dissociative disorder—with the weird visions, anxiety and out-of-body experiences—though none of them truly knew for sure what was going on with me, because my case was rare. And rare was an understatement; just like the incident on the bus, it was something out of this world.

“Does your mom know about him?” I quashed my ricocheting mind.

“Enough about me. Tell me about your he-friend.”

“Ah, sorry, that subject is dead. Don’t have one.” Not that I was against it. My weirdness stood in the way of me becoming a twosome.

“What do you mean?” Stephanie asked.

“Just what I said.” I cracked a smile. Should I tell her? Tell her that I was mentally crippled? Explain how I wished I could erase the past few years so my life would be as it should be. Then it dawned on me: how would that be actually?

There were times I imagined being at the hot chick table at lunch (mostly cheerleaders), chatting away about the boy of my dreams and other unboring stuff. Then I couldn't help wondering if the changes in my life had steered me away from being like them. Mostly I just wanted to fit in. After all, girls at that table were snobby at times.

For a long time, I hated myself, thinking some normalcy would never be restored to my life. Still, it hadn't exactly; but at least now, I had a few friends.

"I don't believe that for a second," Stephanie snapped back. "I think you don't wanna talk about it. You can tell me anything—you know that?"

"I wish—I mean." I lowered my voice. "I mean, I would tell you if I had something *exciting* to tell. Honestly, all the nice-looking guys are here," I said teasingly. "Listening to you makes my life seem less boring."

"You gotta be kidding me."

I frowned at her.

She shook her head but had no problem picking up where she left off about Elijah, whom she insisted she wasn't dating in a biblical way. She went on talking about him as if he was the perfect person to meet.

What? Live dangerously? Suddenly my listeners amplified. Turned out Elijah was in to skateboarding as well.

"Hey, you said all the cute guys are here. Did you happen to run into one yesterday?" Stephanie said.

"Well, funny you should ask because that guy I bumped into yesterday," I patted my bruised arm, "you may know him. Cameron?"

"Umm..." She deliberated a moment. "Don't know anyone by that name, but Elijah might."

"That's okay, it's not that important," I said, not sure if I meant it or not as I thought about that look in his eyes before he disappeared. If I never crossed his path again, the better.

"We'll be meeting up with friends later. Are you okay with that?"

"Sure. I would love to meet your new friends. The more, the merrier," I smiled.

Shortly we were back on the move, wrapping up our day at the mall.

Satisfied shoppers later, we waited outside the mall for the bus. It was making its way around the huge parking lot shadowed by a backdrop of palm trees with trunks stalking the sky. As it did, the world-shattering event that happened earlier flashed in my mind. Of all the weird stuff in my life, that topped them all. And when I realized that I was the only one to witness the event, I was deeply disappointed and wanted to shout, "*The world you live in isn't what you think it is.*" But I was no fool. In my mind's eye I could see a mob of dejected, concerned faces staring at me, and me staring back astounded, frightened even, that I actually put the spotlight on myself like that.

Long ago, standing in front of a mirror, I took an oath to spare myself of such mischief. It was the practical thing to do: The fewer who knew I was a freak, the better.

Chapter Five

The Show

Stephanie and I said good-bye to her mom as we got out at the atrium of the amphitheater. It was 6:30 p.m., and the sound of good music energized the environment. I could feel the vibes of anticipation for the actual show that would start soon.

Many culturally diverse people of various ages were present, in the parking area especially. There were shops, cafés, a souvenir stand here and there, and off from this area was a parking garage. Rows of benches were loaded with no room to spare. So the thought of getting seats took flight, just like the seagulls flying overhead. With that, we decided to mingle or just hang out until the show kicked off.

We started up the sidewalk to the brick wall, which was one of many walls stretching for two miles or so, dividing the spectacular sandy beach from the boardwalk. Since it wasn't as crowded up this way, we moved fluently without walking on someone's heels. We just walked and talked and responded to friendly faces.

Eventually, we stopped at a pretzel stand, ordered hot dog pretzels and sat down at one of the many patio tables along the strip. Neither of us had eaten since the mall hours ago, so we savored the hot dogs.

Stephanie picked up her phone following a sweet melody. "It's Ariana. I'm letting her know where to find us. They should be here in a little bit."

"Good. So I guess you told them about me?'

"Yes, they're looking forward to meeting you."

"Likewise." I smiled as I gazed off into the ocean. I imagined my eyes with wings, crossing the ocean, chasing the horizon, like chasing a never-ending dream, as if life itself was just a dream. I would fly over that mysterious island, stop, and wonder down at it. It too just a dream within a dream, perhaps, though deep within I knew it was far more than a dream. "It's so beautiful," I whispered to myself. I turned, looked past Stephanie, and became trapped in that familiar gaze again.

Not sure that I could trust my vision, I blinked. It was Cameron all right, standing outside of a café across the way.

"Stephanie? See that guy standing in the red and white shirt?" He looked the other way. "Do you recognize him?"

She spun around for a quick glance. "CJ? Is that who you were talking about?"

"Uh huh...he told me his name was Cameron."

She looked uncertain. "I know him as CJ. Could be the *C* stands for Cameron. But listen, don't let his stunning looks fool you. I haven't heard anything good about that dude. Not to mention that he rubs me as weird."

"Why do you say that?"

"Well, I saw him one day and thought he was on something. He was just staring at nothing actually. There was nothing there. They say he hallucinates, and he probably was hallucinating then. I'll admit he seems perfectly normal at times. But please, looks are deceiving. Trust me. You'll want to stay away from him, and I won't be the only one to tell you this."

"I don't know. It just doesn't seem fair to me." I found myself defending him for some strange reason. The accusation touched a nerve, I guess, given my experience with people when they learned of my condition. I knew how cruel people could be; that's why now I kept my mouth shut about my own condition.

"What doesn't seem fair?" Apparently, Stephanie wasn't following.

"Well, maybe he's not as strange as you and others may think. I mean...he has friends." He stared my way again, which distracted me. "Do you think his friends are strange too? Would you stop being my friend if I...was...something like him?"

"No, that's different."

"How is it different?"

"For one, you're like a sister to me. And I'm much older and older sisters look out for little sisters—"

"And that's what you're doing?"

She sighed and bit her bottom lip.

"What are you talking about? You're older by five months," I said.

"So why are you so sensitive about him?"

I exhaled. "I don't know."

"That's okay. I'll look out for you." She looked around. "Here comes Ariana and Cristina now."

I watched as they approached, eyeing the cute strappy sandals with sequins one of the girls wore. Both wore pastel tank tops with colorful layered skirts. Also, their closed-mouth smiles seemed to put a signature on their personalities: friendly, yet curious.

"Hi," we all spoke in unison, and Stephanie immediately introduced us.

Ariana smiled and said, "I like what you both are wearing. Somebody just went shopping."

Stephanie and I wore similar sundresses, a dead giveaway. We both couldn't leave the mall without one. At least the colors in our dresses—purple, blue, green, yellow—had unique patterns.

Ariana went on, "I hope the show starts on time. How long have you-all been here?"

"Just long enough to walk up here and eat pretzels," Stephanie answered. "Are you driving?"

"Yeah. I got lucky and found a good spot on the street off from the atrium. They were getting things ready on the stage when we came through there," Ariana said.

Stephanie checked the time on her cellphone. "We don't have to rush. At least we'll hear when it starts."

"I don't know about you, but my favorite group, Boom Rock, is on stage tonight, and I'm going to be there front and center," Ariana said.

"You mean somewhere out there because it's no way you'll be front and center. That's already taken, that's why we're here," Stephanie corrected.

At once, a nice reggae beat changed the tempo of the atmosphere. Cristina swayed her body and snapped her fingers. “Do you like reggae, Pia?” she asked.

“Me? Oh, yeah,” I said, doing little moves with my shoulders and head. “It gets me in the groove, too.” Everyone caught the fever to rock to the beat and hum along to the chorus. It was as if the show had started...for us anyway.

“Hey, how is everybody?” a friendly voice came from behind.

“Hey,” my friends spoke in unison to the three young men who eased around us–a good-looking threesome dressed in neat casual wear. One was tall, looked like a basketball player, with distinct tattoos on both biceps. The other two were slim: one had a charismatic presence about him, and the other one’s eyes were gorgeous. And there was some cockiness in the way they stood that was...kinda hot. Maybe I was being prejudiced because they were good-looking.

“Elijah, I want you to meet Pia. We’ve been friends since forever.” I nodded hello as she went on. “And this is Brett and Josh.”

After the introduction, the chatter among us buzzed merrily. They were such high-spirited people, and it felt right being in their company. And I could see why it was so easy for my longtime friend to adjust to the sudden change in her life. But when Cameron surfaced, the tempo changed. Everybody got quiet. Cameron whispered something to Elijah, and he nodded, “Yeah.” He then excused himself and followed Cameron into the café.

My eyes locked with Stephanie’s as we had a meeting of the minds. Eyes kept glancing over at the café; it was evident Elijah’s departure was a big distraction, but no one mentioned it openly. We continued in light chitchat, mainly reflecting on the show that was starting. Then a screeching sound from the mic went off like a siren. We all snapped to attention one way or another showing approval of the music. My fingers drummed lightly on the table to the beat, as curiosity drummed in my head to an entirely different beat. I wasn't the only one to hear the beat, I knew: We all were hell-bent and curious about Cameron and Elijah's involvement with him.

Before long, Elijah reemerged with a folded piece of paper in his hand. "CJ is good with computers—repairs, web design—if you ever need help," he informed as he stuffed the folded paper in his back pocket. "Now listen up," he then sought our attention. "I have a surprise announcement."

"Nah, come on, man, hold up," Josh interrupted. "So everyone knows. I got a basketball scholarship to any college of my choosing." The group erupted in congratulations. The girls hugged him though I didn't. But as I looked over at Elijah, I wondered what was behind the lax grin now on his face.

"Josh?" Elijah said finally. "You just sent your secret to smithereens or should I say you put your foot in your mouth. Just so you know, I wasn't about to let the cat out of the box, not this time. That was all you're doing. Unless you were just ready to put it out there; I don't know. But look, you've spoiled my surprise now," Elijah said, putting on a disappointing face. "But, man, if you're okay with it, I am."

"*Damn.*" Josh was looking dumbfounded the whole time during Elijah's speech, his face rigid, and his shoulders slouched.

"Hey, what's going on?" Cristina asked what we all were wondering.

"Damn. I messed up," Josh proclaimed. "Look, I was going to tell everyone about the scholarship but not now." He exhaled. "I have my reasons."

"Oooh," murmurs echoed.

"Well, it's out there now. There's nothing you can do about it," Brett chimed in.

"And we're proud of you regardless," Elijah said and saluted Josh with an index finger. "Now, back to my surprise. But before I do, any more announcements? A show of hands?" He grinned as his hand went up.

We all laughed and clamored, "Nooo."

"Hey, everybody." Cameron surfaced again in time for another interruption.

All eyes fixed on Cameron once again. In the midst of muted voices, tension was rising, obvious signs of how they felt about his presence. And I felt the same way.

"We all know CJ, right?" Elijah stirred sort of a reaction: a nod here and there and a few heads dropped. But I couldn't take my eyes off Cameron.

He pulled Elijah to the side to talk privately again, leaving us wondering what the hell was going on.

"They seem awfully chummy all of a sudden," Brett commented.

"What do you think is going on?" Ariana wondered.

Moments later, Elijah came forth. "Hey, how 'bout letting CJ hang out with us tonight? Just for the show?"

Stephanie and I faced each other, ignited in awe.

"Why at all?" Brett didn't bite his tongue, though he practically mumbled.

The awe between Stephanie and me was still intact. Uneasy butterflies beat in my stomach. Though I hadn't shared with Stephanie the details of how Cameron and I met, let alone his bizarre behavior, I wouldn't dare tip her off now with the gory details. I didn't want to cause her to lose her cool. With her, all it took was a good old-fashioned excuse to drive her into a bullfight. Besides, if no one else rejected the idea, I certainly wasn't and couldn't have Stephanie doing so, thinking she was doing what was best for me.

"Sure, why not," Stephanie said in a low tone. The way she looked at me, I sensed she was doing this on my behalf. The others, who obviously didn't want him tagging along, gave their Okays in an opposing manner.

"Well, it's unanimous," Elijah said to Cameron, who didn't seem bothered by the muffled growls and nauseating looks of the majority.

"Yeah," Cameron said as he smoothed his hands together, scanning each expression. Then he patted Elijah on the shoulder. "Back in a minute." He then scurried away.

I wondered what Cameron was doing in the café when Cristina's voice cut through the tension. "Was that your surprise?" she asked.

Elijah exhaled then said, "No, of course not. You know me, you know me better than that. It surprised me just as much as it did you. Look, he asked if he could join us. I thought about it and saw no reason to say no. But it'll be cool, you'll see. And if you're having second thoughts about it, then tell me. I can't have you later freaking out on me about this."

"You mean you hope he doesn't freak out on us,"

Brett said.

"Why couldn't you just say no or come to us with this first?" Josh retorted.

Elijah thought for a moment. "You're right. I should've come to you first." He dropped a hand to his side. "Tell you what, I'll go now and make this right. Because I don't want to spoil having a good time with my 'number ones.'" He pointed to us.

"Nah, man, too late for that. What's done is done," said Josh with an unbroken stare.

"So you're telling me not to make this go away. Are you sure? I mean, I can make this right."

"Yeah, it's all right," Brett butted in and gave a flimsy thumbs-up. Josh gradually turned away, nodding.

Elijah was still frowning and looking at each of us in turn. "So what about the rest of you?"

The rest, which was us-girls, were somewhat muted; there were nods and lip movements.

Elijah nodded. "Then it's settled. He's really not as bad as you think. You can trust me on this one."

"How 'bout we just get back to your surprise," said Ariana. Her words brought a smile to his face.

"Yeah, about that. Now don't get ecstatic on me...but I happen to have tickets for everyone," he paused, "to the Miami Heat game!"

"Are you serious, man!" said Brett. And there was no more disappointment or fear of betrayal weighing in each of their faces. They all were so thrilled, and I was thrilled for them, wishing I were a lucky recipient of the surprise, too.

"Sorry. Not one for you." Elijah pointed at me. He then turned as Cameron was coming. "But I'll tell you more about the game later. Now, be on your best behavior. It'll be good, you'll see."

In moments, we all were on our feet, merging with the flow of people hooked by the high volume and beat of reggae reeling us in. The closer we got to the amphitheater, the more people were dancing on the boardwalk. I noticed Stephanie stayed especially close to me. She was monitoring Cameron, who kept glancing at me.

"Stephanie, it'll be okay. No need to be concerned," I whispered. I wanted her to enjoy herself, relax, and think positive, as I wondered and watched this person carefully myself.

Who was he, really? His demeanor in the way he carried himself, as if he was well put together on the inside, mentally and spiritually, because it was definitely showing on the outside, a totally different perception of what they had of him, including me?

Who was this person, really, who had us all on edge?

I watched his every move, trying to detect something foreign about him—but nothing. Not yet anyway. He was nothing like that confused, brazen person I encountered yesterday. This by itself came across as strange. Strange like someone with a split personality. His good behavior had to be a ruse, a front to get whatever he was after.

But what could that possibly be? Whatever it was, I hoped I wasn't making a mistake by keeping quiet about how he treated me yesterday. Apart from that, something else still nagged me, and it had everything to do with him appearing right there in my dream with the island. I was usually alone in those dreams.

The entire area surrounding the theater was jam-packed. But we managed to weave through the volume of people to a spot giving us a clear view of the stage. The band stopped as the emcee appeared on stage to introduce the first act. And the crowd went wild spewing accolades and whistles. I didn't exactly hear what was coming, but whatever it was, the crowd was egging them to bring it on. And the temple of the environment changed when a woman came on stage with long braids performing one of Beyoncé's songs, "Single Ladies," reggae style.

The performance arrested me. It was wholly exhilarating. And I saw in the faces of my companions the same impression. We stood enthralled at one act after another—and there were many. And we were being foolish at times, clapping, swaying, and trying to sing along to songs with catchy lyrics. With the band and the volume of people, we couldn't hear ourselves talk or sing unless it was between shows, so communication among us was at a minimum. But we had no trouble communicating the fun we were having.

About halfway through the show, the woman that seemed to be the heart and soul of the night—the one who performed "Single Ladies"—was back with another hot performance. This time she served up some Taylor Swift—I couldn't believe it, guitar and all. Right after this performance, she began drawing from the crowd, volunteers to join them on stage for a limbo contest. The audience then geared up, clapping in unison and yelling "Yeah, yeah, yeah, yeah...." Many hands in the audience went up, and the man on stage pointed out a couple of them to come up. And ooh the crowd roared as the band started playing, and the contest began.

It was so much fun watching the contestants being silly during the contest. It was so good I thought it was planned or part of the show. If not, then those volunteers actually went out of their way to engage and entertain the audience. And we, with our frolicking spirits, ate it up.

Every bit of the show was a must-see, and I hated leaving for a second when I had to go for a restroom break. I scanned the people around me. I wasn't surprised to see that the crowd had mushroomed more. At this point having standing room meant being treed in. It was just that tight.

However, we were having so much fun we held our positions till nearly the end when we all decided we needed a breather. By then the crowd had dwindled, and we were able to make our exit with ease. We ended up on the lit-up strip, at a café where we could use the restroom, get something to drink and still enjoy the music as the show drew to a close.

Cameron stood beside me as I ordered iced tea.

"I'll have the same," he told the waiter. "And I'll cover hers."

I looked at him and said, "You don't have to do that."

"It's the least I can do...after...yesterday."

"Like I said, you don't have to."

"It's only a drink." His brows joined as if he was studying me.

"What? Thinking about trying me again?" This slipped out. Yet maybe that person I saw yesterday would show up.

The clerk handed us our drinks, and we both held stern stares as we stepped away.

"Try you? No." He stared into my eyes. "I wouldn't think of it. I mean, what would be the point...after such a lovely evening?" He smirked somewhat. "And, um—what would you hope to gain?"

"What happened to that person I met yesterday? I'm inviting him to this lovely occasion."

"Sorry. He can't make it. He's off tonight."

"Precisely!" I attempted to bolt, but he grabbed my arm.

"Hey, wait, I'm sorry. I'm sorry, okay," he pleaded as I yanked my arm from his grip. "My behavior"—he was slow coming with the words—"it was just an accident. Just a weird accident I can't explain. I didn't mean any harm." He dropped his forehead and began massaging it. The confusion I saw in him yesterday, I thought I saw now.

But I didn't let that weaken me. "It was more than an accident. It was strange, inappropriate." I lowered my voice as a couple went by. I then looked around to see where the others were: outside chatting.

"I deeply regret it. You just don't know. Look, I won't try to stop you if you choose to tell them. But really, why would you now?"

Right again. It didn't make any sense. I should have said something at least to Stephanie from the beginning. Spilling the beans at this point was bad timing, and I wouldn't look credible at all.

"Pia, come on," Stephanie beckoned. I held up a finger.

"Pia. It's Italian and have a Latin origin," he said and I gave him a "so what" look. "Well...I know this because *Pia* was my mother's name."

My mind rippled at this piece of news, but I

wouldn't let it distract me. "Look, Cameron—CJ, whatever you want to be called. You practically accused me of causing the accident."

"Now how could you have done that?"

"That's my question. You want something—what is it? You didn't barge your way in this little affair for nothing."

He nodded. "Yeah, you're right. I needed to apologize...again. And, um, I just wanted a chance to get to know you."

"I don't get involved with strangers," I said.

"That may be the case now," he said smoothly, sounding assured of himself.

I was now certain he had a motive. Yet I didn't like my mixed feelings about his sincerity. To avoid further discussions, I moved past him and thanked him for the tea.

"Not a problem," he said, trailing me into the night air. It was much cooler out now. As we approached the others, they were talking about the surprise Elijah unveiled to them earlier: the Miami Heat game on Monday.

"Sounds like an excellent way to spend a Sunday," Cameron said.

"Monday," Elijah corrected. "And it's going to be a blast."

Their excitement about the game hadn't died one bit, and I felt a pang of disappointment. It sounded like it would be so much fun I wished I were going, too. I had never been to a pro game.

"You think we can sneak Pia in somehow?" Stephanie asked.

"That would be the only way given the short notice,"

Elijah said.

"It really sounds like the place to be on Monday. But that's okay, really. I'll be thinking about you guys having so much fun." I pretended to weep, sniffing, a finger dabbing an eye.

"Here, my dear," Cameron said in an English accent. His offering of a napkin for my fake tears took me by surprise. I smirked. And we all—including Cameron—burst into laughter. And then real tears formed in my eyes, so I really had a use for the napkin.

We had settled down at a couple of patio tables to hang out for a while until we finally decided to part ways. As our togetherness winded down, Stephanie called to inform her mother that Ariana was bringing us home. The others were getting in last-minute talks and inching toward leaving. And Cameron, in his last minute before departing, popped the question.

"How 'bout you meet me for lunch or dinner tomorrow?" He angled his head to see my eyes, hands stuffed in his pockets. I felt a gentle breath brush my neck, which could have been his; he was that close. The idea that I should be offended or afraid crossed my mind, as I recalled my first impression of him: how explosive it was, enough to blow anyone off for good. Though now I felt far from that. He was setting off my adrenaline without a flicker of fear. But still, I had good reasons to be cautious, and extremely curious.

"Just think about it," he went on. "Here, take my number."

How convenient. I took the business card. In my periphery, I noticed Stephanie watching with folded arms. I ignored her, squaring my eyes on the blue printing on the card: his full name, Cameron Jacks, and his business, computer repair. The last four digits of the phone number were an acronym of his last name, which made it very easy to remember.

"How old are you?" I frowned.

He sighed. "Nineteen, but only for one week now," he said. I guess he was hoping that that would make the situation better somehow.

"Hey, CJ, are you coming?" hollered Elijah.

"Yeah, I'll be right there," he yelled back.

"Look, I, uh–" I wasn't sure how I felt about going out with him.

"You don't have to decide now. Just think about it and call me," he whispered and then whisked away to catch up to the other boys.

I faced Stephanie, standing very near with the other girls. "See, it wasn't so bad," I said.

"That doesn't mean anything. I still say stay away from him." She rolled her eyes.

Ariana asked, "Do you like him?"

"No," I exhaled. "It's not what you guys think. Besides, he's nineteen, and it's not like I live here. I'm going back home next week," I said as we moved along slowly.

"But you like him. Are you going to see him again? I mean he gave you his number," Cristina said.

"And a lot can happen in a week," Stephanie noted.

"Yeah, like you could see him again," Cristina said.

"But he's drop-dead gorgeous. Kinda hard to resist. But you should. Resist, I mean," Ariana pointed an assuring finger.

Getting the third degree from these divas had

already become annoying.

"Come on...it's not that serious," I said. *Was it really necessary to be that protective? Elijah didn't seem to think so.* But it was obvious they had no regard for Elijah's evaluation of Cameron.

Stephanie stopped cold in her tracks. "Okay, then tear up the card," she challenged me. "If it's not serious, then tear up the card."

I stared at her, then at Cristina and Ariana. I played with the card between my fingers. It didn't matter if I took the dare or not: I had his full name and number memorized. I also knew that if I did, it would be to please them only—and why should I? I sneered, opened my purse, and slid the card in a securely tight pocket.

"I *knew* you wouldn't do it," Stephanie said. Grinning, we all picked up pace, heading for the parking lot as another interesting topic transitioned for talk. And we bantered over various topics ranging from boys to future expectations until our fun-filled evening finally ended with words of farewell.

Chapter Six

A Divine Truce

On this gorgeous afternoon, I sat stretched out on the back porch in a hypnotic mode. The sun peeped in and out of nomadic clouds making way for a clear blue sky. I was up at nine after reading long into the night. My parents and I had breakfast together and made small talk. It sounded and felt like old times here again. Afterward, I cleaned up the kitchen and tidied up my room; my parents did other things. Now here I was, stretched out.

I glanced at the table next to me and realized I had left my journal in the room. I got up quickly to go get it and returned just as quick. I opened it and began writing:

Sunday, March 21, 2010

Dreams flooded my sleep last night, and as usual, I couldn't remember any of them clearly, except for the ones I always dreamed about. Last night it was again about the glass house. Cameron was in it again too...

Flipping the pen, I pondered why he was appearing in my dreams all of a sudden. How did he fit in...? After a brief stance, I continued:

...I was in the glass house when I heard the sound of a plane moving overhead. I rushed out, ran across the lawn to this velvety road, which I think was a huge driveway. I was frantic, swinging my head from side to side. Obviously I was Iooking for something or someone. Then there it was, a very small plane. I began shouting, waving as it taxied up the road, stopping at my feet. The door dropped open and there he was, Cameron. I knew it was him. It had to be though I couldn't see his face. I had been waiting a long time for him to come. Slowly he exited the plane but then suddenly stopped. We both looked toward the house and saw the light. It grew brighter and brighter, so bright that it erased us–the entire scene–like Whiteout clearing a picture on paper.

I woke up immediately, my heart not racing but I was annoyed and felt strangely serene for some reason. And I was baffled that it was different from what I was used to. Things are definitely changing. And it could be because I've had enough horrible dreams to last me a lifetime. Or was it because of him? Can he really fly a plane? Probably not. Just another weird clueless dream not meant to be understood. I hope this won't always be the case. And how can something so meaningless play an important part in my life for so long anyway? Could it be that I'm really insane? Could it be my desire to write about it? And if I stopped writing about it, will it be less meaningless? I love writing, so maybe it's a good thing...

I gave the pen a rest when my phone vibrated, which reminded me that the ringer was off still. It was Stephanie.

"Hi, Pia. What are you doing right now?" I knew she had something brewing in that head of hers.

"Ooh, hanging out here on the back porch. What's up?"

"Volleyball. You wanna go? There's a game later on the beach. I know volleyball isn't your thing, but I thought it'd be fun just watching us play."

"Well, yeah, sure. Watching from the sidelines is fun." I smiled, recalling the last time I tried to play. I landed face down, getting much sand in my mouth.

"So that's a yes, good."

"Uh, it's a maybe. My parents haven't said anything, but they could be planning something as we speak."

"Ooh, um...I didn't mean to eavesdrop, but I overheard my mother talking to yours earlier about the game, and I asked Mom about it. She said your mom was interested in playing."

"Really? Well, I haven't heard anything. But I'll see and get back to you."

"Okay, get back to me."

I got up. "Mom, are you playing volleyball later on?" I moved through the house and found her in the living room and told her about Stephanie's invitation.

"Well, I think so. We don't have anything else planned, and it's a beautiful day for a game of volleyball.

Are you thinking about playing? I hope so," she said as I trailed behind her to the kitchen.

I stopped and rested my elbows on the edge of the kitchen counter as Mom moved from the pantry to the cabinet under the sink. She was apparently searching for something.

"I don't know. Maybe, maybe not."

"Well, it'll be fun. You know how much I love playing, as do your dad."

I squinted. "Where is he by the way? And what are you looking for?"

"Oh, your father's around here somewhere. You know how he is. Always have to find something to get into." She came out of her stooping position. "I can't find the soap I just bought at the store."

"So that's what you're looking for. Maybe you thought you bought some."

She nodded. "You know, you might be right. Then again, maybe I left it in the car. I should go out there and check. Also, I've decided to go with your father to the convention, which starts tomorrow you know."

"Yeah, I remember. But you don't have to worry, Mom. I promise that I'll be just fine and on my best behavior."

She grimaced. "I think you will. Mr. Jenkins retired recently so he'll be around the house for the most part and be keeping an eye out. And Ms. Saunders will be home until about two when she leaves for work. We'll be getting out about three, no later than four. If you hang out in the back, make sure the front door is locked. And just keep your phone on you at all times so we can reach you."

"And Stephanie, she'll be around," I reminded her.

"Yes, you guys should keep an eye on each other," she said, coming out of the kitchen.

Back to our original topic. "Does Dad know about the volleyball game?"

"Not yet. We don't have definitive plans so he'd likely be interested. I'll talk to him about it as soon as he gets back."

"Should I call Stephanie back to let her know something?"

"If you do, just tell her we haven't confirmed it with your father yet," she instructed, moving nonstop for outdoors.

"All right." *I might as well wait then.*

I went back outside, picked up my journal, and began writing some more until I ran empty. Then I closed my eyes and thought about how well behaved Cameron had been. I wasn't surprised he asked me out at the end. Did he have a motive going out of his way to befriend me? And not once but twice he popped up in my dreams. It was all strange to me.

Later Dad came out and assumed my cozy, languid state in the seat next to me. Mom had left to run errands in time for the game.

After a while, Dad broke the silence in exchange for a little dialogue. "Did you have a good time last night?"

I smiled his way. "Yup...it was the best show ever. *A really good show.*"

"Tell me about it," he said, looking extremely

relaxed.

"Well, they involved the audience more. They spiced it up with a limbo and karaoke contests—singing only reggae because after all, it *was* reggae night. They clowned their butts off last night, Dad. You would've enjoyed it. But my favorite part of the show was when a woman with braids down to here"—I pointed to my butt—"came on stage with male backup singers. And they put on a show. *I mean a show,* singing one of Beyoncé's songs reggae style. It was over-the-top good. We had such a good time, Dad." I could have gone on and on.

"Sounds like *the* show to remember. I'm glad you had a good time." He looked over at me. "So how have you been feeling?"

"Oh, fine." Immediately, I reflected on the two incidents I had yesterday—while on the bus *and* at the show—and realized I wasn't telling the truth.

"But?" His instinct called me out.

"I had, um...just one episode since we've been here. That's about it." I decided I wouldn't alarm him with the bus incident because we would be fast on the plane back to Texas. I also wouldn't mention the little incident involving Cameron yesterday. The vision I had at the show while in the restroom would be better.

"A mild one?"

"Yes, thank goodness. Before the one yesterday, it had been a few days since I had one. But now, it's happening all of a sudden. Why do you think that is, Dad?"

I knew he wouldn't have an answer. But I asked anyway, hoping somehow he would see things my way for a change, because I always thought it was more to it—far more than what any doctor could explain.

"Well, to begin with, it has never stopped. Because you're getting better doesn't mean you won't have setbacks. Besides, it's only been a few days since your last one. It's probably just a mild setback being back in this environment." He exhaled. "Maybe we should've discussed this with the doctor."

"Yeah," I said, not really meaning it.

"Dreams too?"

I nodded. "Yup, the usual." Still, I didn't want to give him full details. My dad could be unpredictable at times, and I wasn't ready to flee...not yet.

"Describe this image you saw." His tone struck me as a demand.

"Well, I was in line at the restroom. As you know, the tension is usually at its peak when I see 'em. This time, it was different. I saw me, just as I was, in line waiting to use the restroom. Can you imagine that–and no symptoms? It was like looking at myself in a mirror. It's so confusing." I paused. "It's like it's getting better and worse at the same time."

His concerning eyes gazed at me. "Strange hallucination," he called it. As he always had. *Hallucination* was the psychological term they easily identified with. Frankly, I didn't like it.

"Yeah," I said, still not fully agreeing. No matter what the doctor thought, I knew the visions were something more than hallucinations. And it bothered me to feel I was alone in thinking that. But I went on, "Dad, I know there's more to it than hallucination. I just know it."

"You still think so? Explain it to me. What else could it be? I've taken you to all sorts of doctors, and they all have the same diagnosis."

I lowered my forehead in my palm as I entered deep thought. This was where they got me every time because I couldn't explain it without sounding crazy. I didn't have the answer, but I knew. Deep in my gut, I just knew. If only I could remember something about that night, I believed I could prove them all wrong.

God help me.

I lifted my head. "I know it's hard for you, Dad, and truly, I understand your position. Even though I can't explain it, I have a position, too. So I'll just try harder to keep my belief about this to myself"—I looked over at him—"because I know it's better that way and it doesn't do me any good anyway."

"I want you to feel free to talk to me about anything, especially this—regardless. It's hard, I know. You can't help believing what you believe. It's what makes you, you, because you're entitled to your belief. And your beliefs are true to you. Honey, I respect that. You know, it's kind of like the way we believe in God."

"Yeah...kinda like that," I began softly, "because I have no way to explain it. And just because I can't doesn't mean it isn't so."

"That's right. But listen, baby girl, if the episodes continue or get worse, I'll take you in to see the doctor. Better yet, maybe you should see the doctor as soon as we get back. It's been a while since your last visit."

"Ah-ah, Dad...that won't be necessary. Besides, I probably will be back to normal when we get back home. And just like you said, I'm probably readjusting to being here again." I was willing to accept this since no logical explanation was available. For now on, I would keep my mouth shut. I didn't want to worry him, especially while on vacation and if it wasn't going to make a difference anyway.

Besides, I didn't want him to think he wasn't doing enough to help me. Just the opposite, he was a wonderful father, and I knew how much he wanted to believe my claims, and he did in his own way. He and Mom both, from the start suspected I would start having nightmares–and they were right, except the visions were something else entirely. They didn't know exactly what it was I going through. And, I supposed being realistic was vital. Otherwise, we all would have been seeing a shrink.

"We'll see," he said, looking out of the corner of his eye.

Settled comfortably now, I eventually dozed off.

Chapter Seven

Twists in the Game

When we arrived the net was up, and people were warming up in a practice match. The light breeze stirred around the flavor of barbecue from the temporary stands set up for today's game. Off from the stands were large canisters of cold beverages. Everything seemed in place. As I looked far off in the distance, I saw nothing on the horizon to interrupt the game.

People flocked all over the place. Some were up on the hill stretched out on huge beach towels. Others on chairs and mats below the hill, even some lay on the naked sand. Many just stood around; I assumed some were players wearing team colors: yellow tops and blue tops. Yet people wearing those colors were still coming.

Mom and Dad hung around talking to team leaders and other players while I secured a spot slightly up the hill with our beach towels. I spotted Stephanie and her mother coming down the hill and waved. Now that I was getting a good look at Mrs. Burke, Stephanie's mom, I saw that she hadn't changed a bit. She was still a beautiful, full-figured woman. Mrs. Burke went toward my parents, and Stephanie came toward me.

"Hey. Are you playing?" She'd been trying to encourage me to play since she heard we were coming.

"Mmm. I don't know...maybe later on."

"Okay, well. I have to see who's in line to start the game. I'll check back with you later."

"Okay," I said, then she padded away to meet with others players, particularly those around her age.

As they got the teams together, I saw that they were balancing the playing field with equal numbers of adults and kids, especially with so many wanting to get into the game from the start. Scorekeepers and referees were being appointed. I plugged in my iPod to listen to music as they got organized. Mom was on the team with Stephanie and her mother, and Dad was on the other team. I counted as they formed on both sides of the net...sixteen players to each team. After tossing the coin to determine which team would serve first, a heavyset man from Dad's team released the ball from one hand and bumped it with the other, and the ball went sailing over the net. The game was off to a start.

I watched as the ball sailed over the net. No one was gunning for it because it headed straight to a short man in line for a perfect play. He moved forward, his hands in ready position to bump the ball. But then he stooped low and stopped cold, and the ball landed smack on his forehead. Boos roared throughout the crowd, and there were some cheers in the mix too, but the Boos were louder. And as the Boos and cheers continued, the little man just danced and danced like a playful little kid having the thrill of his life. All people, on both teams, were excited right along with him, laughing at this adorable, frisky old man with impressive bow legs; he was so much fun to watch. For now, he had the stage all to himself, having surprised everyone with that capricious stunt. All in all, it was a pleasant diversion to starting the game.

His tempo changed when he raised his arms straight up, yelling, "I'm sorry, I'm sorry everybody," running in place and still wearing a huge smile. "I'm so sorry, everyone. Now let's get this game started!" A heated game of volleyball followed, and from that point on, I watched him play a fantastic game.

All the players were good, though, including my parents. They loved volleyball and made a point to play whenever they got the chance. I was impressed at how Stephanie had mastered her skills. As I watched, I couldn't see myself getting in and spoiling it for everyone. I was truly lousy at the sport. My main problem was my inability to maneuver in the sand. Walking in it was laboring enough, but I would rather walk in it than get out there and embarrass myself. With volleyball, you have to run or move quickly, which almost always caused my feet to trip over each other–two left feet–and I would end up on the ground more times than I would like to.

So far the ball was going across the net at a steady pace until Dad upped the ante by tapping the ball just enough to send it over the net. I could almost feel heart rates accelerating as a tall slim man angled forward, trying to catch the ball with a detonator that would gut his team to bottom first if the ball hit the ground. As the ball did, he landed flat on his stomach, the ball ultimately bouncing off his fisted hands. His miss ignited the greatest accolade throughout the many onlookers in awe over the failed play. Dad and all his team members were just as ecstatic about being the first to score after a steady and intense beginning.

That first legitimate score pressed the players to compete vigorously: slipping, falling, jumping, skidding, all to get the ball up and back over the net. Gunning to be the winning team inspired more creative and surprising moves, which raked in points on both sides.

"Show me what you got," "Serve you up for dinner," "In your face," "Gotcha," and many more phrases were spoken to express their fun-filled emotions, and not-so-pleased emotions, some of which I wouldn't dare repeat.

I took my eyes off the game, scanning my surrounding. But when I turned for a quick glance on top of the hill, something apparently changed in that moment. I started hearing "Omigods...Holy molys...What the hell..." So when I turned back to see what was happening, all eyes were on this scary-looking twister that formed out of the blue in the water. Nearly everyone just stood around looking, amazed by it suddenly being there. Very few made an urgent attempt to get as far away from it, though that changed when the wind picked up as it moved closer to shore. Everybody scattered every which a way out of its path. I jumped to my feet, looking to make my escape up the hill as everyone else, and behold, my anxious orbs landed dead on Cameron.

What is he doing here? I was sure he read me loud and clear, glaring at me. *The waterspout,* I remembered as his attention moved off me. To see how far it had come, I quickly turned. What! Where did it go? Strange, it was as if it was never there. It looked now as though the game had stopped only because a woman was down with a sprain ankle. *What on earth happened to the waterspout?* I was freaking out in wonder when Stephanie's voice startled me.

"Hey, girl. Are you okay? You look like you saw a ghost."

Judging from the expression on her face, I supposed I did look like that.

"I, uh, yeah, I'm good." *Cameron*...I looked up to where I thought I saw him. "Just that...I thought I saw–"

"Cameron? Yeah. What was he doing here?" Stephanie said obnoxiously. "I've never seen him at one of the games.

"Mmm." At this point, all I wanted to do was just sit down and think about what just happened. Of course, Stephanie had something else in mind.

"You know I'm here to get you in the game. So are you ready?"

I shook my head. "Nope, this is bad timing."

"Bad timing? This is the perfect time, see." She pointed in general at the surroundings. To me, it wasn't perfect timing to get in the game.

I sighed. "How can you ask me to get out there and make a fool of myself in front of all these people? You don't need someone like me coming in and screwing things up. I *suck* and you know it."

"Don't worry about that. It's only a game. It'll be fun, and at the same time, you'll be getting practice. Besides, we have plenty of good players out there to take up the slack."

"Ooh," I muttered. "So it's okay to do what, screw up the game?" I simply didn't want to give in.

"Aah, c'mon." She grabbed my hand and pulled me

forward.

"Okay, okay, okay," I said to get her to stop yanking my arm off. By now, I was leaning to a yes, just to get it out of the way. Stephanie would only keep bugging me.

Stephanie stood with both hands on her hip, her dark eyes begging me to get up.

I huffed, "Oooh, okay."

She grabbed my hand again and got me moving. Mom, wearing a smile, clapped her hands as we drew closer. I took a position next to Stephanie, praying to walk away from this without looking ridiculous. So I kept my eyes on the ball at the start. It was my way of preparing for my contribution to the team. I was mentally coaching myself: *When the ball comes my way, I'll just hit it, not straight up but horizontally, at least get it going toward the net so someone else can be in a better position to assist. Piece a cake.*

With me in it, the game got started and went pretty well although other matters roamed around in my head. Our team scored two points, and I was still on my feet. But now as the ball soared directly toward me, I became a little excited. *Here comes the moment of truth,* I thought. I made a fist, keeping my eye on the ball as I stepped forward and thumped it. It angled upward, not straight up, but in direction of the little man that had done the dance before the game; he knocked it over the net. I breathed a sigh of relief. *Thank goodness.* Mom and Stephanie were beaming, sending me thumbs-up.

I felt good about the play, but it was still early in the game as far as I was concerned. I couldn't shake the thought of doing something awkward that would spoil it for the team. Why couldn't Stephanie just let me enjoy the game from the sideline? I thought as I ran a few feet sideways to hit the ball a second time.

"Whew." I gawked as I sent the ball well over to the other side. The opposing team fumbled the ball, we scored a point, and the audience went wild with cheers and whistles.

It felt good scoring for the team, and the immediate attention I got from the team members gave me a little morale. Especially Stephanie, saying, "You go, girl!" as she gave me a high-five, and we bumped fists. And Mom yelled, "That's my girl–good come back."

We were back in serious game mode as the ball again soared over the dividing web. I looked around me, noticing larger gaps between the players, which was why I had to run a little to meet the ball. *The waterspout, Cameron–did he see it? Could he be the key to everything'that's going on*?–I just couldn't get out of my head.

The ball now was coming fast between me and another player. Feeling confident, I moved quickly in line with the ball, a clear communication to my teammate that I had it. She slowed down giving me clear access to make the play. But doggone it, I fumbled and began falling. Still thinking about the ball, I swirled around and came face-to-face with the ball as it smacked me dead in the face. I felt humiliated.

Oh no, here I go again. It was time to get out of the game. Another one of those attacks was coming on. All I wanted to know was why. Why so frequently now–like everything else? Maybe this time it was the combination of the ball hitting me in the face and me panicking.

"Time out for me," I said to Stephanie as I got up.

"Are you all right?" Stephanie began walking with me off the court, and Mom joined us.

"That's okay, Stephanie, I've got her," Mom said. "You go back and play."

"All right, I'll be over there in a little while." Much concern was in her voice.

"What's happening? Are you having an attack?" Mom asked as we made our way up the slope.

"Yeah." And when we got to our spot, I flopped down on the beach towel and lay on my side. Tension was rising: small quakes sprouting through my insides from limb to limb, my head wishy-washy.

Mom settled down next to me. "I'm right here, honey." She was patient, knowing it wouldn't be long before it passed and I was back to normal.

But I wouldn't be back to normal, not before another freaking scene ran its course. This time it was an image of both Cameron and me. He was trudging through the water carrying my lifeless body. Did I faint? Have an accident—what? I wrestled with this one *hard* because it could very well be a premonition.

"What's happening to me?" I whispered, knowing someone or something had to hear me. And so be it if the little voice popped up and spoke to me. Even if something or someone answered, I felt like lashing out and kicking ass for the unnecessary misery bestowed on me.

The incident of yesterday flashed in my mind, the transparent image of a man—ghost, then the weird scene with the waterspout. Now this! Something definitely had changed since being back here in Florida. Like Pandora's box had cracked open, and Cameron must be the key to it all.

"Pia," Mom whispered, "I want to know if you're having...you know."

"No, Mom, nothing," I lied. I didn't want to explain Cameron to her. And after talking with Dad earlier, I knew it would only make matters worse.

In a few minutes, I was back up, feeling as good as ever. I listened to my iPod and watched the game still going on without me. Naturally, I had decided to set out the rest of the game. Mom had gone back behind Dad. After playing for a while nonstop, he had taken a short recess too.

But I wasn't alone for long; Stephanie came over and flopped down next to me. She was exhausted and finally in need of a real break.

"I'm hungry. You want to go over to one of the stands and get something?"

"Yeah, the barbecue's been smiling good." I got on my feet, and we headed over.

"You know, Pia," Stephanie began, "you shouldn't let a little fall spoil everything for you. We all fall. I do all the time. It's just a game. You just get up, dust yourself off, and get back in there. You shouldn't take it seriously." Stephanie looked and sounded like the big sister she so wanted to be.

"I know—and you're right. Telling you about my two left feet might sound corny, but I do have them. I do when it comes to volleyball anyway. I always get clumsy and fall. You've always known me to fall. But I'm really surprised at how well you play. It would take a lot of practice for me to get half as good as you."

"But that's my point: practice makes perfect."

"And my point is that I don't have the time and place to practice much, unlike you having Sundays here to practice, plus you're on another team. Right now, I just feel awkward playing when I know it won't make much difference, anyway.

"Tell you what I'll do." I smiled. "I'll fall, get up, and dust myself off during something else. Something I really like...like tennis." I chuckled, wondering if I would ever tell her the truth. About me. About everything.

She smiled back wryly. "But you....ooh whatever." She flat out gave up.

At the stand, we both ordered a small Coke, barbecued hotdogs, and sprayed a little mustard and ketchup on top and headed back.

"You know, I think CJ showed up here because he thought you would be here. So have you decided what you're going to do with his number?" She bit into the hot dog and looked at me.

"No...but when I do, you'll be the first to know."

"I was talking to Elijah earlier about you and CJ. I asked for his advice."

"Okay, let's hear it," I encouraged.

"Well, he doesn't see CJ as your type. He thinks you might want to observe his character before diving in. He knows lots of girls who went into a relationship with him blindly and regretted it. His exact words pretty much."

"Well, what happened with those girls? I should know, right?"

"It's just that his personality doesn't quite match his good looks. I mean he hasn't hurt anyone, but he seems to have a better relationship with males than females. No,

I'm not saying he's gay. His problem with hallucination...I don't know. It just seems to affect his relationship with females."

"Oh, that is strange," I said, staring down as our pace slowed.

"So don't call him. Please, do it for me."

What? I couldn't believe her. "Stephanie, Stephanie...this isn't about you. Don't you think you're overstepping your bounds just a little bit? Look, I appreciate you filling me in about him. Really, I do. But you have to trust that *I can* take care of myself. You said yourself, he hasn't really hurt anyone." I breathed. "What am I going to do with you?"

"But–"

"But nothing. No ifs, ands, or buts," I refuted.

After a brief silence, she added, "You know...it's a good thing you're only visiting."

"Um hum...that'd work for me, too."

We arrived back at our spot, sat, and talked as we finished the food, and then she got back in the game. Soon the game fizzled out as players gradually called it quits, as we did eventually.

We arrived home just before dusk.

Chapter Eight

Tough Decision

Today was the start of the three-day convention my parents had been looking forward to, and I was all alone to do whatever I wanted, as long as it didn't fall out of line of the "dos" and "don'ts" my parents had laid out for me.

Stephanie and I had just gotten back from running a few laps at the high school she attended. I woke up this morning with the urge to air out my mind and blow off steam, with a passion I don't think I'd ever had before. I pounded the pavement for three miles to Stephanie's two. Hers was a combination of running and walking. Trying to keep up, Stephanie couldn't figure out what had come over me, saying, if she didn't know better, she would have thought I was training for a marathon. No matter what had compelled me to run and run and run to the max until I lost steam, it felt darn good afterward.

"I'll see you later," Stephanie said, running up to her house. She had so much to do before going to the game later in Miami.

I went on home, ready now to make that crucial next

step: To ease my conscience, I had no other choice.

First thing first though: a shower, a nice refreshing shower. I got undressed, stepped in, dying to wash down the drain the built-up residue of tension and sweat. I was all alone with my mind set on doing the unthinkable. But I had to see it through. That's what I kept telling myself. After showering, I dressed in a cotton dress that tied in the back and ended up out back with a bottle of cold water and my journal in hand. I quickly flipped it open, seeing that my mind was eagerly dictating what to write.

After filling a few pages, mainly about everything that had happened since my last entry–incidents at the volleyball game yesterday and my dream last night–I sat back wondering. *Should I get to the bottom of this thing with Cameron, alone? Yeah, you almost have to.*

I just sat, reflecting on the first time Cameron and I met. Something triggered him to go off on me, a complete stranger, that day, and now he had a strong interest in me that added to my psychotropic troubles. The million-dollar question was "Why?"

Shortly all doors were locked, my heart set on investigating my prime subject. I cut through the back headed for the beach. When I arrived, I stopped and took a long gaze northward. This direction was practically lifeless, not a soul in sight. Then I looked southward, not much going on that way either.

What should I do? Having second thoughts, I could hear myself think, though what brought me to this point nudged me to keep going. Yet the thoughts tripping in my head had me budging at the nudges. Maybe I really needed to go back to the house and rethink this. But that wasn't happening, not by a long shot. Because that drive that got me up for a morning jog resurfaced, and it was scrappy at moving me forward.

So my feet picked up and steered me in my intended direction. Up a ways, I pulled out my cellphone and began keying in the numbers I had memorized. With my thumb on the Send button, I hesitated. My thoughts started running as deep as the ocean, searching for a simple "yes" or "no." Should I or shouldn't I?

I exhaled a deep frustration. What did I have to lose? Nothing, nothing at all. I then pressed the button, slowed my pace as the phone rang. But on the second ring, I gave in to a dreadful impulse and hung up.

I can't do this. I slowed to a halt, recalling that dreadful day I went missing. I didn't want to put myself in position for anything like that to ever happen again. Not that it had ever been my fault.

Frustrated, I still showed no sign of sidetracking. Rather I pressed forward across wet sand like one in pursuit of fetching an arrow already nailed on the bull's-eye. At least I could say I had a good walk on the beach should I decide at the last minute to turn around and head back home, doing nothing at all. Yeah, right, as if that would be satisfying, and as if I really needed a walk on the beach after running three miles already today. I was only fooling myself. And as sure as I was aware of my frustration, I knew it would just eat me alive if I went on fighting the urge to call Cameron.

I was on the verge of insanity, that's where I was. But lucky for me, the urge *to do* overpowered the urge *to resist.* So once again, I pressed the button, stood still, and began counting the rings.

"Hello," he answered on the fourth.

"Cameron?" I said.

"Yeah. Who is this?"

"This is Pia." I raised my voice a bit for confidence.

"Pia? Well, hi. It's nice to hear from you. You called a moment ago?"

"Yeah, I did. A bad connection, I suppose."

"I'm glad you called back."

"Yeah, well. I thought I'd take a chance and call you." *Since I can't get you out of my mind, that is.* I was starting to feel awkward, like this was a bad mistake. But I ignored it; I had to see this through.

"Good, I'm glad you did. What are you doing right now?" he asked.

But before I could respond, he said, "I think I hear birds in the background." He was spot-on, for there were birds flying over me.

"Yeah, I'm outside," I said. "So where are you?"

"At the café...the same place from the other day. I help out here part-time."

"Yeah, I remember the place."

"I recall asking you to join me for lunch. You know, the offer still stands."

"Gosh, um, I don't know. It may not be safe–I mean the right thing to do."

"Look, I'm not going to pretend I don't know where you're coming from. I'm sure you have heard some things about me. But I'm not as bad as some people portray me to be. And I think you kinda know that. Really, if you give me the time, I will clear up whatever you have on your mind. Just give me a try."

"Why...um...why the interest in me?" I stuttered, asking what I needed to know before moving forward, before making up my mind.

"Why you?" he repeated.

"Yes, me." I refused to elaborate.

"Besides you happen to be incredibly gorgeous, it's kinda hard to put into words. It's just that...ever since that day with the skateboard, you've been on my mind. I know it's strange, but I felt I had to get to know you. Especially since we got the chance to really talk that night at the show. Call it fate, intuition–whatever. I won't go as far as to say it was meant to be, but something's there. For me anyway. So how am I doing so far?"

"Umm, I...I–" Under normal circumstances, I probably would say horrible. But this wasn't normal.

"Look Pia, maybe none of that impressed you. The bottom line is that I like you, and the last thing I want to do is scare you off."

"Well, I don't scare that easy," I said as words he used–*strange, intuition, fate*–piqued my curiosity. Fate how? I wondered.

"Then have lunch with me today," he continued, revealing a softer tone.

"Uh, where exactly you say you are?"

"At the café. Riverview Café."

"Then how 'bout coming out of your hiding place so I can see you?"

Chapter Nine

The Meeting

"What, you're he–?" He emerged from the back with an astounding look on his face. "Hey, I'll talk to you later," he said into the phone.

"*I'll talk to you later.*" I smiled at those words as he made his way into the sunlight. His gaze caught on to mine, and it lasted until we were face-to-face.

"I apologize for sneaking up on you like this," I said.

"Yeah, you surprised me all right." His shoulders relaxed as his hands slid into his pockets. "But I'm glad you're here...really. But I sense a little secrecy."

"Secrecy? No. More like me being cautious. I wanted to be sure that meeting you was the right thing to do. Because I'm still not sure what I'm dealing with. You know what I mean?"

He shrugged. "Mmm...enlighten me."

"Well, should something happen to me, my cellphone will show that you were the last person I talked to–just playing it safe. You of all people should understand."

"Wow. That's quite impressive. You think you've covered everything?"

"Oh, and um, I told Stephanie, too," I lied. Though regardless of her criticism, it probably wouldn't have been a bad idea informing her. Gosh, I wished I had a Taser.

"Look"—he placed his hands on my shoulders—"I'm perfectly harmless and would go all out to protect you, be your personal bodyguard even."

I stepped loose of his hold and crossed my arms. "Like I really need one," I sassed.

Chortling, he looked off, then stepped aside, his hand making a gesture. "Shall we?"

I drew a breath, and then led the way across polished tile floors inside the café to one of the booths in the far corner; pop music was playing low in the background. Business at this hour was as light as air with an immediate smell of food on the grill. Cameron retrieved a menu and handed it to me; in moments, he sat across from me.

"What's your favorite?" I asked, not wanting to settle with the usual: a hamburger.

"My favorite? The grilled tilapia over a bed of yellow rice with steamed broccoli."

"Yuck...to the broccoli. I hate broccoli. My parents would worship anyone who got me to eat broccoli," I noted as I continued looking over the menu.

He chuckled. "You can always switch it out for something else."

I looked up from the menu. "The fish tacos with fries sound good. Yeah, I think I'll have that."

"Good. Another one of my favorites. What are you

drinking?"

"Ice tea with lemons."

He got up. "Be right back."

Shortly he was back with a plate of celery and carrots centered with a small beaker of Ranch dip.

"Appetizer," he said and winked. He picked up a piece of celery, dipped it in the sauce, and stared at me before biting a piece off.

I picked up a baby carrot, and I too dipped it in the sauce and took a bite. "Delicious...I love carrots," I said and returned the wink.

"I'm really glad you decided to have lunch with me. It gives me the chance to really get to know you." He glared into my eyes. "You have beautiful eyes. I bet you hear that a lot?"

"Not often...but thanks."

"Well, now that I have you all to myself, tell me, are you from around here? I mean, I can't imagine you being around all this time without me noticing."

"I can say the same to you."

His head tilted back slightly. "Really?"

"Really. I've been here; well, not exactly here, but on the boardwalk lots of times." Of course, it's been a good four years since I was here last. "We have a vacation home up a ways about a quarter mile. And I've never seen you. Not until recently. And yesterday...I was surprised to see you at the volleyball game. Do you hang out there much?"

"I haven't much lately."

"And you didn't for long yesterday. Why did you take off so fast?" I studied his eyes, the muscle movement in his face for truth, or the lack of it, since I couldn't come right out and question him about the waterspout.

"Sorry for leaving without saying hi. But something came up as soon as I got there."

Now that wasn't going to do, so I pressed on. "Did you think I'd be there?"

He didn't come fast with a response. Instead, his absorbed smile pried my soul, my insides felt tensed, like a queen tiptoeing around the edge of a chessboard, wholly vulnerable in a game she knew nothing about.

"I was hoping," he expelled. "Is something bothering you?"

"What?"

"You had a vile look. Did I say something to offend you?"

"No, you're imagining. I'm just wondering what it is you want from me. I don't think our meeting was a coincidence...it's like weird."

"Neither do I," he said, ignoring my last remark.

"Really? So you won't mind telling me why I'm really here...in this situation?"

Cameron grunted, rested his back against the red vinyl, and smiled without actually smiling. "Pia, who do you think I am, really? A maniac? A stalker? And what is 'this situation'?" He bent forward, spread elbows on the table, and continued, nice and easy, "Look, I'm not here to confuse things. I'm here as a friend. I would like to think that's why you're here. I'm grateful we're together, finally, alone. Can you say the same?"

"Alone?" I stiffened a little. I intended to mock him. Or did I? Anyway, I couldn't resist being sarcastic. "I'll say you're the nice guy that ran me down with the skateboard and tried to blame me for it and still you haven't exactly explained what was going on with you. But I was *so* grateful to have met you, just hoping I'd run into you again. Suppose you were grateful then, too?"

He bowed his head. "You're still stuck on that I see. Just what can I do to get us past that? Look, you're here, so there has to be something."

I was here; I could give him that. For now, I decided to change the subject, knowing I couldn't snap my fingers to get him to spill his guts. I had to get my thoughts together.

"So you say you're from around here?"

"Actually, I've been living in the area for about four years now. I live not too far from here with my uncle. And I've been a part-timer here at the café for over a year now. So where are you from?"

"Sugar Land, Texas. It's in the Houston area."

"I've been there a couple times, not to visit, just passing through. How long are you here for?"

"About a week. Spring break." I paused. "You said you've been in the area for about four years, with your uncle?" I was curious about his parents.

"Yeah...well...both my parents are," he smacked his lips, "deceased."

Before I could speak, he raised a finger requesting a moment; our order arrived. In the meantime, I wondered about his emotions, so raw, upon mentioning his parents' death–as if, it had happened recently. The day of the show when he mentioned his mother, he hadn't shown any emotions then. Now I was eager to learn more.

We got prepared to eat by removing napkins from our silverware and covering our laps with them. I spooned mild taco sauce over my tacos before biting off a portion. Cameron put a chunk of broccoli in his mouth; slowly chewing, he looked to have strayed into deep thought but then snapped out of it with a smile.

"How do you like the taco?" he asked.

"It's really good, actually."

"Good," he said curtly.

I wanted to continue the talk about his parents but didn't want to be the one bringing it back up. I didn't want to miss this opportunity of knowing more about them either. We chatted a while about other things until I couldn't prolong the urge of bringing his parents up again.

"So finish telling me. Where are you from?" I nudged kindly.

"Paris, actually. I was born there and lived there until I was five years old. After the age of five, we were back and forth from Europe and the States. You see, my parents were engineers, and they traveled a lot."

"And you managed to not have an accent."

"Well, I do and I don't. I mean it's easy to turn it on and off. For example: It's a splendid day, wouldn't you say?" he spoke in a British accent. "See, on and off, just like that."

"Aah, I like that." I paused to eat a little more taco. Then I proceeded on a more sympathetic tone. "Cameron...I'm sorry to hear about your folks."

"Thanks—but really, it's okay. I always think about my parents." He wiped his mouth with a napkin. "You see, their bodies were never found. Nor was the ship they were on. The ship—and everybody on it—just vanished without a trace."

"What—I mean, how did that happen?"

"That's everybody's question. Have you heard of the

Bermuda Triangle?"

"Well...yes, I think so..." I paused briefly trying recall what it was I knew. What came to mind was a place in Bermuda called Devil's Hole, a sinkhole of rising and falling water where cries echo; some people believe to be cries from Satan. Quickly I shook that out of my head, as I recalled something else. "Oh yeah...about disappearing planes and ships."

"Yeah, that's right. The Bermuda Triangle is one big mystery, has been for quite some time now. You see, my parents are victims of this great mystery.

"You think?" I leaned forward; I was all ears.

"That day, there was a distress call about the engines dying and that they were surrounded by this strange fog with flickering lights. They were about ten miles off the coast of Florida. They were coming back from the Bahamas with friends–they all worked together. But when the coast guard made it out there, they had vanished, just like that; out of nowhere they were completely off the radar."

"That's incredible." Obviously I was stunned, couldn't talk, and couldn't think with my mind going wild. What I could do was drink. I reached for my iced tea, began sipping it through the straw.

Just like that, his parents disappeared, their bodies never found. That's just too strange: mainly because it happened recently, just four years ago, to the dear parents of this person in front of me. And because I wasn't reading about this in some ancient history book about black magic and witchcraft, and other strange phenomena that science helped to unravel. No. I was hearing this straight from the horse's mouth and he wasn't joking.

I ended up sipping a great deal of the tea, almost emptying the cup, before placing it back on the table. Cameron was pretty much finishing what was left on his plate. Quietness hung between us for an unmeasured time. Cameron glared over at me, his mouth gapped open as if he was about to speak, though it took a minute before he did.

"Talking about my parents and the Bermuda Triangle, must come as a shock to you?"

I shrugged. "I suppose so. I wonder about you, what you've been going through, how you've been coping with it. It must've been driving you crazy. I mean, how could it not?"

"You're right, it has been. I started having problems after that. I miss my parents so much. It's almost impossible to forget what happened to them. They're still part of my life. My passion for computers has a lot to do with my parents."

"How so?" I fumbled with my fingers. I was more nervous than I realized.

He covered my nervousness with his hand. "I didn't mean to make you nervous, scare you if that's what you're feeling."

And I was. It was beginning to sink in that we had a lot more in common than I would've imagined. His hallucination, and mine–though I chose not to call it that–and his parents' turning up missing around the same time I did.

"I'm fine, really. I don't know what came over me," I said, knowing fully well that I did. "I really want to hear more about this. To be honest, I find it fascinating. But there must be a logical explanation for what happened?"

"You would think. But nothing made sense. They radioed...They were very concerned about the fog. But that night the sky was clear, and there was nothing in the atmosphere that would have caused foggy conditions.

"All sorts of possibilities floated around. That something from out of space beamed them up, maybe captured by pirates. But they would have to have been clever magicians. The boat was just a few miles from shore when it disappeared from radar. There are theories, scientific ones, but nothing provides any real answers. And I'm not kidding, but there are weirdoes who think the Loch Ness monster swallowed them all including the ship." He shook his head to that.

Thoroughly engrossed, I sat back, itching for more; I couldn't get enough. A strange disappearance happening around the time mine happened–what did it mean? Could somehow both be connected?

"You said this happened about four years ago. Do you remember the date?"

"November 19, 2006. How can I forget?"

Days before I came up missing. But no...how can an incident with a boat have anything to do with what happen to me? I attempted to brush off the possibility of the two somehow being related–but what if...

"You look like you saw a ghost."

The mentioning of "ghost" snapped me out of my mind and back to the person requesting my attention. "No, I'm just fascinated by all this. Did any other strange things happen around that time?"

"No...I don't recall. You know, you really do seem interested in all this. Come home with me. I can show you all the research that I've compiled on my website and other sites on the subject."

"Really, you have a website about all this?"

"I do. This whole mystery about my parents' disappearance really inspired my interest in computers, from repairs to designing web pages. I run a small business from the house."

"That's great, Cameron. But as much as I'd like too, I can't come home with you."

"Remember, I'm at your disposal solely to protect you. I'm your bodyguard, and my uncle is the sheriff."

"Sheriff?" I frowned in disbelief.

"Well, ex-sheriff. He's over the fire department now."

I smiled. "You're incredible, Cameron, really."

"It means a lot you think so. Let me interest you more. Come and let me show off the kind of work I do on the Internet. You can trust me. We are well-known in the community, and you couldn't be in better hands."

"Really?" I was still in disbelief.

"Absolutely."

I faintly shook my head. "I don't know. You have to do some convincing first."

"What do you think I'm trying to do?"

"Okay. How 'bout you explain to me why certain people feel uncomfortable around you."

"Not Elijah," he emphasized. "I admit I've had my share of problems. It's been hard, missing my parents and not knowing what really happened to them. I guess you can say that I've been sick because of it. My sickness made me paranoiac and prone to other things, hallucination for one. I was an emotional wreck after losing my parents.

"But I've never hurt myself or anyone else as far as that goes. I'm a brand-new person compared to how bad off I once was. The bottom line to your question is simple. Because *some people* have a problem understanding what was really going on with me, they labeled me the weird guy. But you don't, Pia. And that makes you special. I know you wouldn't be here now if you didn't want to understand...me. And you don't have to be afraid, I wouldn't hurt you."

"We just met...but then, you think you know me and why I'm here. How is that?"

"It's...it's all in how I perceive you. You're different, Pia...special." He placed my hand between his rather smooth hands and lent a sincere look.

I didn't say anything for a while, studying the structure of his face. And then I traveled through a perfect set of marble eyes that came to still darkness over a sea of lava. Something was there, I was sure of it, only I couldn't see it, could only feel it, a feeling of him holding something back.

He lowered his head a little, maybe to allow me time to digest all that was said, or maybe to break from my stare on him. But he couldn't take my silence any longer apparently because—

"What more can I do to convince you, Pia?" he urged.

Lowering my eyes, I nodded faintly. "Nothing...I'll go with you. But not for long, we have to make it quick." For what it's worth, I had to take the bait and follow my gut feeling. He was hiding something—I was sure of it, so sure that it somehow had to do with all the mystery surrounding me.

"It won't take long, you have my word," Cameron said and quickly excused himself from the table.

I got up and went to the ladies' room while he took care of a few things before leaving. I called Stephanie, but she didn't answer the phone, so I hung up without leaving a message.

I probably have nothing to worry about, I thought, making my decision final.

We left the café shortly after, and as we pulled away in his red GMC pickup, I perceived a little voice. *This is the right thing to do.*

The voice sounded like mine.

Chapter Ten

Mysterious Island

We were at his house in no time. As he got out of the truck and came around to my side, I admired the pictographic two-story house, white with black trimming, palm trees, and a long driveway stretching to a detached garage.

A few doors down, a woman's voice echoed in calling Cameron's name. He quickly turned and waved, calling her Ms. Helen. He then continued opening the door and helped me out. Seeing the curious expression on this petite woman's face, I couldn't help but smile. She was out watering the flowerbed. Cameron didn't hesitate to introduce us. I spoke kindly, feeling very pleased to meet her. I think she gave me a sense of security. She was palpably up in age; her voice alone was sheer proof of that. Yet none of that belied her dazzling charm, her youthful witty spirit that I marveled at the whole time during our chat; then we finally entered the house.

Mmm. I stepped in looking the place over. The place was simple in style, definitely had a woman's touch. The color coordination and patterns, from the wallpaper to select pieces of unmatching furniture, showed that someone had a particular eye for tying things together.

"I love how your aunt decorated the place," I assumed.

"Thank you. We hardly ever use these rooms. We hang out in the den. Uncle pretty much keeps these rooms intact, in memory of his wife, Aunt Michelle."

"Ooh, I'm sorry."

He nodded. "It's been two years now, an aneurysm."

"Your parents, then your aunt. It's a lot to go through in such a short time."

"Yeah." There's a moment of silence.

"So, in what part of the house do you run your business?"

"This way." He led me up a flight of stairs. Before reaching the top, I could see the entire room almost. Roomy with paneled walls, the space was ideal for his line of work. On one end of the room was a queen bed. Next to it was a chiffonier stained with colors of green, yellow, brown, and the top was black, which happened to be the color of the bed. Computers were stacked in a corner close to the stairs; closer to the bed was a computer desk with a hutch, with a few file cabinets in the wing. Everything was neatly situated under the vaulted ceiling, other than a few computers here and there that looked like work in progress. What impressed me though was an oak bookcase loaded with books.

"Have you read all those books?"

"Just about. I enjoy mostly science fiction, mystery, and suspense—anything I find interesting, and the tech books to stay up-to-date."

"Have you ever taken computer classes?"

"Not really. Either I teach myself or I get help from other people who know more than I do. I keep up with computer nerds."

"What about college, have you thought about it?"

"Somehow I knew that would come up," he said, booting up the computer.

"And?"

"And yes, I have."

"And?" I moved closer to him, predicting a "but."

Leaning over the chair, he waited for the login screen to load. With lips folded inside his mouth, he glanced at me, then eyes back on the computer. I waited for him to fill my ears with anything he deemed appropriate.

He turned to me again, snickering.

I crossed my arms and said, "That's okay, I'm not here," then inched toward the bookcase.

"You're even more beautiful when you get uptight." He stood straight up, then came over, and brushed the back of his hand over my cheek.

"Don't do that." My head turned in a swift motion. "What do you think you're doing?"

"Didn't mean to offend you. Sorry." He moved back over to the computer and proceeded online. "Come take a look at this," he urged shortly.

I eased over his shoulder. "Wow. You did this?" The graphic and sound at the website was awesome. It reminded me of a game site, icons urging, *click here,*

here, and *there* to explore endless possibilities. It was just that exciting and unbelievable how one could learn to do something like this on their own.

"It's my latest design. As you can see, my customer sells music and other stuff. Let me show you another one," he said as my phone rang. It was Stephanie calling back.

"Hold up, it's Stephanie." I stepped away for some privacy.

"Hey...just me calling back. Everything's okay?"

"Oh, sure. It's all good," I said mostly for Cameron's ears, still wanting him to think she knew about our meeting. If Stephanie knew where I was and who I was with, the shock in her voice would send Cameron crashing to the wall not knowing what hit him.

She was in the middle of something else, so our conversation was rush-rush. I tucked away my phone afterward and stepped back over to see what he had on the screen now.

"For a long time, I had no desire to go to college. But I never ruled it out." He surprised me. "When I graduated from high school, I needed time to find out who I was and what I wanted out of life, not what everybody else wanted for me. I didn't want to go immediately into another setting where I had to abide by rules and be stressed out with books. I needed to be free of the hassle."

"About your parents, eh?"

"Yup. But lately, it's been different. I mean...working with computers served a purpose, and it's been fun, interesting. Most of all, I've proven to myself that I can do it. But now, it is time for a change."

"College? Or are you talking about teaching yourself something new?"

He smiled. "Let's just say I haven't ruled out college just yet. Hey, check this out."

"Omigod, this too! You're so good at this." This was pretty much my expression for all of the websites he showed me.

After a while, Cameron had grabbed his laptop, suggesting we go downstairs for something cold to drink before looking at sites on the Bermuda Triangle. By now his interests, talent, and ability to ease—my conscience for the moment anyway—made me feel I could snuggle up with him, like having a good book with the perfect storyline that kept you turning the pages for more and more. And there was more to his story, of course. As we drank ice water, he started again by introducing me to his family, by way of photos, beginning with his uncle Michael.

"My, he's a spitting image of my English teacher. He's not a twin, is he?" I asked.

"Not Uncle Mike," he assured, grinning at the thought. Next to that picture was one of him and his late wife, Michelle.

"Uh, she was such a lovely woman, and it's a beautiful picture of them together. He looks younger here."

"He's in his late forties now. This was taken...umm...I want to say five, six years before Aunt Michelle passed."

Then we came to a photo of his parents. I sensed anyway. They were posing in front of a ship, and it was the only one Cameron lifted from the mantel.

"My parents. They really loved traveling, by boat especially. Always going on cruises, whether a daylong cruise, it didn't matter. They loved it so much they should've owned a cruise line. And yeah, I loved it, too." Sadness washed over him once more as he stared at the photo. He mumbled, "Maybe they're still cruising. I wonder sometimes."

"I think I know what you mean," I said softly, as we both gazed at the warm faces in the photo.

"When you don't have all the answers, it's much harder to find closure. There were times I begged the universe to reveal its secrets and take away the pain. That must sound lame," he said.

"Why? Were you hallucinating then?" I asked, recalling what Stephanie had said.

"Not really. That was different."

"Meaning what?" I tried encouraging him to go on.

"Meaning..." A pause. "Meaning I don't want to talk about it. It's not one of my favorite subjects."

"But–"

He shook his head and I let it go. He placed the photo back on the mantle. "Come, have a seat. I have more to show you."

He circled the oversized ottoman strewed with assorted magazines, sports magazines especially, and sat down on a grayish sofa flanked by cherry-wood tables. Cameron grabbed the laptop off the ottoman and placed it on his lap. I settled down next to him as he worked his way back online. Soon we were at the website he'd designed strictly for his own personal interest called MissingParents.com. I thought the name was ingenious and straight to the point.

On the first page of this site, smack in the middle, were pictures of his parents. Instantly the page reminded me of a eulogy though it was much more than that. Cameron made that clear.

"This site is dedicated to my parents' memory and the others that vanished too that night. Here on this site, I've gathered a lot of information about other strange happenings in the Bermuda Triangle, a.k.a. Devil's Triangle. And throughout the page, including here at the bottom"—he scrolled down—"are links to other sites with even more information."

"Gosh. Has that much happened—I mean, is it that strange of a place?"

"You'll be surprised. But not all bad since some lived to tell about it. During my research, I found that the first reporting of this place was in 1492 by Christopher Columbus. Even back then, the Triangle was considered cryptic."

"You're talking about, uh,"—I quickly calculated—"over five hundred years ago."

"I know. Amazing, isn't it? Get a hold of this." He clicked on one of the links, and another page popped up showing a list of reports from other people about strange experiences in the Triangle. We read one story of a plane disappearing into thin air, where dispatchers heard the pilot trying to make contact. Eventually, the pilot's voice faded out and static, sounding like blowing wind, came in its place. There was nothing in the pilot's voice revealing distress. Instantly, the plane disappeared from radar and was never found.

Story after story we read about unexplained incidents that seemed unreal. When Cameron clicked on a link opening to a story about a mysterious island, the phone interrupted. He got up to answer, paced the floor for a second before going into the next room as he talked.

Curious about this story, I began reading on my own. The story began like the others: a clear, perfect day or night. This was one of those perfect-night stories: The ship was about two hundred miles off the coast. Suddenly, something strange appeared on the radarscope, resembling a mass of land that shouldn't have been there. Curious, the crew moved closer to check it out. A half hour later, flares went up from this mass of land. Someone signaling for help, they thought. They sailed even closer, close enough to shine the searchlight on it...

"Hey," said Cameron, looking a bit crestfallen.

"What's going on?"

"Gotta go to work. One of the workers had to leave, and Brent needs me to cover. I told him I'll be there in fifteen minutes. I'm sorry."

"No, that's okay, I understand. Hey, I was just reading this write up about this mysterious place...." I guided his attention to the screen as I picked up where I left off.

...They shined the light on it. As they drew closer, the area around the boat grew darker even the searchlight dimmed. Suddenly the engine started making strange noises and losing pressure. The radar and other controls started going haywire, too. They knew to get out of there immediately. As they did, the engine regained pressure and all the other controls started working gradually. When the radar was back working entirely, it still showed the island there. But not for long, it faded off the radar, as though it had never been there.

I turned my cogitating face to Cameron. "There one minute, gone the next...?"

"I know. It makes you wonder, huh?" Cameron closed the laptop. "I'm going to run this back upstairs. Be back in a sec." He clutched the laptop at his side and took off fleeting up the blanketed stairs, giving each a strong pulse as he climbed.

In the meantime, I went into a pondering trance. How can something like an island be there one minute and not the next? Everyone on the boat had seen it. I wondered did they have trouble with people believing their story because no one believed my sighting of an island. Could be that I was the only one seeing it, which made it insanely complicated. *It's all in your head.* That's what everyone really thought and I was so sick and tired of it. *But someday, somehow, I'll prove them all wrong and they'll–*

"Are you ready?" Cameron snapped me out of it. I didn't hear him come back down. He'd changed into a black T-shirt I noticed.

"That was quick. Yeah, let's go." I got up thinking that something had to give: I just couldn't see my life going on as it was until the end of time.

As he drove up the street, I gave directions to the house from the boardwalk since I didn't know exactly where I was.

"I hate having to end our date like this on short notice," said Cameron. "Maybe we can get together later?"

"I repeat, not a date, but it was interesting. I can't help wondering about that mysterious island. What do you think? Do you really believe the story?"

We came upon a group of people at an intersection (tourists, I suspected) blocking traffic as they crossed the street headed for the beach.

"I admit the story is different from the rest—a place that's not supposed to be there just appears then disappears, just like that, like a submarine in a way."

"You don't believe that story, do you?" I asked.

"Yeah, I guess. I believe they saw what they saw." The road was clear now, and Cameron continued through the intersection.

"Then you would believe just about anything?"

He hesitated, throwing me a quick, puzzling glance, not sure what to take from my remark, I assumed. Then he nodded. "I suppose you're right, Pia. You know, I saw my parents—wait, hold on, let me finish. I saw them at this place by the edge of the water, waving, calling out to me. I'm out in the water, trying my damnedest to get to them. My feet moving, but I wasn't getting anywhere, and I got so frustrated, feverish, burning sweat running down my face—"

"Wait a minute—"

"Just hold up." He demanded. "I honestly believe there's another world or another dimension within our world and wonder about my parents trapped in such a place, somewhere like an island. Well, every time I tried to reach them, I wasn't on a boat, or a raft of any sort, and I certainly wasn't swimming. Believe it or not, I was standing on water. *Three times...three times,* I saw them. The last time something told me to look down, and when I did, I saw the water below me moving like a treadmill. And you know, in a strange way it explained why I could never get to them."

"But that's incredible, unreal. It's like a dream."

"Ha, ha, ha." He turned with a smile. "Yeah, a dream. You really think I walked on water? Now who believes anything?"

"I didn't say I believed it."

"But you thought it was possible. It was all over your face."

Was I that obvious, wanting it to be real? It would've meant I was on the verge of a breakthrough, if what he was telling me was real. *And he made it all up to rattle my brain?*

"So your dreams stopped just like that?" I now asked.

He nodded. "It was the meds the doctor put me on. Haven't had another one since."

"What about when you ha–"

"Never. I never hallucinated anything that elaborate."

"You are second-guessing me, reading my mind?"

"Isn't that what you're thinking?"

"You should've waited to see. Don't pass up the street!"

He slowed down in time to make the right turn, then came to a stop midway the block. He shifted the gear and then stretched his arm over the backside of the seat, torso twisted accordingly. "You know what I want?"

"What?"

"To see you again."

"I don't know. Let me call you."

"Will it be okay if I called you? I might need your take on something important."

"You mean you might need a woman's opinion?" I

didn't bother asking about what.

"Yeah, that works."

"Okay." I opened the door and landed a foot on concrete. "Well, I'll see you when I see you."

"Soon, I'll call you."

I got out, closed the door, and waved as he pulled away.

I started walking, thinking about the island I just read about. *Could it be? No, probably not. But what if...? No, that was then, this is now. The island couldn't possibly be the same one I've been seeing. But...could it be?*

Chapter Eleven

Plans, Plans

Cameron called while I was having dinner at an Italian restaurant with my parents. Lousy timing. I had just put a fat, juicy meatball in my mouth, and my parents were sitting across from me, a perfect setup for eavesdropping. "Who are you talking to?" or "Who was that?" or "What was that all about?" No, answering Cameron's call wasn't a good idea. However, the phone beeped, letting me know a message awaited.

"How was the first day of the convention?" I asked for talk.

"Mmm..." Mom nodded, not able to speak right away with a full mouth.

Dad spoke up, though. "Good. But it got boring toward the end. I couldn't wait to get out of there."

"Can't be getting bored; we have two more days left. Besides, it'll be interesting tomorrow: with another surprising agenda that's always worth the wait," Mom said.

"Yeah. They're good with surprises," Dad replied.

"Can you remember what it was the last time?"

"Honey, that was two years ago." Mom smiled at Dad, then looked over at me. "After the convention we'll be flying to Bermuda," she said. "There's a get-together for your Aunt Iris, celebrating the publication of her cookbook."

"Whoa, we're going *cross dee pond* to party," I said playfully and raised a glass of ice water. "I'm there already."

"Me too." Mom's glass clicked mine. "I can't wait for the tree frogs to put me to sleep." She closed her eyes and exhaled like one stretched out under a parasol and I giggled. To me, Bermuda meant spending precious time with my cousins Regina and Prince; I could stretch out with Mom over that.

As Mom and I rambled on, Dad lightly elbowed Mom's arm. "Sounds like my girls have gone to Bermuda without me." Mom and I laughed, mutedly to not draw attention to our table. But then I got the urge to embellish what Dad started.

"Omigod! Mom, turn this plane around. We forgot Dad."

"Oh no. We can't go back. We're almost there," Mom said, shining a smile on Dad. Speechless, Dad just shook his head, smiling. Mom reached over and landed a kiss on his cheek.

Moments like this with my family, full of joy, I savored the most.

"I'm going for a walk," I yelled to my parents all tucked

away in their room. I figured they were homebound for the rest of the evening; they had another early start in the morning. For me, it was too nice of an evening to be stuck around the house. I had to get up and move and was glad my parents didn't hassle me. "Don't go far" was all I got. Not a hassle at all.

When I got around to calling Cameron back, he was going to a hardware store with a friend. We didn't talk long, and since he was somewhat busy and it was late, we decided to touch bases tomorrow and work out a plan to meet.

I cut through the backyard, down the steps I flew. I couldn't wait to breathe the entire view of the ocean. As I began my stroll, I smiled thinking about Stephanie. I could see her having the time of her life in a rowdy arena resonating with others as they did that thing, rising and falling, section by section, to create a fluid wave in full circle. So much excitement. And here I was surrounded by tranquility. I smiled at the comparison, acknowledging that I was a little jealous. But I had my iPod. I took it out, and the noise from it instantly satisfied me.

The music stimulated me to pick up my pace to a light jog as I observed everything along the way, scuba divers, in particular, plunging into the ocean off a yacht. A young man playing Frisbee with his dog, his smile spoke to me. With the music grounded in my head, I couldn't tell if he said anything. I only smiled back and waved as I did in passing others. Many were out taking advantage of this divine evening. Up ahead was a group of people, about where we played volleyball yesterday. To satisfy my curiosity, I would go that far to see what was going on.

It didn't take long to reach the crowd of people

gathered for another game of volleyball, which I expected beforehand. A few of them I recognized from yesterday's game...good players. I thought about hanging around to see them play but decided not to. So I headed back.

About midway back, music coming from the boat with the scuba divers got my attention again. *They must be partying.* At this point, I settled down on the cool sand and removed the earplugs. Not so I could hear the music coming from the yacht clearly, and I wasn't tired from jogging. It was just time for a break.

I brought my knees together and hugged them, giving my head a firm resting spot. Again, not because I needed a break. At this moment I was feeling frustrated, sick and tired of this creepy thing inside me, bringing me down once again, not knowing after all this time why it was happening. Trying to fight it off, I was no match for stopping it altogether. It's always been that way, but for once, right this instant, I wanted *my good* to defeat *this evil.*

I lifted my head. Seeing nothing weird before me, I sighed then began gazing out at the boat. *How nice it would be to sail far, far away...away from everything,* I thought. I closed my eyes and repositioned my head between the knees, realizing that that wouldn't do me any good. The very thing I wanted to get away from would only follow me. Inside me, now it felt like a slow virus spreading through me, slowly shutting my body down, taking my breath entirely–it could if it wanted to. This rare form of tension, stalking me this very moment could do just about anything.

What is it? My eyes blinked open as I lifted my head. Nothing was in front of me, but as I turned to my right—yeah, to my right it was hazy, but I could make out colors. The yellow top and dark-colored jeans I had on, my face a total blur.

"Go away, leave me alone," I whispered. I wanted to badmouth it. Squinting, I saw another image materializing, of not a thing but a person. Who could that be? I tried to make out. These visions were changing, getting stranger and unpredictable by the day. I strained my eyes to fill in this vague outline of a person. *The ghost.* Suddenly a flash in my head, of a ghost turning my parents to stone then whisking me away, only to take me on a play date, I sensed this. And I sensed it didn't mean to hurt me or make me suffer all this time.

I sniffed, blinked my watery strained eyes, and lowered my head to my knees. *It'll be over soon. Soon it'll be over,* I repeated quietly, and then I found myself wanting to grab another peep at the image. Or did I just want to find it gone already? Regardless, I had to turn back to it. And it was still there, yet the fuzziness, going away. I started to feel better as it did, my vision glued to it. Gradually coming to focus was—I couldn't believe it—Cameron?

"Cameron?" I called out.

"Ah, look at the lovebirds," someone said.

I swirled around, came face-to-face with a young couple, holding hands and smiling directly at me and at—I turned quickly—at Cameron. It was really him, in the flesh, right before my eyes. Our eyes locked as he inched forth and kneeled down beside me.

"Where...where did you come from?" I studied his muddled expression as I waited for a response.

"'*Come from*?' Pia, what's going on?" He smoothed

his fingers over the ridge of my chin.

The young couple's whispers and giggles distracted me again. They were watching us, smiling. Maybe because they thought we were having a romantic moment, a time made in heaven. They couldn't be further from the truth, although there was no mistaking the aura of love-butterflies hanging around them.

"What do you mean 'what's going on with me'?" I probably looked like I had seen a ghost, and sounded disgusted, but I didn't mean to.

"Well, look at you...obviously something is going on with you. What is it?" He crooked his neck some; had sympathy all in his face. "I have this strange feeling that I...cannot explain. Is there anything you want to talk about? I'm here, would love to lend an ear; that's if you can trust me. You know already I'm in no position to judge anyone."

The breeze fluffed the fabrics of his still frame as he waited for me to say something–anything that would appease the curiosity written all over his face. But I was trying to figure out whether it was he I saw in the illusion right before he appeared. It seemed weird that he showed up when he did, insisting that I had something crucial to talk about and should fess up–now. I couldn't bring myself to just be surprised to see him. Under the circumstances, I was highly suspicious.

"So you're saying this strange feeling you have has to do with *me,* and you want me to–what?–explain this feeling you're having?" I blew a torch, I supposed.

He turned, stopped for a moment to think.

"See, I'm fine, just surprised to see you. What more do you want from me?" I then added, "What is this really about?"

"Can't explain it. Was hoping that you could. It looks to me that something spooked you."

His eyes narrowed then, looked as if they were begging me to tell my most precious secrets. My eyes returned a hard stare. He should feel me wanting the exact same thing from him. It was time to come clean and reveal the mystery that brought us together once and for all.

"Cameron, what is it–what's on your mind?" I spoke gently now to the same bothersome look he wore on his face the day we met. "Tell me," I pleaded.

He flattened his bottom on the ground, elbows propping his upper body, and he just stared off into space. "The sky is beautiful," he voiced.

Ignoring me? I couldn't believe it. I adjusted to a more comfortable position myself and waited for him to stop staring at the sky and see that I had no interest in how beautiful it was. One thing for sure, he was good at disconnecting and shutting down cold, therefore, good at pissing me off. And I had to remind myself why I was putting up with this bull. Eventually, I took my eyes off him and gazed out into the ocean. The whole picture was beautiful, no doubt about that. Though to the south, the sky was ominous. A storm was moving in.

"Do you believe in ghosts?" I asked, still gazing off into the water. "They walk the earth. Do you think they walk on water, too? Maybe even dive in to cool off, take a long refreshing swim? Mmm." I took a breath then released it quickly. "Can you imagine them going as far as the ocean floor, walking it? I wonder why some seem not bothered by us while others haunt us and scare us out of house and home, try to hurt us even. I saw a ghost once." I turned to him now. "I want to know: do you believe in ghosts and all that creepy stuff?"

He stayed still, continued to ignore me. Until finally, his stillness came alive with a heavy sigh. "Here, all around us are all sorts of possibilities of the universe. All that you can imagine in another world is here in this world. It's to say that I firmly believe everything isn't what it seems and that anything is possible."

I rolled my eyes and fired, "You know you can be quite stubborn at times. And I'm sure you've been told *that* before."

"What? You didn't like what I said? Look, Pia. I don't mean to blow your top, get you all upset. And I'm not this weirdo you may think I am. Am I being rude—what?"

"*Duh.* You're annoying and obnoxious and you know it. Look how long it took you to open your mouth. Was it that hard?" I thought I saw a hint of pleasure in his eyes at how I blew my temper.

"I suppose I'm not an easy person to get to know. But I promise, once you really get to know me, you'll come to appreciate me more."

"I'm trying to understand you now," I said, thinking I didn't have time to get deep.

"I know. And, Pia, I truly, truly like you, a whole lot..." He pressed his lips together. "More than I can say. I mean, whatever this is between us, has to be fate."

"Fate? What are you talking about?"

"Well, let's see if I can explain." He propped his body to one side. "Say I'm wandering around, uh...in a maze. And I think I'm the only one trapped until I come across you. The two of us stick together because we both realize that we have—let's just say *a common goal*, if you will. And this common goal is to find our way out. And while we're trying to find our way out, we get to know each other. You see, right now we are still in this maze, and we're sticking together to the end until we find our way through it."

"So we find our way out, then what?"

"Then...then it'd be good we made it through a difficult time. And we'll be happy. It's what I feel: fate."

"Mmm. Interesting. This maze, how do you see it? Draw it for me right here in the sand."

He smiled. "No problem."

With his finger, he drew a square. Then he drew intersecting lines at various lengths inside the square. He pointed to one of the longest lines touching the square and said that it was the exit.

"Some maze," I said, "not very complicated."

"Well, I don't want 'getting to know each other' to be complicated."

"I don't get it. You looked so happy the first day we met. How do you think you got trapped in this maze?" I questioned.

"Like I said before, I can't explain it."

I nodded faintly. "And the way you see it, we're still in this maze?"

"Yeah, it's only the beginning. As I said, we're still finding our way through. Our coming together was fate," he repeated, sounding assured of himself.

"Well, I wish you could tell me why. Why don't you get this thing call fate to shed a little light on that for us?"

"Mmm. I suppose in time it will."

"Yeah, hope it does soon," I said as another thought came to mind. "Hey, what are you doing here anyway? You were supposed to be doing whatever with a friend."

"I wanted to see you."

"Wait a minute. How did you know I would be here? I didn't tell you I was going to the beach."

"Yes, you did. You don't remember?"

"No...because I didn't say anything to you. It wasn't until after I got off the phone with you that I decided to take a walk."

"Then how did I know, hum? You think I'm psychic or something?"

He was mocking me again, trying to make me look like a fool, but I knew what I knew: I didn't tell him. "Could be that you are, or something," I growled.

A brief silence hung between us. Then he got up, reached for my hand, and pulled me up. "We better head back. That storm headed this way looks mean." We started walking. "Let's just say I assumed you would be here and came, hoping to find you. Was it wrong for me to show up?"

"Why didn't you call first?"

"Because we agreed to talk tomorrow, and I was just following a hunch."

I locked my arms. "A hunch, huh?"

"Look, it's all I've got. I have nothing else to offer."

I rolled my eyes. "So just take it or leave it? That's what you're telling me?"

"Okay. What do you want me to say, that I'm a psychic? All right, I'm a psychic. Does that make you feel better?" He was doing that again, mocking me, trying to make me feel ridiculous.

I studied him; we studied each other actually, as we treaded along. I turned away slightly, then turned back and said, "I suppose that'd do for now."

He bobbed his head wearing a half smile. "So tell me something I don't know about you, if you don't mind?"

"Sure. Like what exactly?"

"Well, what things interest you?"

"Um...I like the classic stuff: shopping, movies, tennis, reading, writing, a variety of music." I smiled a dull smile. "The Classic."

"All right, '*the classic*.' So how old are you?"

"Probably too young for a nineteen-year-old. Does it really matter?"

"Whoa...now you can't be that young." His brows furrowed together. "Fourteen, fifteen?"

"Nah, not that young. Sixteen. You did all that talk about us in the maze, my parents would consider me way too young for you."

"Sweet sixteen." His smile grew. "Yes, your parents probably would. But for me, it's not an issue. Because I'm only hoping for something that will last forever. Like friendship. I can see us way into the future, looking back on this day and toasting to it with a real drink." He then sniggered, and I couldn't help smiling.

"What? Wisdom at nineteen? You are such an optimist. So this is a prelude to the Cameron I'd get to know, huh?"

He slowed down. "You like?"

"Well...it's getting better, and it's definitely an improvement from that first day we met for sure."

He tightened his jaws. "I'm sure you've been told

this many times, but it's interesting how your entire body moves. Kinda like your whole frame is made of Jell-O. Ahem, hope you like Jell-O."

I shook my head. "Yeah, I do. Interesting choice of words, though. It seems today that you're full of it."

"Yeah. Now that I think about it, it seems I was describing you as *wobbly*, and that's not what I meant at all."

"That's okay, I know what you meant. I've been complimented on my walk before. Someone once said I have a free-flowing spirit in my bones that reflects in my movement."

"Exactly! Now why couldn't I come up with something like that?"

I laughed. "That person was my mom. She has a way with words."

"Mmm, that she does." He nodded and we both grinned. A brief silence followed.

"Get a hold of the clouds. The storm's coming fast," he said. As we looked off into the angry sky approaching, dark and with capillaries of lightning striking through it, the air felt more saturated, and the breeze was growing stiffer.

"How 'bout we plan something for tomorrow? In the morning I have to go to Miami to see my cousin. Business. Maybe you can ride with me, and I'll show you places I like to hang out at. Maybe we can have lunch, see a movie—whatever you like."

"All the way to Miami? Oh, I don't know. What time are you talking about anyway?"

"About ten. Come on, Miami isn't that far, about twenty minutes from here. Let me pick you up?"

I folded my arms, played with my lips. "I don't know, Cameron. I probably shouldn't—I shouldn't, no." This wasn't going the way I had expected; I was really starting to like him. And I thought, in a charming way, he was fogging up my mind with this friendship stuff when all I wanted to do was get to the bottom of why he was so interested in me. I thought his concept about the maze was a muddled way of confessing that we had a secret connection and that he had the answers I was seeking. And that in due time, fate would allow him to hand them over to me. Something like that anyway.

Fate. I wondered what would become of it.

"Oh c'mon. I would love the company, and if you like, we can come straight back after I finish my business with my cousin, which shouldn't take long. Look, I'm won't push you into making a decision, but will you at least think about it?" He asked as we both acknowledged the drizzle by brushing our arms.

"Yeah, I can do that," I supposed.

"Good. You can let me know whatever you decide right before I get on the road in the morning. I'll call you, say, around nine, nine-thirty?"

"Okay."

He took my hand and cuddled it. "And don't worry, you'll be in good hands with me," he declared.

"You're not parked too far are you?"

"No, not too far."

"Well, you better hurry." I stopped at the path leading up to the house. "Here's where I get off."

"Okay," he said, grabbing my head only to land a quick kiss on my forehead. Then he headed off in a sideways manner, waving. "I'll call you in the morning,

Pia."

"Sure...in the morning," I yelled after him, waving back.

I headed up the sandy slope. It wasn't clear to me now, but I felt the mystery unraveling right before my eyes, and that all I needed was time to see this thing for what it was. To see the whole picture.

Chapter Twelve

To Miami

I vaguely remembered my parents moving around the house this morning. Surely it wasn't a dream. To prove it, there should be grits, sausage and eggs in the microwave waiting just for me.

On that note, I rose and checked my cellphone for the time. It was 8:30 (early still). I hopped out of bed. The thought of instant breakfast just a microwave away had my appetite screaming.

There was a note affixed to the oven: *Thanks for being such a good sport through all of this. Love you.* It was Mom's handwriting. I opened the microwave, and there's breakfast. After warming it up, I placed it on the table with a glass of milk. I sat and ate, chugging down milk bite after bite until the plate was empty.

With breakfast out of the way, I mulled over past events—my first meeting with Cameron, *Cameron, Cameron,* and everything that happened that seemed connected to him, not to mention that ghost. Who was that ghost? Who was Cameron? He held the key to something vital I just knew it. And when—if that was in his plan—was he going to tell me? When we find our way out of that so-called maze? Which shouldn't be long: that maze didn't look complicated to find your way out of.

My cellphone rang and I rushed to answer. Cameron, more likely it was. The ringing had stopped before I got to it. I saw that it wasn't Cameron after all but Stephanie, and there was a text message from my best friend back home. She'd finally returned my text from last night. Quickly I read it and giggled lightly. *A gamble to the end* and so on, she messaged. It was an inside joke. *Our* inside joke. I texted her back immediately, then returned Stephanie's call.

First thing first, "Hey how was the game yesterday?"

"It was the best exhilaration ever..." she started, going on and on. Miami Heat won, and she wished I could've been there, and I happened to mention my jealousy while walking alone on the beach and she pretended to weep for me. Our conversation ended with plans of going waterskiing later today, something I enjoyed doing a lot. She had things to do, including a doctor's appointment around noon.

I went straight to the bathroom, grabbed my toothbrush to start the process of getting ready. The phone rang while I was in the middle of brushing. I spat out a full mouth of toothpaste to catch the call.

"Hey, good morning." Cameron this time.

"Good morning."

"My morning would be better if you'd ride with me to Miami." He sounded romantic.

"Again, how long you think you'd be?"

"Til about one thirty. Maybe not that long. Like I

said yesterday, I'm going on business, then I would like to show you around."

"Yeah, well, maybe we should shoot for one o'clock getting back. So when can I expect you? I mean..." I hadn't decided where to have him meet me. Where he dropped me off maybe? No...the bank parking lot.

"What?"

"Nothing, nothing. I'll be waiting."

"Waiting where?"

"Yeah right. There's a bank over from where you dropped me off. Meet me there in the parking lot. Give me about thirty minutes?"

"Sure, I'll be there," he said.

For a minute there, I had second thoughts about going. All the way to Miami? I didn't want to pass up the opportunity but was struggling with guilt; I was about to break my parents' rules big time. But what they didn't know wouldn't hurt; this thing—or Cameron—was irresistible.

I placed the phone on the bureau, closed my eyes, and said a brief prayer for all to go well. Because at the end of the day—or end of guilt—I knew what I was about to do was exactly what I wanted to do. With no one around to stop me, I put my trust in the hands of fate.

Cameron was already waiting in the bank's parking lot when I arrived. I opened the door of the red pickup, got in, and said, "Hi."

"Wow. You look nice. That color really becomes you." I was wearing a mustard-green blouse, ruffles along the front, and blue jean shorts.

"Thanks." I pulled the seat belt across me and clicked it.

"Mmm. Whatever you're wearing smells magnificent, too."

"I'm testing some of Mom's cologne. It's called Angel. So you really like it?"

He bent for a closer sniff of the scent. "Oh yeah. It passes the test all right."

I smiled. "You don't look so bad yourself." And he didn't, wearing a crisp short-sleeve, white shirt, and jeans with stiff creases. Starched jeans? Now you don't see that often. Blushing, I wondered was it all to impress me.

"Thanks." He sounded pleased enough. From the corner of my eye, I could see him smiling as he yanked the gearshift to drive. In seconds, we merged into traffic.

"So what grade are you in, tenth, eleventh?"

"Eleventh. One more year left. One very long year."

"It'll fly by before you know it. Time is like that."

"Time flies, but eagerness slows it down."

"What got you so eager?"

"I don't know. Well, just to get it out of the way and be done with it." *To be done so I can start fresh at a new school, in a new environment, with new people.* Mostly a new outlook on life and peace of mind I looked forward to; if at all that was optional under the circumstances. I suppose I was looking forward to a new outlook on life and peace of mind; if this was optional under the circumstances. I wasn't sure what would become of my life.

"I'll start college after I graduate to get the prerequisites out the way. I'm not sure on a career yet." I paused. "Getting the requirements out of the way won't hurt, you know?" I hinted.

His lips formed a thin line. He caught the hint. "You

have a boyfriend?" he asked.

My first thought was not to get on this subject but..."Boyfriends, yes, sure. Aren't you kinda like a boyfriend?" I danced around the question instead.

"I am? Uh, yeah, but c'mon...you know what I mean. You're trying to mess with my head?"

"Not nice, is it? Since being around you, I've picked up on bad habits not common with me." I looked into his eyes. "And you got it bad, ignoring me when I'm talking to you."

"Okay, okay. Suppose I need to work on that. Now can I get an answer?"

"No...not really," I answered.

"I don't believe you. Are you serious?"

"I'm just like you. You don't have a girlfriend, right? Ah, wait a minute–I don't believe you," I continued to play around.

"Fine...you have boyfriends. Are you going with anyone? Can I get a straight answer to that?"

"Since we're on the subject, let's hear about your exes."

"I guess not," he said with a look of annoyance and disappointment. "You don't really want to talk about my exes, do you?"

"Well, not if you don't want to," I said.

"Have it your way, Pia. Just so you know, I'm satisfied with my current situation. I have no need for a threesome." He winked.

"A threesome." I chuckled. "Whatever."

We switched the topic, talking about sibling; neither of us had one turns out. I had suspected that. He hadn't mentioned one prior nor did he show a picture of a sibling. Perhaps he assumed as much about me. As we talked, I devoted attention to the beautiful scenery: the trees, the small lakes scattered here and there, and the fabulous buildings jutting out like kings and queens of the land.

"It really means a lot that you decided to come. It shows trust."

"So far so good," I remarked, and he just smiled.

"You said one of the things you like is writing. You write poetry?"

"Not exactly, but I manage to write a few lines once in a while without really trying. I surprise myself sometimes. But I keep a journal to keep up with things happening daily. It's better, at times, to release your thoughts on paper than out loud."

"Really...a diary? Will you allow me a sneak peek? There must be a few lines in there about me," he teased devilishly.

"You're practically salivating, Cameron, stop it. No way are you getting your hands on all that juicy stuff I've written," I teased back. "And your name's not on a single page." Of course, I lied to burst his bubble and to deviate from the subject.

He frowned curiously and mumbled, "How did you manage to not write about me in your diary? Did you miss a few days?"

"Excuse me?" I pretended to not hear.

"Uh, forget it," he said tersely. We both then hushed and looked straight ahead. We were going through an area that reminded me of a country town with buildings close to the sidewalk, or street, linked together, and people were hanging out.

"You know"—we turned to each other simultaneously—"I had a dream about you last night," he said.

My mouth had gapped open before I realized it.

"Are you surprised?"

"Ah, yeah. We hardly know each other."

"Yeah, I know. But the dream I had was awfully weird. You were wearing the same thing you had on yesterday, earplugs in your ears. It was clear in the dream we didn't know each other; we smiled at each other and kept going. For whatever reason, I turned around. Maybe to check you out," he said jokingly, but then became dour as he continued. "When I turned, something horrified me, and there was this strong force of wind coming from somewhere. And as horrified as I looked, or was, I was trying to run against this force. My cheeks were fluttering, face caving in. And then, that was it, that was all of the dream." He glanced at me. "Weird, huh?"

"But what did you see that horrified you?"

"That's just it. I didn't see what it was. That's how weird it was."

"Then what do you think it means? Did you go to bed with something heavy on your mind?"

"Nothing."

"Do you have dreams like that often?"

"Nope. No nightmares for a while now."

"I suppose you had a lot of them after your parents...?"

He nodded. "I had more than my share."

The bus scene instantly popped into my head and showed on my face.

"What's wrong?" Cameron wondered.

I looked to him, unveiling curiosity. “Can you imagine time standing still?”

His dark eyes sparkled. “Have you ever seen time move…really move?”

“You know what I mean—with us in it, as still as death or statues?”

“I don’t know how you come up with this stuff, but if that happens, it would really be something.”

“Exactly…‘really something,’” I said and just dropped the subject.

“We don’t have that much farther to go,” he said after a while.

“You must be reading my mind: I was just thinking that.” My view took to the road again. “This area looks familiar. Like that building ahead.” A two-story, quaint building, huge front windows, magnificent trees around it, even looked like a stone dolphin, a black one, on the lawn. “I think my parents have taken this route before.”

“Probably so. A1A runs a good ways along the coast. It’s the Scenic Route.”

I shifted to a more comfortable position, resting my elbow on the console. Might as well relax and be content regardless of my failure so far to get him to talk. I hoped time didn’t run out on me. Besides, he was tolerable, likable even. It appeared he was really rubbing off on me.

As we got closer to Miami, Cameron pointed out certain landmarks, telling a short story about each. When we came to Diplomat Landing, I suddenly recognized the crosswalk running over the two-lane street we were on that linked two buildings together. The street had a median, decorated with various shrubs and flowery orange trees. In this block were chromatic-type buildings, of equal stories for the most part. We came upon another road curving overhead and a train flew across it, startling me.

"It's the Metrorail?" Cameron said.

"Yeah, I know...I just forgot about it."

He smiled. "It really startled you," he said in a dainty British accent. Then his cellphone came to life in a cartoonish melody. I thought it was cute in a macho way.

As soon as Cameron put the phone down, he hit the right blinker and looked through the rearview mirror. When there was an opening, he veered into the right lane. Sensing something had changed, I looked for him to comment.

But out of the blue, I got an image of him, which diverted my mind completely.

"Do you skateboard often?" He was merging onto the expressway now. Seeming to welcome the topic, he smiled.

"Yeah, I do often enough. It's interesting you asked."

"Ooh?"

"Yeah. Wave Skatepark...here in Miami...just happen to be one of my favorite spots I plan to show you. You will love this place. Have you ever skateboarded?" he asked as his phone began ringing again. "Uh." His finger requested a pause as he glanced at the caller ID. He then apologized for having to take the call.

By the conversation, he obviously was talking to one of his friends. Perhaps one of the guys he was with the day we met: Anthony. He mentioned the name just now. The conversation went on, much longer than he expected, based on how he contorted his face at me. It appeared serious somewhat though I couldn't really tell from the "Oh my Gods" and "Are you serious "

I looked out the window to distance myself from his conversation somewhat, taking in more of Miami's breathtaking and not-so-breathtaking scenery. The trees especially. Compared to Florida, Houston has hardly any trees, I thought. If only I could take some back home with me. Of course trying to put my mind on the scenery didn't work. Cameron's phone conversation was too distracting. More verbal expressions of "You got to be kidding me" and "Then what..." spilled from his lips into my ears. I was involuntarily in this conversation wondering what the heck was going on and waiting for something else to roll off Cameron's lips to give me a clue.

"Whew," he said after the call ended a short time later. He was quick in telling me that his friend had sprung an ankle and won a $500 prize doing it. He then apologized profoundly, promising not to answer another call. "It was okay, really," I said. It was after all.

About ten minutes later, we were following signs to Kensington-Dade Airport. As we entered airport property, our moment of silence ended.

"The airport?" I asked.

"I guess today is full of surprises, eh?" He was referring to the conversation he'd had with his friend.

"More like a disaster," I replied.

"Ah...but a good disaster. I didn't plan this, though. I forgot to mention: the first call I got was from my cousin, asking me to meet him here instead...at Hertz Aviation." The sign was visible as we entered. "So we're not exactly going to the airport," he clarified.

"Technically, it's still airport property," I corrected.

"Yeah, if you want to be technical," he expelled, looking off in a distance. "I wonder what the fire trucks are doing here."

I followed his gaze across a vast area, noticing many T-hangars and larger hangars and a few planes coned off, and I wondered as well what was going on. There was no smoke, but it was wet.

He proceeded to park directly in front of one of the small buildings. "Well, he should be in there. Come on, this shouldn't take long."

As soon as we walked through glass doors, a young man about Cameron's height and build, in a tailor-made uniform, his name calligraphically stitched on the shirt pocket, was standing behind a desk on the phone. He smiled and beckoned us to come closer. Naturally, I assumed this person was his cousin.

The building was bright with lights and few windows. To the left was a small area for lounging. Along the wall was a cabinet with a full coffee pot and a microwave on top, and a little frig tucked perfectly between cabinets underneath. To the right were more seats, and a few cubicles partitioned through the back of the building.

"Hey, who is this you got with you?" he asked, hanging up the phone.

"This is Pia." Cameron presented me with his hands.

"Well, hi Pia. I'm Brian." He offered a handshake, and I casually accepted. "It's nice to meet you."

"It's a pleasure to meet you," I responded graciously and tied my hands behind me.

"I hope it wasn't too much of a bother for you to come this way instead?" Brian said.

"Nah, don't worry about. It's okay. Say, what happened over there? I noticed the fire trucks."

"There was a fire in one of the hangars. But it's nothing to worry about. It's under control now."

"That's good," said Cameron. "Well, we don't want to keep you. I'll just get the computer and we'll be on our way."

"Don't rush on my account. I'm waiting for the instructor to get here." He glanced at the clock on the wall. "In about twenty minutes...he's running behind."

"So are you training today?" Cameron asked.

"Uh...not today." Brian sounded uncertain.

Bubbling inside, I had to ask, "What exactly do you do here?"

"I'm a technician. I mostly inspect parts of the aircrafts."

"Wow, that's great. I have an interest in aviation...well, sort of." I faced Cameron after this admission, letting him know too since this was his first time hearing it. At the moment, I was curious, impressed even, by Brian having a position with an aviation company. He appeared awfully young.

"Really? I think it's great you have an interest. Maybe you'd like me to show you around?" Not quite the response I expected, and from the look on Cameron's face, neither did he.

"I don't think so, not today anyway," Cameron passed.

And I chimed in, "Yeah, he's right, maybe some other time." I wasn't even sure about that given I had just met them both and was just here visiting.

Cameron then turned to me. "Why didn't you tell

me you were interested in aviation?"

"I don't know. I guess it just didn't come up," I spoke in a low tone.

"Yeah, or maybe you just neglected to say, *big time.*"

I supposed I could've mentioned it when he asked what I liked to do. Or even what I wanted to do after I graduated. Maybe he thought that was the appropriate time to mention it. I still say it just didn't come up, so maybe it had not been the right time then.

"*Wait a minute,*" Brian stopped us from being too carried away in our discussion. "How long have you two known each other?" he asked, adjusting his cap.

We faced him and spoke simultaneously. "A few days."

Brian gave us an awkward look, shook his head slightly as he stepped back behind the desk to answer the phone. I could only imagine what he was thinking.

"You know, you're so secretive. You don't tell me anything unless I ask. I mean, you could've told me you were coming to see your cousin at the airport," I growled whisperingly.

"You mean to tell me that all of a sudden you're upset about a last minute change that shouldn't matter at all? You knew I was meeting with my cousin, so here we are," he growled back.

"Still, I have to press to get anything out of you. You keep things from me. And I know you're holding back on something crucial–you're not fooling me," I said this knowing I was reacting from a place that he probably knew nothing about. But if it came down to it, I would bet my life that my instinct about him was dead on.

He snapped back. "I'm not having this round with

you in front of—" He hiked his thumb in Brian's direction.

"Is that what we're having?"

With squinty eyes, he gave a stiff nod. "Not now."

I opened my mouth to speak but—

"Not here!" He stopped me cold, reminding me of Dad.

I then nudged his arm with my shoulder and grimaced.

Brian hung up the phone and attempted to pick up where we'd left off. "Soo...only a few days, huh?"

"Yeah, that's right," Cameron said but then quickly changed the subject. "Look, we're going to get out of here. I want to show Pia around while I can. So if I can get the computer, we will be on our way."

"Yeah, sure." Brian came around the desk. "It's out in the truck."

"In the truck! Do you want to finish it off? Leaving the computer out in the car is like leaving a defenseless child in a heat chamber." It sounded like Cameron was kidding, chuckling, but he probably wasn't. "You better hurry like someone's life depends on it," he went on. We all laughed as Brian brushed past us to open the door, Cameron and I right behind him.

Cameron started up the truck and turned on the air-conditioner while I waited inside the truck; he stood against it waiting for Brian. He was back with the laptop in a flash, and they talked briefly before diverging.

"Hey, it was nice meeting you, Pia." Brain waved, headed back inside, and I said it was nice meeting him as I waved back.

Cameron placed the computer behind his seat after getting in, and then we were on our way.

Chapter Thirteen

Confusions

"You really surprised me back there. But of course you already know that. So how long you been interested in aviation?"

"For a while, I suppose. And it's not like I intended to keep it from you."

"So what inspires you?"

"Well, my parents. They both are pilots." In my peripheral vision, I saw his bottom lip drop low, and I faced him. "Don't think that, Cam. And by the way, we have a plane too...named after me."

"A plane named after you, really! That's huge, Pia. And you want to chastise me for keeping a tight lip?"

"It's kinda like how you didn't bother telling me until the last minute that we were going to the airport to see your cousin, who happens to work with planes. I mean, you probably would've just gone in, had a little chat with him, got the computer, and left."

"But you don't know that because you didn't give

me a chance to tell you."

"That's my point: You didn't give me the opportunity to tell you–and you know that. Gosh, you act like we're married." I could feel steam on my face now.

We settled down as though we were two people miles apart as we brooded about our disagreement internally. For what it's worth, I was determined to stay true to my stance. And this stubborn standoff between us went on for a while. From my peripheral holding a tight lip, not once did I see him look my way. To be honest, I couldn't believe we had come to this point, like longtime couples feuding. He didn't have any claims to me; we hardly knew each other. This was ridiculous and it was time to put a stop to this kind of treatment. Hoping he'd agreed to break the ice by meeting me halfway, I turned, stared at him for few seconds before turning away, furious. He wouldn't let up on giving me the cold-shoulder treatment.

"Just how long do you plan to keep this up?" I demanded.

"Keep what up?"

"Nothing! Forget it."

"Look, I told you about my parents because I wanted you to understand and trust me. I took you to my house to make you feel comfortable. Learning about you and your parents like that was like a slap in the face."

"Mmm. I didn't know you bruise so easily," I retorted, and he chose to ignore me a while longer.

"Brian didn't mention it, but he's also a pilot," he said finally.

I gawked though I shouldn't have been surprised.

"Yeah, that's right. He studied aviation to do what

he's doing now, then afterward decided to go for his pilot license. Now he's training to be an instructor."

"So that's why you asked if he was training today? It crossed my mind then that he might be a pilot. I can't get over how young he looks."

"He just turned twenty-six actually."

"I repeat: *young*. You two look to be the same age."

"I'm sure he would appreciate the compliment."

"Dad learned to fly in the air force. He taught Mom. She seldom flies, though. She teaches English full-time."

"A teacher and a pilot, that's great. That explains your interest, but not as a career choice...why?"

"I don't know. Maybe because Dad can teach me all I need to know about flying. He has given me lessons already. And I've studied the manuals and the simulations. They feel so much like the real thing. In a way, I have my wings. My next step is to really get them by flying a plane–and I will. "Your career should be something you love but"–*but this weird condition I have prevents me from doing what I love*–"let's just say I won't rule it out just yet," I finished.

"Sounds familiar," he said. He then took my hand and held it. "I like this...talking about things that matter to us."

Nodding, I reflected on us trapped in that maze he spoke of again, wondering how much longer before we found our way out.

Kneading my hand with his thumb, he said, "Promise me if there's anything I can help you with, or if you need someone to talk to, you'd think of me. Because I'm your friend, Pia, for however long you will have me. Just because we'll be hundreds of miles apart won't change a thing...technology...I'll be a click or a phone call away."

His expression had a gentle sense of sincerity that I couldn't accept at face value.

"Tell me. Why do I feel there's something going on with you that you're not telling me?"

He came to a gradual stop at a red light, lifted my hand, and smoothed it over his soft cheek–my mind screaming, *Why?*

"Have you ever wished that you could share something significant without doubting whether or not you're doing the right thing for fear of being prejudged?"

"Yes, don't we all?" I was even more confused now.

"Then you know how important it is to have that one person there for you no matter what...always in you corner. Kinda like looking into a mirror and seeing that person's reflection."

Weird. And the profound look on his face was weird, too. "Yeah...I suppose. But what does that have to do with anything–you think I'd judge you?"

"Mnh," he shook his head, "never mind." He was trying to cast it off as if it didn't matter after all. But I wouldn't let it fly that easy.

"Wait a minute. You wish to look in the mirror and see me instead?" I paraphrased.

He chuckled. "Sounds like another bad analogy to me. I really need to take a page out of your mother's book." Sweeping my question under the rug, he dodged answering me again.

"You have to know that you stand a chance of ruining things for us." I paused, pressing my lips together. "I don't know. Maybe seeing you in the mirror won't be so bad. Because I know something's going on with you and you need someone to confide in. I can be that person. What's going on with you, it's not all about your parents, is it? Is...what's bothering you...have to do with me?"

"You're trying really hard, but I know we'll get there," he said calmly. "Because I'm attracted to you, more than you can imagine." He looked me in the eyes and said no more.

Suddenly he hit the gas pedal to beat a changing light, and then, when a car ahead put on its blinker, he swiftly changed lanes, passed that car then jumped in front of it. Embracing my body, my eyes stayed glued to the road until he was finally satisfied with his position in traffic.

Did he suddenly get an adrenaline rush? It didn't take much to aggravate him, but I didn't see the urgency for that move.

"Oh, I get it. You were trying to scare me," I said bitterly.

"No." He flatly denied it.

"You know, you really know how to get a person's attention by the odd way you communicate, then you turn around and pull a stunt like that. What are you doing, playing a trick on me, maybe screwing with my head with these ridiculous mind games?"

The smile on his face melted away. "No tricks or mind games here. But I understand. If I were you, I would probably think that about me."

"Yeah right." I turned away frustrated. He was too good at driving me to a dead end. So for the rest of the way to the skate park, we rode in quietude.

Later he pulled into a sizable parking lot outside a red-bricked building. He shut off the engine. "Well, this is it: Wave Skatepark." He cracked the door, and I was about to do the same when he ordered me to "hold up." Not knowing what was going on, he proceeded around the truck to my side then opened my door. "Just so you know, chivalry is alive and kicking," he said, wearing a proud grin.

I grimaced. He's a die-hard act to follow, I thought—meaning, he was unpredictable, complex, and full of surprises. I swung my legs around and landed feet on the ground, as he reached for my hand. "Thanks," I accepted.

He shoved the door close then slid a hand in his pocket. He assumed a handsomely sane facial expression that promptly accessorized his attire. As we proceeded toward the entrance, my hand hung in his clutch. Upon entering the building, I was amazed how much larger it was on the inside than it appeared on the outside. And even before entering the area where all the action was, through huge windows, you could see how the building situated right below the expressway, cars flying by. And the walls at the entrance had all kinds of posters associated with the sport. And off the way was a store with all the goodies a skateboarder would ever need, I assumed.

As soon as we opened one of the heavy steel doors to enter the park itself, the sound of thunder emerged. There were two viewing levels in this area, with wide open space from top to bottom. We entered on the second level, and I could see right off that mostly standing room was left. I was so amazed, given that this was my first time ever at a skate park, and the ones I've seen in movies on

TV was nothing like this.

"Wow. This place is awesome. And the dome ceiling–just look at it." Rubbernecking, I couldn't get enough of the immense fascination. Cameron smiled, looking up also until we simultaneously settled our attention down below on the skaters.

"Look at that. They're dangerously good. Desperate in a way."

"They are, but they really know their stuff," said Cameron.

"From what I saw, you're no wimp yourself. Are you that good?" I looked off at one flipping off a rail, landing perfectly on the skateboard.

"Nah...not like that. It requires a lot of practice to get as good as these dudes are. Me...nah, I just do it for fun, for recreation."

"So how often do you come here?"

"Once...twice a week. I have another spot I go to closer to the house, but it doesn't compare to this place."

"Again, I think you're good. In spite of that little slip-up," I said softly.

"I heard that. Again, a freak accident; it just came out of nowhere."

"What came out of nowhere?"

Cameron sighed. "The accident. What are we talking about? Forget it." His hands went up and dropped in one wave. "You're right about one thing. I'm better than that little slip-up."

"Exactly what I was saying."

He hunched over the wall. "You're not going to let me off the hook about that, are you?"

"Should I, after all that talk you did on the way here,

about needing someone to talk to? Remember, we're together in this so-call maze, and I wonder how we ended up in it in the first place."

He pinched between his eyes, nodded his head. "Yeah, I know. You can't help but wonder. How it came about...well.... You're right. I should practice what I preach. Just bear with me, please?"

I agreed for now.

We continued to watch the activity below. A man came over a loudspeaker announcing the competition would start in twenty minutes. Skaters were still in full swing, flying over staircases, railings—all over the place, actually. One particular skating area, with a broad bottom and steep sides, shaped like a bowl, captured my attention—and why not? It was where skateboarders reached the edge flying high. It was in the bowl where the most persistent skaters had the place in a sonic boom.

Cameron now had an incredible glow on his face looking down. I rested my forearms on the wall, as the animated part of him came to life. The part of him I wasn't used to seeing, like a youngster marveling over a new Big Wheel, or an older one over a new sports car, or, in this case, over incredible skaters who seemed to pop in out of nowhere. Out of nowhere because a couple of them I hadn't noticed before certainly had my attention now. It was the whole environment actually—the flickering lights, loudspeakers, cheering crowd—that his spirit mingled with; and being so close next to him, my spirit was in the mix, too.

Suddenly he remembered I was there, I thought. He turned and put on a fresh smile just for me, and it shined just like a spotlight.

"What? What now?" I said.

"Nothing. It's just that all this excitement can grow on you. The fellas are in the zone today. See that one there in the red shirt." I followed his gesture. "He made it twice to the Maloof competition. I don't know if you've heard of it, but the event is televised every year. First place winner wins one hundred grand. Although he hasn't won it yet, it's rewarding to be that good to be in the lineup. He's the best I've seen locally. I would put money on him."

"You can bet in the competitions?"

"Some do, but for me, it's just a figure of speech." His mind wandered off below as to collect his thoughts, and he continued. "I remember when I had as much enthusiasm to be competitive. After getting my first skateboard, I was around eight then, I practiced around the neighborhood and eventually began practicing at a place like this. Not quite as nice as this one, but it was *the* place to be."

"So what changed?"

"Life." He grimaced. "I lost the desire to attain pro status. And, uh, it's mainly to do with what happened to my parents, the toll it took on me. Like I said, now it's all for recreation, and I just love being in this environment."

"Again, I'm sorry about your parents. The more you talk about everything, the more I realize how hard it really was for you, and still is apparently." So much so I wanted to console him by letting him know that standing next to him was someone just as weird as he thought he was, that we were actually two peas in a pod swimming around for answers. But it wasn't easy to do. I couldn't let my feelings cloud my judgment because I wasn't sure about anything...about him.

"I have to be okay, and I am. I need you to get that."

"Cameron look—"

"It's what I want for us. I can't change anything. God, I would if I could. All we can do is look ahead, whether we see what's coming or not. There is no going back..." Lightly his head shook as his thought trailed off.

I emanated a mild breath. "You, Cameron Jacks, are so theatrical, today especially. I'm trying so hard to understand, but you don't make it easy for me."

"I know...I know." He took my hand then, and landed a gentle kiss on my forehead. For a time unmeasured, no words exchanged between us as we watched the action below.

A strange feeling came over me as we did, not that of an attack coming on, though it was cool and tingling, like warmth melting ice, radiating from clasped palms, our palms. I imagined them unfolding, only to settle flat on a surface, side by side, touching, waiting for a reading for our future. Fate...right in the palm of your hand, I wondered.

"Yeah!" Cameron let loose of my hand in excitement.

"There have to be names for all the tricks they do? I know the Ollie but the others..."

He chuckled. "Now I'm surprise. See, that's something else you didn't bother telling me." He grinned. "Nah, just kidding."

"Well, I am and I'm not. I just think it's cool and cool to watch."

"So you think you know an Ollie? Show me," he said, suggesting I identify an Ollie right then and there.

I searched about the few skaters still left on the rank before the real competition started. "Okay, wait a moment." Moments later, I glanced Cameron a smile, mused some more to spot anyone during an Ollie.

"Time up," he said.

"Already? You didn't give me a chance," I rejected.

"Look, see the guy with the dreads–that's an Ollie. Watch the one with the ponytail...see, that's an Ollie. It's confusing because there are so many ways to do the trick," he enlightened me.

"Oh, I see. And when they fly over the railing, the wall even, that's like a trick on top of a trick, isn't it?"

"Yep, and the more tricks incorporated in the moves, the greater the risk. Whoa, now get a hold to that." I quickly focused on the subject. "See how he's holding the end of the board. That's a risky move. Now if he'd leaned too far and lost elevation, we would've heard fingers go *crunch*."

"Ooh...how lovely," I said, loving his hyperbole.

"No, really! That's what we call the Broken-Finger Trick." He laughed, and I couldn't hold back busting out laughing, too.

The loudspeaker blared. The time had come for the competition to start. I scanned the place, noticing that more people had gathered. My cellphone vibrated, which reminded me that my time was limited. I checked to see who was calling, hoping it wasn't either of my parents.

Stephanie. I had better call her back.

"Hey, I have to step out for a minute." I left the loud arena and ended up in the ladies' room where it was much quieter and called Stephanie.

"Hey, what's going on? Have you seen the doctor

yet?"

"It's a dentist appointment actually, and no, not yet. My appointment is at 11:30. I'm outside of the office waiting to be called in. What's that noise I hear in the background? Are you at home?"

"Uh, I'm in the bathroom talking to you. I hear something, though. Maybe it's a bad connection." I hated this but Stephanie wouldn't understand.

"Well listen up. Ariana and Cristina think we should get together and go waterskiing and invite the fellas to go with us. I told them you love waterskiing. So what do you say?"

"Yeah, it's not like I've changed my mind since you asked last."

"Well, there's someone else going for sure, and he wants to meet you," Stephanie added. "How do you feel about that?"

"You told him about me?"

"Not exactly. He saw you the night of the show and has been asking Ariana about you."

"Oh...that's nice," I said, not sure what to say.

"So we'll pick you up around five if I don't see you before then. I have to go now. Talk to you later."

When I surfaced from the restroom, there was Cameron, lurking around wondering where I'd disappeared to. "Oh, there you are."

"Hey, has it started yet?"

"It just started. C'mon, let's go back in."

I checked the time, 11:30 on the nose. "Okay...for a few minutes, then we should be heading back."

A door opened, releasing noise of excitement as a couple of people came through. One of them held the door open for us and I mouthed *thanks.*

Fifteen minutes ticked by, then another, and another. Nearly an hour had gone by when we finally hurried out of the building thrilled by the performances we had a chance to see. I kept giving in to Cameron suggesting "just a few more minutes" because it was hard even for me to walk out on such great performances. Eventually, we forced ourselves out, exhaled exhaustingly as we made our departure. We wanted so much to see the entire show to the end.

Traffic flowed without any delays on the way back. As Cameron pulled into the parking lot he'd picked me up at, I felt relieved–off the hook–for making the trip without telling a soul and making it back safely and in good time.

"Thanks, Cameron. I have to say I really enjoyed it."

"So did I. We have to do it again."

I nodded. "Well, I better get going. I know you have things to do."

"Nothing that can't wait. My whole day is open to you if you like."

"I wish," I said regretfully. "We're going waterskiing, Stephanie and some of her friends a little later."

His head dropped slightly. "Waterskiing...sounds like fun. Maybe we can talk later if you find the time?"

"Yeah," I mumbled.

He gave a relaxed look. I reciprocated with a smile, remembering his bizarre moments from earlier, which felt not so bizarre now.

"Look, don't let me hold you up. I'm just not ready for this to end. But I'll be okay...I'm a big boy, I'll survive," he said in a refreshing tone.

I patted his hand. "Of course you'll be fine."

He covered my hand and squeezed gently.

Sympathy, I believed, was what came over me when I suddenly extended my lips only to land a quick kiss on his cheek. But he was swift, catching my lips with his, his hands grabbing hold of the back my head and locking me in position. And I believed, still, that sympathy pressed me to indulge, though just for a quick moment. As I tried to part lips, I found myself shoving and pounding his shoulders to break from his now suffocating hold on me. And when he finally let go, I swung at him but he intercepted a burning slap upside his face.

"You don't want to do that now, do you? You kissed me back."

By now, thoughts swimming in my head should've knocked me unconscious, not being able to channel through that familiar outlet called "my mouth" fast enough. My lips moved, but words came tumbling out. "I didn't...What the hell...what the hell you think you were doing? I, um, I was just–I don't know–not trying to kiss you like that, that's for sure. You were forcing yourself on me."

"Wait...I'm sorry. I didn't mean–I just thought you were feeling it too."

"*Feeling it*! Are you crazy? How could you've thought that? No! You went too far you creep." I forced the door open and he grabbed me.

"Pia, no, wait...don't. I can't let you go like this. All right, I was wrong. You can't hold a little kiss against me. Come on, now...I'm sorry."

"I have to go." I yanked loose of his grip and got out.

He pleaded, "We can't leave it like this, Pia."

I turned away as he ranted.

"Okay, that's fine. We'll just settle this later. Okay? Promise we'll talk about this later."

I turned to him, stared as if I was looking through him as fresh feelings of betrayal generated confusing thoughts. *This is all screwed up. Fate? I don't think so.* With tight lips, slowly I shook my head, not exactly in response to his last appeal, for there was no immediate response for that, except repeating myself.

"I have to go." I then slammed the door close; he cracked open his. "Don't even think about it," I vetoed, and he just glared as I took off in long strides.

I could feel his stare creeping up behind me as I approached the curb. The running engine suddenly went dead. I turned to see what was going on. Before turning completely, somehow I knew it was just a trick. Kill-the-engine trick, I assumed, given that he was a skateboarder, and skateboarders have a bag full of tricks.

I met those eyes once again still showing remorse. *I'm not going anywhere,* was the expression I read, as if telepathically. Sensing we were on that level, I telepathized back, *I know you're not going to sit there all day.*

I showed my back, dropping the connection. I leaped from the curb to beat the coming traffic. From there, up a block and around the corner, I would be home.

Chapter Fourteen

Deluded Not

I surfaced from my room as my parents came through the door. They had gourmet pizza, a small case of Heineken, and a Coke for me. I assumed they were set to be around the house for the rest of the evening. Could be the beer hinted to that. They were cheerful, wrapped up in a discussion about what went on today at the convention. I assumed they had a good day.

"Hi, honey. We got pizza," Mom said.

I spoke, not putting a damper on their discussion. Mom opened the box. The pizza ladened with cheese and toppings looked better than the tantalizing aroma–oh, can't see smell.

"Go ahead and get some." Mom gestured. I just maneuvered around them and their not-so-private conversation and gathered in one hand a couple slices of pizza on a plate and a Coke in the other. Then I scooted out on the back porch.

After things had quieted down, Mom came to the door. "So how was your day?" she asked.

"Um...not bad. Sounds like you and Dad had an exciting day today," I said to divert the subject from me. I didn't want her to ask anything I wasn't prepared to answer.

"Yes. It was quite an interesting day." She smiled, not offering details, however.

"I'm glad. At least you guys don't seem as worn out today as you were yesterday." I finished the last piece of pizza and got up. Mom slid open the screen door for me to cross back into the kitchen. "Good pizza, Mom."

"Mm hum...there's more left," she said. "Well, just one more day left," she added.

"Yep. Now aren't you glad you went?" I said.

Dad entered the kitchen before she could say anything. "Tomorrow we'll be getting out right after lunch, and we'll be leaving for Bermuda. So be around the house *and* be ready when we get here," he said.

"That's right, honey. So if you need something washed, get it out for me," Mom added.

"Okay. By the way, Stephanie and her friends want me to go waterskiing with them. Can I go since we're leaving tomorrow?"

"I don't see why not. What do you say, Isaac?" Mom sought after Dad's input. He'd wandered into the living room.

"At what time?" asked Dad.

"Not too late...around five," I grimaced, hoping for a *yes*.

"Where?"

"I'm not sure, but it should be in the area. They're planning to be here around five. We can get the details then," I said, thinking I could call Stephanie to find out.

But I kept that idea to myself. "I'm sure it's not far, Dad," I recapped.

"I'll give you an answer when they get here then," he concluded.

I moved to the front door, gazed out and began thinking, again, how much I loved it here. Before I knew it, I opened my mouth. "Dad, why don't we live here in Florida instead of Texas?" I uttered softly.

"What...why, what's going on?"

"Well, I was just thinking how easy it would be for you to transfer your job here—even Mom. I really envy Stephanie. She has the perfect life here, whether she knows it or not, and she has such great friends."

"But we have a great life in Texas," Mom entered the conversation. "It's home, and for the most part, we've been happy there."

Dad agreed with Mom, adding, "I don't quite understand your logic. You even said yourself your symptoms are more frequent since we arrived on Friday. Maybe it's not such a good idea. What's the real reason you want to move here?" I could hear his suspicion growing. "Would this have anything to do with a new boyfriend?"

Awestruck. "What...a new boyfriend? Now come on, Dad. We haven't been here a week, and you're talking about a boyfriend." It entered my mind that someone probably mentioned seeing me with Cameron, but then I thought better. Dad wouldn't hesitate to bring it up. He didn't operate like that.

"Well, you talk about Stephanie's friends."

"Oh, Dad, nah, nah, nah. That's not it at all. Is it that difficult to believe in me, and besides, would it be so bad if I was interested in someone?" I glanced from Dad to Mom, back to Dad.

"Look, honey, your dad and I, we're just trying to understand. You have to admit it's surprising to hear. And this isn't the first time we've broached the subject about boys. You're at that age, and it's a parent's right to stay on top of things. So don't ever think you can't come to me about a particular young man that sparks your interest. That's what mothers are for—and don't worry about your dad," she said, peeping around the corner at him. "I'll work with you in the boy department. Isn't that right, dear?" she teased Dad.

Dad gave a disapproving look, didn't say anything.

She went on...and I imagined sitting down, having that conversation with her about Cameron. *Okay, Mom, there's this person I've met and been seeing—and in fact, just today I went with him to Miami. But I don't really consider him a boyfriend. I mean, I don't really think he's my type. He's kinda weird. Would you believe he forced a kiss on me today?*

This definitely wasn't the right move. Nor the right time for this type of confession. All hell would break loose, and I would be chained in an iron cell made just for me—for life. So under the circumstances, my logical response was "Thanks, Mom. But at this time I don't need to have that conversation with you because I don't have anyone that I'm interested in like that." And this was no lie, or it was too early to tell. "I just like it here, always have. And since Stephanie is living here now—and she's like a sister. I just think it would be nice to be close to her. She's like a sister," I reinforced.

Listening to myself, I was amazed at how I was

handling the situation. Not for my obvious omission of Cameron, but for being true to myself whether my parents would have seen things differently or not. And surely, they would've shown their disapproval one way or another had I alluded to seeing Cameron behind their backs.

Besides, if anyone was deluded or confused at this point, it was me. Cameron was so complicated. It was hard to get a footing on what to think or how to feel about him with him wanting to move fast as if he was racing with time, and at times, seeming off, mentally. Though for the most part, he was engaging, smart, and talented. And there had not been a dull moment with him—not ever.

Yet to say he was my boyfriend in my parents' way of thinking wasn't true at all. I hadn't determined how he fit in my world. From the obnoxious stunt he pulled earlier to the first day we met and every weird thing in between, how should I feel for a person I suspected was holding something vital to me. We were leaving for Bermuda tomorrow, and on Sunday for home. With time flying by, so was hope of ever unlocking the mystery.

A little chic four-door sedan, carrying Stephanie, pulled up. Early I may add. When she got out, I recognized Cristina behind the wheel. She waved and I waved back. Stephanie closed the car door and came forth nimbly. She was wearing a colorful one-piece bathing suit, red boxer shorts, and flip-flops. All ready for some waterskiing, so I thought.

I swept open the screen door. "Hey, you're here early."

"Yeah," she deflated, and I grimaced in concern. "There's been a change of plans. Hi, Mr. and Mrs.

Wade," she immediately spoke upon entering the foyer.

"Hi, Stephanie," they spoke back.

"We're going paddle-surfing instead," she continued. "It was too short notice to get a boat to take us out for waterskiing. And Ralph's brother"–I had no clue who Ralph was, but okay–"was going to take us in their boat but something came up. So we decided on paddle-surfing instead. Have you ever paddle-surfed?"

My head twitched. "Not really."

"It's fun. I think you'll like it," Stephanie said, and I frowned. "And don't worry it's easy to learn. You'll see."

"Okay," I said, turning to Dad. "What do you say, Dad?"

"Paddle-boarding, where?" he asked.

"On the beach. There's a place right there on the boardwalk that rents everything we need for paddle-boarding...including life jackets." Stephanie was eager to relate this to my parents, hoping they wouldn't deny me the opportunity.

"Oh, that's good. How much?" Dad asked next.

"Forty dollars. For two hours."

"'Forty dollars?'" he reiterated acerbically, and my heart skipped a beat.

"I got it right here, Isaac," Mom intervened, saving me from a huge letdown.

Dad got up and took a quick glance out the door, to see who's in the car, I assumed, as he moved from the living room to the kitchen. I made a face at Stephanie as I trailed behind him to retrieve the money from Mom. Before disappearing in the bedroom, Dad instructed us to be safe and keep a close eye on each other, especially in the water, regardless of how well we could swim.

Mom handed me the money and prompted me to gather up clothes I wanted to be washed. Bermuda tomorrow...how could I forget? Shortly after, while Stephanie was having a chat with Mom, she yelled for me to put on my swimsuit. Little did Stephanie know that I was changing into one as she spoke. I then grabbed a beach towel.

After that, I was set to go.

Chapter Fifteen

Close Call

With the car parked, the three of us piled out and trailed up an alley-like street toward the boardwalk. As we approached, the vast ocean beyond the white brick wall looked like part of the blue sky. Ahead on the corner was the surf shop, situated between an apparel shop on the right side of the street and a charming patio-style motel directly next to it on the left side. The others, Brett, Josh, and Ariana, whom I recognized right off, were standing at the wall having fruity drinks. Stephanie and Cristina yelled to get their attention, and we all waved as we entered the shop.

The shop was sizable and stocked with everything you could imagine for water sports and more. We went straight to the attendant up front to be equipped with everything we needed to hit the water. I had extra money after the transaction and wondered where to keep it. Of course, big sister Stephanie had an instant solution: wrapping the money in plastic and stuffing it down my bathing suit.

Getting all the necessary gear we needed for paddle-surfing didn't take long.

On our way out of the shop and back to where the others waited, I noticed someone else all set for paddle-surfing had joined the group.

"That's who I was telling you about. Remember?" Stephanie whispered. *"His name is Colin."*

I flashed a smile...I had no instant remark to share with her about Colin. Instead, I asked, "Where's Elijah? Is he coming?"

"I don't think so. He's tied up at the moment doing something else. I doubt he'll make it," she said, revealing such disappointment. "How long have you-all been waiting?" she said to the others as we approached.

"Not long," Josh replied. He, Brett, and Ariana quickly finished their drinks and trashed them.

"Let's hit the water," said Brett. And we set off, trudging across the sand, hauling paddles and surfboards. The surfboards had a built-in handle, which made it easy to tuck firmly underneath the arm and carry.

The fella Stephanie pointed out earlier came up alongside me with a friendly smile. "Hi."

Towering roughly six inches above me, I met the eyes of this slender frame and spoke back. "Hi."

Stephanie, at my other side, suddenly spoke up, "Oh, I'm sorry. Pia, meet Colin. Colin...Pia. Colin's part of the volleyball team, too," she added.

"Ooh...nice to meet you." I glanced up at him again. *Wow, I don't think I've ever met so many good-looking guys in one area before*, I thought. This added to my case for loving Florida that much more. And if my parents could hear what was going through my mind, they would be convinced that my reason for wanting to move here had every bit to do with, well, boys.

"My pleasure," he said immediately. "Are you new to paddle boarding?"

"I am, actually. This is my first time."

"Good—I mean, I can help you get the hang of it."

"That's right," Stephanie assured. "He's the only one that has had any real training. You can say he trained us all."

"Sounds like you're the man then," I said.

A smile then graced his lips. "Uh...you probably should go ahead and put on the jacket."

"Oh, okay. I suppose this is lesson number one," I said like a vivacious student raring to learn.

We stopped at the top of the slope to put on our jackets, Stephanie and I, before continuing down the hill to catch up with the others.

As we came to the water's edge, we all paused to make sure all of us were ready to enter the water, and Colin smiled at his new student. "Now, lesson number two, which is to go out past the waves to reach calm water."

"Mmm, this is getting catchy," I aired openly, referring to the lessons.

"Yeah, quite catchy," he rejoined. "You'll see how calm the water is. It's important. We can't have the waves knocking us off the boards every time we get on our feet or in a steady position."

"Oh no, we can't have that. I wouldn't stand a chance," I reiterated, and he laughed in agreement.

We endured the medium-force waves as we proceeded. I dropped the board and guided it afloat.

Others hopped on their boards and began hand-paddling. At the point where the water concealed half of me, Colin suggested we get on the board as well. By then, we were near still water.

The others wasted no time standing up on the board and began paddling after reaching the exact spot. It looked simple enough to me, so I got to my feet like a wobbly-leg toddler standing solo for the first time. In a hot minute, I lost my balance and fell overboard. So then, I learned another lesson right off, and that was to wait for my instructor to introduce the next lesson.

Colin helped me back on the board and said, "Lesson number three...newcomers should kneel first before standing. Give yourself time to get used to being in the water on top of the board. You'll see it's different and will take a little getting used to. You can use the paddle in that position to help guide you."

"Yeah, right." I grabbed the paddle and started paddling. "How long you think I'll be in this position?"

"Not long. You'll be up and going before you know it. Try paddling from side to side. That way you will go straight. That's lesson number four."

"Gee thanks. I'll have my certificate before the day is over."

Stephanie had paddled a stretch and was now on her way back to us. The others were a little farther. She yelled, "Hey, what do you think? Isn't this great?"

I yelled back, "How long did it take you to get the hang of it?"

"This is as good as it gets in one day," she exhilaratingly exhaled, not missing a beat.

With a big smile, I watched as she drew closer.

"You're not going to pass out, are you?" She seemed to be struggling to me.

Colin started laughing, which had me thinking I'd said something silly without thinking.

"What?" I simpered. But he just shook his head.

"Nah...I'm just kidding," he finally spoke.

"I'm going to try again," I said, meaning I was about to stand again on the board. I managed off my knees to my feet in a stooping position.

"You're doing good, but spread your feet to the width of your shoulders." Colin was back to instructing.

I did just that and continued rising from the board, very easy until I was standing straight up.

"Whew, way to go," the cheery voices of Josh and the others echoed from a distance.

"Okay, now start paddling," said Stephanie, thrilled.

"That's right, you're doing good, but keep your knees slightly bent," said Colin, as he got on his board and began paddling beside me. "Easy now."

"Hey, Pia, you want to race," hollered Josh.

"Whew...yeah...you go...hurrah" were some of the cheery sounds expressed by the others. I was on my feet paddling and had not fallen off the board again yet. I was making progress, which I thought was worthy of their cheers. But as far as racing, I wasn't sure about that. So I consulted with my instructor.

"They got to be kidding...right?" I chuckled.

"They're nuts. But, um, I think you're good to go for now. How do you feel so far?"

"Uh, so far good, as long as I'm not falling off."

"That's about it, managing to stay afloat on the board. Now, you will start to feel it in your upper body, especially your abs, after a while. You're in for a good workout. You'll see. Just take your time and go at it at your own pace." He then gave me a merciful look and said, "Don't worry. I won't leave you behind."

"So how far are they racing, anyway?" I asked, wondering if I could make it.

"See that palm tree down there?" he pointed, and I looked, estimating the tree to be about a block away.

"Oh...that's not too far," I concluded. "Go 'head and get in the race, I'll be fine," I encouraged. "I won't be too far behind."

"All right, but don't overdo it. When you get tired, just lower back down on the board and float. That's all you have to do. And if you happen to fall off, just remember the water isn't deep, and just stand up."

"I'm a pretty good swimmer, so you don't have to worry about me panicking."

He held up a balled fist, said "Great!" and we advanced forth to get in line for the race.

My paddling gradually came to a halt to reserve strength as the others drew closer to meet us.

Stephanie was already perched on the board...resting up. She looked tired in a peaceful kind of way. But she was right: paddle boarding was fun. The others gathered around us, and we all took a moment to breathe and kid around before starting.

Before long, we were back up and in unison counting down to the start.

At the sound of *go*, I was empowered to do just that. I was so excited to be up on my own without guidance. And the calmness made me feel as though I was walking on water. *Walking on water*, I instantly imagined us as a tribal clan that was in pursuit to conquer—in this case—*that palm tree.* It tickled me embellishing the image of the palm tree full of coconuts, berries, and lots more goodies, and we sneak up on it and savagely stash plenty of the goodies down our clothes and in pockets and then scat in thin air.

But the image faded in a matter of seconds as my stride to reaching the palm tree became a huge struggle. The others were ahead of me; still, I wanted to give myself a chance to stay in the race. But my trying to maintain balance while paddling was getting sloppy. I kept trying but I was getting farther behind. So far behind I had to come to terms that I was officially out of the race. And I confirmed this by yelling, waving, and yelling some more to the others, "Hey y'all. Don't mind me. I'll see you when you get back." So I gave up paddling and returned to my knees, in the novice position. This proved to be a soothing and refreshing position after all the hard work.

I was feeling especially relaxed, and for once, the surroundings drew me in. The racy sound of boats towing water skiers across the water particularly got my attention. I would love to be waterskiing about now and not bothered by all the water splashing me in the face. That's part of the thrill, I thought. And farther out there was another boat pulling a foursome. I looked over my shoulder and saw that the other one was coming up not too far from me now. The skier appeared to be a pro, zigzagging over the water. But so was the boat, zigzagging through the water and at an alarming speed.

Something about this picture just wasn't right. As the boat got closer, I realized that the skier was trying to get the driver's attention, by signaling with his hands to slow down, and his loud cries weren't signs of a thrilling moment. At this point, I got very nervous; the skier was heading too close in my direction. I picked up the paddle and began stroking the water laboriously, trying to get out the path of the helpless skier in the hands of this lunatic behind the wheel. But I wasn't getting out of the way fast enough, as the skier was certainly dead center in my path.

With fear and tension mounting, I had to do something fast. As tension began feeling like elastic cutting across my forehead, I knew what was about to happen and at the worst time ever. Quickly I abandoned the board to try to make a run for it, as fast as I could, against the massive volume of water. I was moving faster than I would have, had I stayed on the board, yet it still wasn't fast enough. In my race for safety, time managed to get away from me as soon as a wave caught up to me and took me under. I seemed so helpless when I resurfaced and saw that another big splash was coming at me. But ahead of it I got a good glimpse of the skier, so close that he was definitely on a collision course with me and was very much contributing to the wave about to swallow me whole.

He let go of the rope, I told myself, seeing that his hands were free before plunging beneath the wave. I thought I heard the boat far in the distance though at the same time I was fierce at the skier. Why couldn't he have just let go sooner? He would have spared me the horrific agony I was now experiencing.

A wave of panic, tension, passed through my body by the second. *Tick tock, tick tock, tick tock*; a vague sound I could hear all around me. The humming sound came, slowly fizzled out the sound of the ticking clock. By now, and with all my might, I dragged myself closer to dry land, slowly but surely. Regardless if I couldn't feel, I knew my legs were alive and fighting for me.

I made it, yes! Through my blurred vision, there were figures that certainly looked like people coming toward me. Or was I moving toward them. I tried to blink away the salt water stinging and blurring my vision, afraid to use my hands for the sand. But it wasn't happening as quickly as I wanted.

I stumbled to the ground, and then, unexpectedly, very strong arms came to my rescue, scooping me up. "Eric, go get the board and paddle," the agitated voice commanded. A voice I thought I recognized.

"That was horrible. I can't believe what happened out there. Are you okay, sweetheart?" another man asked.

My head brushing against the shoulder blade of the person carrying me, I muttered, "Yeah."

The voices of anxious, furious people resounded like a cloud of commotion settling over me. Distinctive voices saying, "That was a close call," which seemed to be the voice of a wisplike male. "Oh my God, you think they were drunk," I heard another say. "Thank goodness she got out of there when she did. It could have been worse," a voice of a middle-aged woman, whom I assumed was caressing my arm. So many wispy voices seemed to scan and ventilate through me.

I was still trying to open my eyes that were burning like hell. Unless something foreign was in the water, why was I having problems with my eyes? In a panicky situation, I tried rationalizing. Yeah, it had to be from too much eye contact with the water. Either way, my eyes had never burned so badly.

Safe from mayhem, he eased me down on the ground. "You see that? The nerve of that jerk running off like that. He didn't even have the common decency to see if she was okay. That creep! I would love to get my hands on him and on that one driving the boat." His tone was fired up.

"Yeah, they both ought to be reported and to think they might get away with this. They could've seriously hurt her," the other male sounded off with much disgust. "I wish I had gotten a better look at the boat. Did you manage to get anything that might help find them?"

"Unfortunately, not," he said to the other guy. "Are you okay?" he then asked me.

The distinctive voice I was still trying to make out, at the same time thinking, *it couldn't be.*

My eyes squinted open enough to see a frame over me; however, my sight was still experiencing the effects of trauma. "Except for my eyes, something must've gotten in them," I said. "I don't know why they're burning so bad. Everything's blurry. And the sun isn't helping."

"Just give it a moment. Don't worry," he comforted.

"Do I know you?" I asked, feeling sure I recognized his voice. But I wouldn't jump to that conclusion in case I was wrong. On second thought, I hadn't thanked him for coming to my rescue and didn't want to come across as rude. So I recanted, "I'm sorry. I should be thanking you for coming to my rescue." But as tears began forming, soothing my eyes like a fire extinguisher, I would soon see this person.

I started blinking my eyes, effortlessly now as this person smoothed a hand over my hair. I made a swift turn to my left as if not to lose another second of seeing who was at my side the whole time. Eyes wide-open, I looked into the eyes of this gumptious soul, whom I wasn't sure I wanted to see again, ever. But here he was.

I straightened up pronto. "What...what are you doing here?"

"Hey, man, I think I'll give y'all some room," said the other fella.

"Yeah, all right. I'll catch up with you later," said Cameron, and the guy walked off.

"All this time it was you, and you didn't say anything?"

He studied me for a second. "You had a close call out there. I'm just glad I was here. You could have been seriously hurt."

"You didn't answer my question. What are you doing here?"

He sighed heavily. "Look, I'm not going to stand here and pretend that it's just a coincidence that I'm here. The fact is I just thought it was a nice evening to get out and walk the beach to see what's happening."

"Mm, hum. I call it stalking."

He turned slightly, giving me the silent treatment.

"You know something...it seems awfully funny how things or people want to crash into me when you're around."

"Now here you go again!" Obviously, he wasn't going to be a punching bag for insults. "How can you even say that? That's a low blow and you know it. No way in hell do I have a connection with those lunatics that hauled ass and didn't even bother to look back or even stop to assess any damage they may have caused. You really think—"

"Pia!" Stephanie yelled as she and the others ran toward us. Breathless, she dropped to her knees before me. "Thank goodness you're all right."

Ariana, Josh, Cristina, Brett, and Colin gathered around showing a softer side of the horrific expression upon their faces.

"I'm okay, really. I survived with a scratch," I said. But from the look on their faces, they weren't convinced.

"Yeah, but you could have been seriously hurt. I shouldn't have left you out there alone," said Colin. He reached for my hand and gently squeezed it, his glances at Cameron, grating.

"It's not your fault," I said, hoping the words would penetrate right away.

"She's right, you're not to blame," Cameron concurred at once.

Stephanie stared at Cameron with her lips balled. "Where did you come from anyway?"

For a moment, I didn't think he would bother to answer. But he mustered up something. "What do you mean? This is a public place."

It was a rhetorical question. I knew Stephanie well enough to know she wouldn't respond to that directly, because overall, she's a rational person with lots of common sense for maintaining peace at all cost. At least, that's what I was hoping at this moment.

"Now, Stephanie," I cut in, guess I had second thoughts. This was Cameron, after all; she just may go off on him given Elijah nowhere around to control her.

"Well, she's in good hands. You can go now." Oh well, Stephanie just couldn't help being snobby.

I looked at Cameron. "Maybe we'll have a chance to get together later. Thanks for pulling me out of the water."

He gave me a strange look. Behind it I imagined a multitude of thoughts swirling around in his head, and that he was trying to deal with each one of them at once. He rose to his feet. "Okay, we'll have it your way." I looked up at him, thinking he'd come to a good solution rather quick until he added, "Can you meet me at the same place and time, tomorrow?"

"What!" Stephanie jumped to her feet, then bent over me. "You gotta be kidding me. You've been seeing him all this time?"

Cameron butted in, "Wait a minute...all this time she didn't know?"

Eyes and mouths opened wide, I stared up at Stephanie, then at Cameron. My speech was paralyzed, and I felt mortified. All I could do was shake my head, eventually covering it with sandy palms. I didn't want to face or even answer Stephanie about my deceiving her. Nor face Cameron, he knowing now that I had deliberately set out to deceive him. Right before everyone, I was caught...caught red-handed in a fat lie.

I looked up to face everyone. They all were still wearing stunned, disapproving looks. Even Cameron, though I knew was for a slightly different reason. He wouldn't have cared less if I had told Stephanie or not. We'd agreed to be honest with each other; that's what he cared about most.

And yes, Stephanie was still demanding answers but not with words; her body language–tilted head with a hand resting on the hip–spoke loud and clear.

"Look," I spoke. "Don't let me spoil the rest of your evening. You spent good money for two hours of paddle-boarding, and that's way too much to waste. Now all of you, *go*—just go. Have fun without me. Please, just go, I'm not going anywhere. I'll be right here when you get back."

Stephanie glared at me, then Cameron. "That means you too," she said, her finger stabbing the air.

Cameron pointed back. "Don't you worry about me."

I chimed in. "Stephanie, it's fine. We obviously need some time to talk."

It was a cue for Stephanie to let it go, and I hoped she would without trying to convince me otherwise. Her arms flopped to her side, and then she turned her back on me. She took the cue well, leading the others away in a march across the sand to the ocean for whatever time they had left for paddle-boarding.

According to my estimation, a good hour left to go.

Chapter Sixteen

Unbelievable Paradox

I glared at Cameron as he lowered down next to me. The kiss he forced on me earlier somehow didn't matter now. I just wanted to clear the air between us. "I know what you're thinking," I lead off.

"No. I don't believe you do," he said starkly. He then turned away, looking off into space. I just let him be, I couldn't press him in the slightest way, though I had an urge to do so. He needed a moment, and I allowed him that much.

"I didn't mean to snap at you," he whispered.

"I understand," I replied.

"We need to talk–I mean, *really*, talk." He was still facing the ocean, his voice sounding adrift. "I don't think I can keep going on like this. It's time that I get something off my chest, once and for all."

"I'm sorry, Cameron, really I am. I don't know what more I can say."

"That's not it I'm trying to tell you. You trusted me enough to give me a chance. That alone satisfied me.

None of that other stuff matters right now."

"Okay, then, what is it?"

He folded his hands, rested arms over bent knees as he turned his head slightly toward me. "What's on my mind is what's been on my mind since the first day we met. And what I'm about to say may sound insane *and it is*; I will be the first to admit it. But I have to talk about it to at least try to understand what's going on with me."

"Okay...I'm listening." Could this be the moment I'd been waiting for? I couldn't help wondering.

"Remember the day of the skateboard accident, how I went off on you apparently for no reason? How can you forget, right? Well, for the record, I plead temporary insanity."

"*Temporary insanity.* Hmm, I buy that."

"At that moment I lost it because I wanted to but couldn't explain what happened. That day I saw something obviously no one else did. This thing, Pia, appeared out of nowhere, causing me to panic and lose control of the skateboard." He began fumbling with his hands and continued. "But here's the weirdest part about all this: the thing that got in my way, causing me to lose control, came from you."

"From me? *Oh please.* You're back at square one blaming me for the accident? You really are out of your mind."

"No, now, wait, let me finish."

"Let you finish? You're putting it all on me still. You want me to finish listening to someone who is obviously insane? How in the world–"

"Will you stop and let me finish!" His high-pitched voice shattered over mine, bringing about a momentary stance of calm, and we both looked around to see if we had captured an audience before he continued. "You're right, it wasn't you...not directly anyway. But it came out of nowhere, some sort of apparition, and I crashed right into it, or through it."

"A freaking apparition? Don't you mean you had a hallucination? And why you're trying to hand it over to me to claim as my own is beyond me. I can't believe this; you're so full of it. Just listen to yourself. Can't you see? Something's wrong with this picture."

"Believe me, I understand. But it's been like a train wreck happening over and over in my head thinking about this. Look, I wouldn't have brought this up if–" He drew a deep breath and released it.

"If what?" I tried to remain calm though I pounded a fist on my lap.

"No way would I have brought this up if I was not convinced that that thing generated from you and that it wasn't a figment of my imagination and thank goodness for that. For one thing, it was impossible. That's why I'm telling you it came from you, Pia, even though you didn't see it yourself."

I shook my head, honestly thinking that he was delusional. His sick confession had us goggling at each other for a minute. I couldn't believe what I was hearing, and I supposed he couldn't believe what he was saying either. My emotion felt savage, but I wielded a civil tone.

"Okay, I get it. You desperately need someone to talk to and to help you sort some things out–I get it. This is what you were trying to say to me earlier today. Your right, it's crazy. But think about it: how could I produce something like this thing you're talking about?"

At this point, I was more than willing to lend an ear, to take the position of a therapist in which I was all too familiar with, given my sessions with one, and given I felt forced to take the position now. Also, it gave me the conduit I currently needed to release the fury and not run away from this. After all, he was calling me a freak whether he knew it or not about all this, and I had to defend myself. This was his craziness, not mine. Having the table turned on me in this way—well, this simply wasn't going the way I had expected at all. My theory was being blown to smithereens.

He glared at me. "So that's how you want to play it? Listen, you want an answer to something I don't have the answer to."

"Then how can you be sure about anything?" I asked calmly. My rage settled to the crux of empathy as I framed my mind to listen and console.

"The question is how did I come to the conclusion that it was yours and not mine."

"*Whatever.*"

"I have a theory."

"Okay, let's hear this theory."

"Now follow me," he pointed a finger. With the finger, he drew a square in the sand, saying, "This is the big white screen in a theater." He then drew another square: "And in this square are all the people, sitting, watching the movie on the screen. And by the way, I'm in this square watching the movie too. Now imagine this being my first time in a theater, okay?"

"Yeah, I'm following you."

"My first time *ever* in any theater," he emphasized, "and I'm looking around excited like anyone would be in an unusual setting for the first time."

I exhaled in exasperation.

He continued. "Now let's just pretend I'm an alien from another planet and don't know a thing about movie theaters. And say I'm extremely curious about where the movie is coming from or how it's appearing on the screen. I know, I know, just bear with me," he responded to my hurried expression then proceeded. "I'm so curious that I turn around, look up, and then see the light shining out of an opening; this light shining directly on the big screen. And then I say, uh-huh; that's where it's coming from. Remember, I'm an alien?"

"Will you just get to the point?"

Next, he drew in the sand a stretched-out triangle, being the light shining from the opening to the screen. Then he pointed to the opening again. "You are here, Pia, in the opening, because that day you were the movie projector. That thing just popped out of you. Not to mention it was in 3-D."

Speechless, I had to take a moment to digest this crap. No way could I accept his bizarre theory as proof of anything other than he was insane and I didn't like any of this not one bit. This had to be one of his mind games, but I couldn't understand why. And no way could I give in to it (that would mean admitting to being a freak) or let him get away with it. He simply couldn't be trusted.

"Say that your theory is right. Why did you see it and not me?" *Let's see what elaborate excuse he comes up with now.*

"That's the million-dollar question. I can't explain why I'm able to see the images coming from you. Let me ask you this. Do you or have you ever seen anything like that?"

I gawked. "Don't even try it. You got a lot of nerve. It's not like you haven't hallucinated before. How are you so sure you didn't then? The point is you saw it, not me. You cannot pin this thing on me."

"I had no physiological changes. Yes, I've done my homework. As for my mental state, it doesn't add up because I was in a damn good mood until I ran into you."

I narrowed my eyes at that.

"Pia, look...I haven't had a hallucination in over a year. And Friday was different. It was nothing like what I had ever experienced before, except for in a sci-fi movie. It was like you blew up the whole scene of me falling off the skateboard in a bubble. You have to believe me. I've never had a hallucination like that before."

"What! You in a bubble? And it came from me?" I had been experiencing some crazy things since being back here but this, no. He couldn't be 100 percent sure that it wasn't his delusion. After all, there's a first time for everything. And by admitting at this point that I did experience such things would have easily got him off the hook.

No. This whole thing was too suspicious.

"Seeing yourself fall off the skateboard, was that all you saw?"

He frowned. "Yeah. Obviously I was the only one to see it. My boys went right through it. I tried to avoid it but lost control. You know, I read up on out-of-body experience. It's strange like that. But you see, I don't fit the profile," he said warily.

"But I would, huh? Look, Cameron, why did you go out of your way to pursue me if you thought I was a freak?" *Freak*: The word slipped off my tongue again. I hate that word.

"I don't know. Suppose I couldn't help myself."

"What do you mean you couldn't help yourself?"

"I felt a strange need to protect you."

"Protect me? What is it about you? Are you obsessed with damsels in distress?"

"Is that what you think you are? Besides, that's not it at all. I will admit that the skateboard incident brought us together; by fate, I would like to think. No matter what brought us together, the feeling I have for you is real."

"But you did a good deed for today by scooping me out of the water. You should feel good having rescued this damsel in distress. Funny how you just happened to be here." The words rolled bitterly off my tongue.

He looked at me in disbelief and turned away to the ocean, resisting the urge to slam my bitter attacks, I knew.

But I charged on. "Answer me this then. Why bring all this up now?"

"I have my reasons."

"Yeah right, you have your reasons. Enough of this I have to get up and move around." I got to my feet, brushing sand off my hands and from other parts of my body. Looking down at the paddleboard next to my feet, reminded me that I had to return it soon. Immediately I picked it up and tucked it under my arm.

"Let me get that for you. You grab the paddle. You're not planning to surf some more are you?" Cameron asked as he got up. The board readily transferred to Cameron, which he locked under his arm.

"No. I'm going to turn it in." I grabbed up the paddle, and we padded toward the shop. Not much was said during the trip over. And it wasn't until we were leaving the shop that I broached the topic again.

"I really would like to know why you come to me now with this."

"Well, I'm thinking now that it probably wasn't a good idea."

"Okay, if that's how you feel."

After a moment of silence, and as we strolled closer to the water, he changed his mind. "You were in danger, and I realized I couldn't live with myself if anything happened to you; that's why now."

"What do you mean?"

"Just as the disaster with the water skier was happening, another one of those images appeared. Except this time, I was determined to make real what I was seeing. And to do that, I, the real me, had to run out to rescue you. I didn't think twice about it. I just ran right through it regardless of the consequences."

I glared at him as he continued.

"It was a bold move, so I closed my eyes going through it. When I was sure I made it through, I opened them. And you were right there for me to grab into my arms. Now, however strange this may seem, the rest is history. And, um...now that I think about it, I'm not sure if I grabbed *you* in the image or *you* out of the image." He then chuckled. "I hope I got the real deal."

I smiled. "What do I look like to you?"

He looked off, grinning.

Caught in the waft of this unusual tale, I grew speechless as we strolled closer to the water. Passing through something as creepy as that, would have looked rather cartoonish I thought. How could something so remote, so riveting, be happening here in our world. What is imagination, really, if it took on a life of its own outside of you?

No, no. I quickly pushed the thought out of my head. I knew all too well that kind of thinking would only drive my mind outer space, and leave me feeling discouraged.

I stalled now to let the water splash high over my knees. "So, as you were going through it, you didn't think you would disappear into another dimension or something?"

"Yes, but I didn't think it was likely to happen. Like hallucinations, it wasn't real. That's what I told myself anyway."

"You just admitted that it could have been or was a hallucination."

"I never ruled out hallucination. Just that it wasn't mine."

"But it's all in the mind of the person having it. How can you explain that?" I challenged.

"As I said before, I do not deny how strange all of this is," he replied.

As I waded along the shoreline to meet the coming tide, my eyes met his. "Was that the only two you saw?" I wasn't sure why I assumed there was more.

"You would be surprised– Hey, are you about to take a swim?" he raised his voice to my moving farther into the water.

"No, just rinsing the sand of my body." Apparently he wasn't coming with me. But in a short while, I was out feeling refreshed.

"You didn't have to stop talking, I could still hear

you," I said as we strolled along the shoreline.

"I know, but I'm serious about all this, Pia."

I faced him, reflecting my sincerity. "Just because I didn't see what you saw doesn't make it any less important."

"But I'm telling you it's serious because you were present every time I saw these things."

"There were other times?"

"Yes...yesterday. Remember on the beach, I kept asking you 'what's going on with you?' I saw something then and thought you did too because you seemed lost and confused. You didn't appear to recognize me at first. So I couldn't help wondering if you saw something that spooked you."

I frowned. "What was it you saw yesterday?"

"You, and me, together in this mirage-like thing–like the others I've seen. Except this one was fuzzy at first, I couldn't make out me but I knew it was me. And when it disappeared there you were. I knew you would be; I saw you right before this thing formed."

"I don't know what to say, Cameron," I said sincerely.

"You know, I wanted to tell you right then what I saw and suspected. If only you had said something, like, *did you see that?* I would have told you. You didn't so I didn't. I didn't want to look, or sound, like a mutant with antennas coming out of his head."

"And that's why you came up with the idea of the maze?"

"Yeah. And after what happened here today, I couldn't keep it to myself any longer."

I nodded faintly. "I hate to say, but it looks like

we're still trapped in that maze." My thoughts went inward then, contemplating the one and only way out of this situation–if not for me then for him.

Our stroll slowed to a snail's pace. Our eyes met and then drifted apart as we collected our surroundings. I closed my eyes for the passing of a stiff breeze. It then suddenly dawned on me: The vision I had of Cameron carrying me out of the water the day of the volleyball game turned out to be a premonition of what happened today.

I hugged my shoulders after feeling a slight chill. I wondered if Cameron had told anyone else. But I didn't bother asking. Somehow, I knew he hadn't. Just as I made up my mind on what to do next, I knew it wouldn't be easy to ignore what he'd revealed to me. Not only that, holding back the truth about me wasn't fair to Cameron. Although I felt that I should tell him everything, I couldn't bring myself to do so. Therefore I, and this craziness I was associated with, was all wrong for him, especially since he was still hurting by what happened to his parents. It was all up to me to make this right–after all, he'd said himself that the visions appeared only when I was around. That he hadn't had a single hallucination in over a year. So what I was about to do was for his sake.

"Cameron." Narrowing my lips, I looked down. "This has to end between us. I mean, I don't think we should go on seeing each other." When he didn't say anything, I looked up and saw him looking off at the others coming ashore, and I knew exactly what he was thinking. "And it has nothing to do with them," I avowed immediately.

He dropped his head slightly. "Then why?"

"Because...you'll be better off without me."

He looked at me in disbelief. "You know I will still dream about you."

"Or not."

"So that's it. You think blaming yourself will solve a problem we personally don't have? All of this is bizarre, I know. But ending it with me won't change anything. It doesn't matter because it's not what I want."

"How can you feel that way? And it does matter. What about how it would affect you mentally?–and it will. It has already and don't try to pretend that it hasn't. And your parents, you still haven't gotten over what happened to them. And I won't have you blaming me if you see another illusion, or should I say, start hallucinating again."

"You're wrong, Pia."

"Hey, you guys had fun?" I said as Stephanie and the others approach.

"Yeah, you missed out big time," pretty much summed up everyone's response.

"Where's your paddleboard?" Stephanie asked.

"I checked it in already."

"Okay, we'll meet you at the shop," she said as they all trod on up the sandy slope.

"I'll be right behind you," I uttered after them.

"We have to talk about this some more," Cameron continued.

"You know I have to go."

"Yeah, I know. It doesn't have to be now. I'll call you later."

"I don't know–"

"C'mon, we're not done with this. I'll call you later."

"It won't do any good so don't waste your time."

"Don't say that. Promise me that you'll sleep on it. I know you'll feel different tomorrow."

"Tomorrow we're leaving for Bermuda."

"Bermuda?" He was starkly surprised. "How long will you be gone? Will you be coming back?"

"We should be back in a day or two," I assumed that was the plan.

We gradually picked up the pace making our way off the beach as I told him more about our upcoming trip to Bermuda. He tried again to convince me not to give up on what we had started, convinced that we would get through it without "casualty." He got a smile out of me with that. But he knew it was hopeless trying so hard in so little time to convince me. I honestly felt I needed the separation and time to process all this. For me, there was nothing left to say. And our final moments together were without words.

As we arrived up at the shop, I intuitively read his tender expression to mean "I'll see you when you get back." For me, it was good-bye. His lips pecked me on the cheek, and the touch lingered as he backed away. Sadness was now prominent in his face. "Call me," I could almost hear him say in his lingering exit. He waved. I waved back. Before long, he was gone.

Cristina, Stephanie, and I left immediately after our cheery sayonara with the others. On the road home, I told Stephanie I had ended it with Cameron. And I snubbed any further discussion on the subject. Thank goodness, I was home in no time.

For the rest of the evening, I went about in a daze. I wanted to share everything with my parents, but how could I? I hadn't been the model daughter they'd extended trust to. And Dad was too unpredictable. Above all, I couldn't get out of my mind how wrong I was about Cameron knowing more than I thought he knew. I wanted so much to pin the mysterious happening in my life on someone, and he was a promising suspect. But as he revealed what was happening with him, it turned out that I was the eerie distraction in his world.

Was that really the case? Me being totally wrong about him? I started thinking about everything that had happened since I arrived. No one had ever been able to see the things I saw...and then he came along. It seemed odd and convenient to meet that unique person—here, now. And I could have gone on forever asking myself "why?"

Time flew by and I was now ready for bed, but not before filling pages in my journal. The first thing I wrote: *What a day this has been*!

Chapter Seventeen

To Bermuda

If there was anything behind the dream I had last night, surely I shouldn't keep it to myself. Not now. Not when I had the opportunity to make a difference. And how could I live with myself if I didn't?

It was around one, and we were just arriving at the airport for Bermuda. After an early dismissal from the three-day convention, my parents were ready to fly away and release. I, on the other hand, was sagging due to a long, restless night, having to do with a dream I had of the plane crashing.

Dad dropped us off at the waiting area while he went to check on the plane, load our luggage, and drop off the rental car. Upon entering the quiet lobby occupied by a handful of people, I crossed the room looking up at the widescreen TV on the wall. Men dressed in suits were surprisingly in a heated discussion, looking as though they would have each other's throats at any moment. I looked around for the remote control to change the channel, but there wasn't one in sight.

"Pia." Mom pointed, letting me know she was going to the ladies' room across the way. I nodded, then flopped down on a black vinyl sofa, cocked my head to one side, resting it on my knuckles, and closed my eyes, thinking.

Cameron, guilt, and the dream were like rummage in my head that needed immediate attention. The guilt had to do with me cutting Cameron loose, not telling him the truth and offering my help in any way that I could. Always, the oath I made with myself got in the way. Because of bad experiences in past, it was just too hard to put my trust into someone else's hands. Like now, doing what I thought was right was too confusing.

Then there was the dream...

"Where's your mom?"

I opened my eyes to Dad's voice. He arrived unexpectedly. "She's in the ladies' room," I replied. "Dad, I have to tell you about the nightmare I had last night...*of the plane crashing*," I whispered partly.

"It must've been awfully disturbing." He sat down next to me. "But it's not the first time you've dreamt of a plane crashing, right?"

"Yeah. It is actually. Does that surprise you?" I said to the contestable look in his face.

"Y-yeah, suppose it does. I seem to remember another time...but I could be wrong."

"On second thought...maybe when I was a little girl I had one but not since...you know?"

"Yeah, I know what you mean. But we're not going to let a dream spoil our plans because a dream is just that, a dream. Maybe you were thinking about flying or something else was bothering you before falling asleep last night—you know how that works. Tell you what...it won't hurt to have them double-check everything before we leave. I'm going to get on that right now. You think that would make you feel better?"

"Yep," I nodded. It was enough telling him just to take a load off me. Because I already knew the dream alone wouldn't halt the trip.

Dad met Mom coming out of the restroom and they both then stepped outside.

Dad didn't ask details about the nightmare, and I couldn't much blame him; it wasn't the time. Even if I had told him, I would have left out the part about Cameron being in the dream.

Resuming my slanted position, I shut my eyes and replayed the dream in my head. The plane was totally submerged in water, my parents were trapped, but I wasn't. Cameron, outside of the plane, was trying to get me to take his hand. Frantic, I wouldn't. I kept shaking my head, looking back at my parents. But he kept insisting that I take his hand. I resisted, shaking my head, turning to my parents. Couldn't he understand that I wouldn't leave until they were freed, too? Until....

Suddenly they were gone, vanished, just like that; bright spots had taken their places.

My eyelids trembled. The footage of the dream turned off and I concentrated on Cameron. If he was mixed up in all of this in ways I wasn't aware of, then how exactly? Besides, he didn't come off as your typical victim, now that I thought about it. Why did he stick around and not run to the hills? That's what a normal person would have done.

Something in the distance beeped, followed by a familiar tone of a text message just arriving. These alerts prompted my orbs open. Mom had slipped back in, was looking over papers from a large envelope. I got up. Our eyes met as I moved past her headed to the ladies' room. I checked the text message as I entered and saw that it wasn't important, given it was from someone I didn't know. All alone in the restroom, I just stood before the mirror, staring at tiredness staring back at me. I was clutching the phone in my purse now.

Should I do this? I pondered a bit. Slowly I lifted the phone out of my purse. *Why not?* I began keying in the numbers—not with eagerness for I was still deciding, so much was at stack—but just as I was about to press the last number, I stopped.

What if?—I mean he could be...

I dropped my face into the palm of my hand; I just didn't know what to do.

If I called, what would I say to him anyway? Nothing. It didn't matter now. It's not as if I'm going to tell him what he wanted to hear anyway. So what was the use? Again, what would I say?

I just put the phone back in my purse and proceeded to use the restroom.

In a while, Dad was back giving the thumbs-up, which meant I should settle my fears about the plane crashing or at least try. He stood holding the door open; it was time to go. We got up, marched out, and hopped on the cart with a man in overalls who transported us to the plane. Breezy and refreshing was the short trip over, passing more planes in hangars here and there. Our plane was out in the open when we arrived, and I boarded first to make sure my things were all there as Mom and Dad got in a last-minute chat with the driver. And I decided I had a little chatting to do on my own before taking off while I still had time and a signal. Guilt was getting the best of me, so I made another attempt to call Cameron. This time the phone rang. Following the fifth ring, voice mail came on—*a sigh*—I was off the hook not having to speak to him directly. Leaving him a voice mail was enough to ease the burden of this guilt trip I was on.

"Cameron, this is Pia. I just wanted to tell you that you're probably right. That maybe there's a logical explanation for the visions you saw." *What was I saying? Nothing about this was logical.* "Scratch that; it's too unreal to be logical. But I hope at least you'll feel better about all this, knowing that I too, just like you thought, have visions. So if—"

Oh, wow. I got that infamous sound of a dropped call, and I had no time to call back. Mom and Dad were now boarding the plane. I held the phone clutched in my hand, wondering how much of the message recorded, until I finally turned it off and dropped it in a cup holder next to me.

Soon we were up in the air, and the mild anxiety attack I usually got was clenching me from the inside. I gripped the armrest until the anxiety ran its course. In two to four minutes, it was over.

The attacks started right when the dreams and visions began. For a while they were so bad I couldn't go anywhere by plane. Dad thought he would solve that problem by buying this plane, saying it would be therapeutic. As it turned out, he was right.

Traveling over the Gulf, I spotted a boat. The white trail it left behind was the reason I noticed it. Instantly my mind went to work imagining the ocean rising, forming into this pleasure-seeking monster, its titanic mouth opening and swallowing up the boat in one gigantic gulp. I shrank and, like an Etch a Sketch, shook away the menacing projection.

However, erasing the notion that any bizarre thing could happen down there wasn't easy, as I reflected on all the strange occurrences reported over centuries in these waters. And that mysterious island Cameron spoke about, how could I not wonder if it's the same one I'd been seeing on trips to Bermuda and in my dreams.

"Ah!" I bounced when the plane hit a bump. Now it felt as though it was riding a tide. *Just turbulence,* I told myself, trying hard not to think about the plane at the bottom of the sea.

Another bump! My heart now pounded as though I had run a 100-yard dash in a split second. I tried to tame my mind to think pleasant things because it was just turbulence, and little turbulence wouldn't cause any harm. *Just a little turbulence. Nothing to worry about.* If only my poor nerves and heart would get the message.

I started to calm down as the fluctuation of the plane lessened, but then we hit another bump, bumpier than before.

"We should be running out of this shortly," Dad promised. But that didn't quash my tizzy state, thinking that the plane would crash for sure. "As a precaution, fasten your seat belt," he directed. Of course, that was the precautionary thing to do, and the turbulence didn't seem to be letting up.

"Dad, what's going on? Are we about to crash?" I didn't want it to come out like that or say anything at all, and I wanted to take it back as soon as I said it.

"Pia, honey, you have to calm down. This plane *isn't* going down. We have experienced turbulences like this numerous times. This one is no different. We've gotten through it before, and we'll get through it this time. Okay? See what you can do, Vivaca," Dad suggested now to Mom.

"He's right, baby. It's going to be okay," Mom assured though there was not much either of them could do under this condition. Somewhere in my mind, I knew Dad was right.

Mom held out a hand, but I didn't reach for it. It was no use. The fluctuation, I just held firm to the armrest and continued bracing myself.

"We've been in worse conditions than this. It's that dream..." Dad's voice came as a whisper over the mayhem.

I glared out the window, my mind thinking loud. *This can't be happening, can't turn out like the dream. It can't be because Cameron isn't here and he definitely isn't down there. So this can't be...my dream.* I turned and saw a glimpse of fear in Mom's face, and suddenly my eyes crushed together and my mind clamored, *Stop!*

What! My eyes shot open. I couldn't believe it. In an instant it stopped, just like that. Was it my cry...?—no, it couldn't have been. It was so unbelievable I didn't know what to think. All I knew was that the plane was a smooth sailing now and the threat appeared to be gone. I couldn't believe it and certainly my body couldn't either; it still clung to a protecting brace. The last breath I took was trapped in my lungs. It wasn't until I released it and began breathing that the tension melted away. And not until then did I feel we were out of the woods.

Shortly I got a strong urge to look out the window and saw that we were coming up on it–the island–as I sensed we would be. It was always there. I couldn't remember a time when it wasn't. And I wondered, as I had many times before, how could this be a state of schizophrenia when it was always there. Was always the same never changing. Was as real as any piece of land on this earth. It was so real to me that all eyes should see it not just mine. Whether it was a figment of my imagination or schizophrenia, it wasn't like the other images I saw, because it didn't appear and disappear like the other ones, but lasted and lasted and lasted. Always the trees looked the same, the hills and the mountains, trees and more trees–it could be a picture of Hawaii, I thought.

Yep, it was there all right. My only problem was proving it. I decided to test the waters, so to speak, since it had been a while since I brought it up.

"I see it, Mom, Dad, the island; it's still there. Do you see it? You have to see it; please tell me you see it." I was practically begging them to see it.

They both began searching for anything that would reveal that I wasn't just seeing things again. And it was taking them much too long to spot what was there as clear as day. For me anyway.

I remembered how desperate my parents were when

I first developed this condition; always wishing that it was something they could do; saying that my condition was merely a bully that pried on the helpless kids—their kid nonetheless. If it were up to them the evil bully invading their precious little girl would disappear, just as easily as it appeared.

I knew they were just trying to make me feel better. Under the circumstances, my parents always had done the best they could. And they had had their share of going crazy mad not knowing what actually happened the night I went missing, therefore, not knowing how my rare condition came to alienate my life, our lives.

"You would think after all this time that rock would have disappeared," Dad said.

Yeah, and why hasn't it? I thought to myself.

"Honey, we just don't see it," Mom said, concerned.

"I know, Mom. Maybe it's a good thing," I said softly. I was now staring down on what was clearly an island with something bright reflecting from the middle of it. I wondered about it.

"You still see it?" Mom asked.

"Yeah." Out of the corner of my eye, I observed a look of concern on her face as she turned away. Could be that we were experiencing more turbulence, however light, and she was concerned how it might affect me this time, too. Again, I closed my eyes as we moved through it and out of range of the island. Though the turbulence was short-lived and wasn't as violent, it was funny how it didn't upset a single nerve in my body this time around.

Cameron came to the forefront as I grew more curious about the Bermuda Triangle and the stories that spawn from it, and I wondered if my parents believed any of them.

“Do you believe the stories about the Bermuda Triangle?” The question went out to no one in particular. Mom, with ambiguous eyes, faced me with her answer.

“I don’t know...I’m not sure about the paranormal part of it. I think there are logical explanations for the disappearances. Other than that”—she lightly shook her head—“I really haven’t given it much thought.”

Mom was careful of what she said, how she said it. Knowing Mom, she didn’t want to contribute to how I was thinking (though she had no proof of what I was thinking) or say anything that would get my hopes up.

“Yeah, Dad,” I suddenly recalled, “I remember you being fascinated with all that stuff at one time. So you must believe some of it?”

“Yeah, I do. Just so you know, that fascination had to do with me schooling you. But much like your mother, I think there’s a logical explanation for some of the things that happened. Now with that said, I also believe in the unknown...say, another dimension of the world we live in, that in certain conditions of time and space, the present somehow aligns with the past or the future, creating a kind of portal. And if you happen to enter this portal, you’re gone forever. I mean, what is the likelihood of you finding your way back?

“But listen, from my understanding, there’s no real proof to all that stuff that happened in the Bermuda Triangle. Some even think that the mystery of the whole thing was manufactured, a hoax.”

“How much of it do you believe?” I pursued.

“That’s hard to say, and it doesn’t really matter because I’m not worried about this plane disappearing, not with us in it."

"You have no fear at all, Dad?"

"None. Never have." His tone was unyielding.

"Then how can you believe the stuff you believe?"

"I can because I don't feel that I'm at risk or that it would ever happen to me. And, because it's the furthest thing from my mind when I'm flying over a large body of water, or any area with a mysterious past. Let me put it to you like this: My belief is this much." He held up a hand, using his index finger and thumb to measure how much. And what small gap between the two fingers. "About 1 percent," he made clear.

"One percent of what?" I smiled.

"Of this." He stretched the fingers apart, forming the biggest gap possible. He probably would have broken them if he could have. He then looked back at me with a big smile, and so did Mom. I couldn't help smiling enormously myself.

"But I disappeared. That wasn't a hoax."

He turned serious. "That was different...although it's still not clear what happened that night."

Mom chimed in, "And you're here with us where you belong. The other disappearances turned up nothing, leaving no clues for finding out what really happened. The Bermuda Triangle is or has been one great mystery. Yes, it's still not clear what happened in your case, but don't think it's like the cases of the Triangle. Thank goodness you're right here where you belong."

"That's right. Your situation has nothing to do with all that and thinking of it on that level is much too confusing," Dad affirmed. "You have to ease your mind of that. Just let it go, Pia."

With that, we dropped the subject and became passively mute. Except silence wasn't so silent in a restless mind like my own. As for my parents, they were still confused and uncertain of what really happened to me that night, so I understood them not wanting to associate it with anything as mysterious as the BT. To me, that pretty much explained their belief being well below 100 percent, 1 percent, according to Dad. Not by a long shot for me though. I was at the 100 percent margin of certainty. Too much had changed in so little time.

*I only wish...*My thought trailed off. I realized I no longer had the right to wish that I had someone to understand what I was going through because, after all, there was Cameron, whether I wanted to accept him or not. I supposed he was as close as I would get to having my wish fulfilled. Maybe I knew that already. Maybe it's why I tried reaching him one last time before takeoff.

How much of the message recorded? I wondered still.

Chapter Eighteen

An Eventful Evening

Uncle John was standing by a shiny black Yukon waiting for us with the backside already open. Spotting him was easy; like Dad, he loved wearing dark shades rain or shine. He dressed in a white button-down, long-sleeve shirt and jeans, appropriate for the slight chill in the air. We knew ahead of time what to expect in the weather. Mom and I had jackets handy on the plane and now had them on.

As we approached, I smiled, glancing between both men, and Mom almost took the words right out of my mouth.

"What are the chances of you two dressing alike? The same shirt on down to the loafers," she said. Uncle John and Dad weren't twins, but they had the kind of resemblances like the Wayans or Jonas brothers. When you look at them, you knew they were brothers. In this case, both were the same height, had the same broad shoulders, and similar smiles.

Uncle John knitted his thick eyebrows together, giving Dad a quick once-over. "You have to give it to us, we're a good-looking pair," he said in his personal Bermudian accent. Then Uncle John fanned out his broad shoulders and gave Mom a gorilla-style hug. "How're you doing, Vivica? It's so good to see you, and you're looking good as ever...And, Pia, come and give uncle a hug." I went into his arms, and he smacked a kiss on a cheek. "How's my girl?"

"Fine, Uncle John." I wrapped my skinny arms around his thick midsection.

Dad loaded our luggage in the trunk as we chattered and gradually made our way inside the spacious luxury truck.

Soon the truck pulled from the curb, maneuvering into traffic, leaving behind a line of stopped cars that seemed to have arrived all at once.

"I trust you had a pleasant trip," Uncle John commented.

"It was," said Dad, "except for a little turbulence here and there."

"Uncle John, where's Regina and Prince?" I slipped into the conversation.

"Prince should be home by now. And Regina went to the mall with a couple of friends. She'll be back shortly after we get there."

"So is Iris all prepared for tonight?" Dad asked.

"Yeah, but she's a bit nervous about being the center of attention." They discussed Aunt Iris for a bit and then began talking about the event itself. This went on for a little while longer as we drove across the island at a slowpoke speed practically. (In Bermuda, the speed limit's around thirty miles per hour). Then the talk rolled over to updates on specific topics and other interests that randomly came to mind. At this point of the conversation, I was aloof, just sitting back taking in the scenery as we cruised over the causeway from St. George's, en route to Paget where Uncle John lived.

No matter how many times I've seen Bermuda; its scenery always presented a warm, delightful feeling. And its historical sights aired a magical feel much like the feeling you'd get entering Disney's Magic Kingdom. Like the Magic Kingdom, everything about Bermuda seemed timeless. So much so that one would wonder if it's being preserved by an invisible time capsule.

Or maybe, just maybe, from the beginning when settlers first landed on the island they took an oath unimaginably. And could be that that oath was to build and preserve a special place, unseen anywhere else. Maybe that's why it appeared timeless and preserved.

I smiled at the crucial realization that my mind could have a loose screw the reason it was running wild with wild possibilities.

Yet the bizarre fancies continued although I tried putting a lid on it, by thinking about seeing my cousins and having lots of fun at the gathering tonight. But the sudden craziness wasn't happening at random; it was leading to a purpose. And that purpose had to do with Cameron, the disappearance of his parents, him seeing my visions, and everything else, which influenced my brain to spawn new ways of looking at things.

For instance, I wondered could my answer be here. *Surely, Bermuda had secrets, mysteries—plenty of it—unknown to the rest of the world. And how did it come to be...really? Could it have appeared one day, perhaps from another dimension? Could my answer really be here? It seemed mysterious enough. And the island, what did it have to do with me since only I could see it?*

If only Dad could hear me, he would say my thoughts about Bermuda were nonsense. After all this time, why would you think such a thing? Just the same, no one could dispute Bermuda's fascinating distinction, like the stunning white roofs, built like steps sloping downward atop colorful buildings replicating flavors of ice cream. Nothing like I've seen anywhere else to this day. And from the air, the view's breathtaking, the white glossy roofs looking like the law of the land.

Nothing about all that was mysterious though, just different. But it had to be a trick to keeping the roofs so clean and white. I was inclined to ask when a couple of men on mopeds jetted by like maniacs.

"What the hell...!" Uncle John blurted. The speed limit sign read 20 mph, and the roads being narrow and winding, they must've been idiots or completely out their minds.

But the distraction was short-lived, for me anyway, as we curved around the Harrington Sound, the main attraction for most tourists. My cousins and I had many times winded around the six-mile-long Harrington Sound on mopeds to take in the sight, which includes a museum, zoo, aquarium, caves, and so much more. At times, we would abandon the mopeds to explore depths of the Sound. Particularly the underground caves and tunnels that required us to explore on our hands and knees. I wasn't looking forward to that this time, though. Honestly, I hadn't for a while now.

I recalled a few times we came across peculiar-looking animals we bolted from like lightning because we didn't know what they were or what to expect. One of the odd-looking creatures I remembered being red. Thinking of this reminded me of Mom, telling me once how red skeletons from particular types of dead animals mix with other things turned the sand pink. Something like that, I couldn't recall the exact details. It had been the first time I noticed the sand here was different from other beaches, as though it had played a quick trick on me and turned pink right before my eyes. I think I was five then. That's when Mom's talent for teaching came to life when she animated a picture for a five-year-old to understand how red things turned things pink.

I know exactly where we are now, I thought. We were approaching the roundabout in Hamilton where Mr. Barnes would stand in the middle and wave to everyone going to work in the morning. Just off the roundabout was a statue erected in his honor. *Hi,* my lips moved in passing. We weren't too far now from Uncle John's house.

In less than ten minutes, we drove up a brick driveway to a charming cottage tucked off the road amongst large shade trees. The house was lambent: a bright pastel green, surrounded by beautiful panoply of plants. Aunt Iris was peeping out of an enormous arched window as we arrived. She then came out on the porch to greet us. She was a slim woman, wearing a ruffled apron and eager smile.

"C'mon," she encouraged us to not waste time unloading the SUV. That's how eager she was. We climbed four to five steps in single file before reaching her opened arms. "Uh, how is everybody?"

"Good...now that we're here" was our natural reply, having made it across the ocean in peace and was now among family. And we all streamed into the house, hauling luggage and other things.

Mmmm. The aroma of something delicious cooking in the kitchen had us sniffing as soon as we stepped on the hardwood floor leading to a roomy living area. A large rug of unique quality was in the center of it. And situated around the rug was the comfort I longed for as soon as I laid eyes on it. At a glance, I saw not much had changed, though the place was as beautiful and inviting as ever.

"How was the trip?" Aunt Iris asked after us.

"Ran into a little turbulence but other than that...a safe flight," Mom riposted.

Uncle John suggested the guest room as usual, and Dad headed that way with the luggage. I was sure I had the choice of sleeping with Regina or sleeping on the pullout in the den.

"We got rid of that old bed in Regina's room and replaced it with twin beds," Aunt Iris informed.

"Really?" Surprised, I instantly made up my mind to share a room with Regina since now I wouldn't fall victim to her bad sleeping habits.

"Sure. Go ahead and see for yourself," she encouraged, and I did right away.

"Mmm...what's that smelling so good?" I heard Mom say as I admired the new twin beds. I also deposited my luggage in the corner.

"I have a casserole in the oven. Come on into the kitchen," she said to Mom just as I resurfaced from the room. "You must be hungry. I've whipped up something to eat, not much, but enough to get by until tonight." Aunt Iris's tone was irresistible in addition to the aroma coming from the kitchen; I had to see what she had cooking.

In my eyes, it was *the* state-of-the-art kitchen, perfect for my Aunt Iris, since her home was in the kitchen. Now she had a new cookbook to show for her love of it.

I sat on a barstool at the granite-top island of the kitchen, foretasting whatever she offered that was smelling so good. Atop the granite island in the kitchen was silver trays and bowls of finger food such as tuna sandwiches, raw veggies with dip, nuts, and potato chips.

"I know you must be hungry, but don't eat much because we're having a big dinner at the book signing later on," she said opening the oven. Carefully, she began removing a huge pan from it.

"Oh my, that's *some* casserole," Mom said.

"Uh, please, Aunt Iris, can I have some now?" I smiled, grabbing chips from the chip bowl.

"Of course, honey, as much as you want—but later," she stressed, smiling back at me.

"So it's going to the book signing," Mom gathered. "What kind of casserole is it?"

"A spinach-chicken casserole. And yes, it's going to the function. Sorry."

"Ohh, uhh," I snuffled. It was disappointing having to wait until later.

My cousin Regina came storming in. "Omigod...you're here already." Her tall, slim frame stooped to give me an ecstatic hug, and then she rushed over to Mom. "Hi, Aunt Vivica," she said and hugged her, too.

"Hi, sweetheart." Mom kissed her forehead.

"Mom, take a break already. I can't believe you...Today is supposed to be your day and here you are in the kitchen cooking," Regina complained to her mother looking at us, then back at her mother. "She lives in the kitchen."

"You're right. All the more reason why I have to garnish the table with one of my fortes from the cookbook...*at least*. It wouldn't be right having a whole buffet of food without something from me. You think?" I didn't know about anyone else, but I thought she had a point. "Besides, it's the least I can do to show my appreciation." Aunt Iris then looked over at Regina with a shifty look. "Now tell them the surprise, Regina."

Regina's thin frame went lopsided, face frowned, looking like "what?" Indeed, Aunt Iris had something sneaky up her sleeve because she was now beaming.

"Mom?" Regina sulked somewhat. "What?"

"I know, I know," Aunt Iris said now, "you don't have to say anything."

And I could see on Regina's face that she was more confused now.

"Come on, Iris, you can't keep us in suspense. Come out with it," Mom spoke up.

"Yeah! Yeah!" Regina and I ranted, fully aware now that this was one of Aunt Iris's guessing games or tricks. She was so good at conjuring up something that got us all worked up. And we loved these times of just having pure fun.

"And I thought you were having a memory lapse or something, thinking you had told me something when you didn't," Regina said to her mother.

"Come on, Aunt Iris, what is it? I sure hope it's some of that casserole because I can't wait to taste it," I said with enthusiasm.

Mom laughed. "You always got something cooking, pun intended," and we all burst with more laughter and lit up the kitchen with scatterbrained comments as well.

As soon as Aunt Iris clutched the handle of the microwave, smiling more now, Mom began drumming the table, "Come on, girls, this has to be good." So Regina and I drummed along with Mom. Aunt Iris then yanked open the oven door, reached in, and brought out–yes–a small pan of casserole. "Whoa! Whew!" we said in unison. Our joy and foolishness soared through the roof, just for the heck of it.

"Hey. What's all the racket about?" the men entered the kitchen, and for the most part, we were too giddy to speak.

Aunt Iris bowed to the pan and said, "Just having a little fun." And then she set the pan on the counter in front of us. "It's only enough to sample. I wish I had more in case it's all gone before you get a chance to get some tonight."

"I know it's good, but don't you think you're just a *little* too vain, Iris?" Uncle John said, chuckling.

Wearing a smile, Aunt Iris held up her hands as if to surrender herself. "I'm only speaking the truth."

"But that was sneaky." Regina smiled at me and then turned to her mother. "That was sneaky of you Mom...pretending I was in on it just to throw everybody off..."

Uncle John then led with something new for discussion. "I'm wondering if we can get out of wearing a suit."

Neither of them wanted to wear a suit and tie. Dad wondered if he could get away without wearing one, given he wasn't a Bermudian and since the event was being held in a reception room at a hotel.

"Now you know better than that." She looked directly at Uncle John. "Tell you what, you can be dress casual but dress up the casual." Then she went on to say that tonight's event was formal to her and that everyone should look proud and the men, specifically, should have polished shoes, heavily starched shirts no matter what they wore. We chuckled to that because we knew she was kidding.

She went on giving more details about the event to Mom and Dad, saying that the gathering was an informal book signing and dinner, arranged and hosted by the book club she belonged to. In Aunt Iris's case, the event was happening ahead of a formal book signing tour she would start in a few weeks.

But tonight, she would have to stand before a volume of people and deliver a ten- to twenty-minute speech; this had her both excited and nervous, even though she had won a few contests and had appeared on television a few times. Apparently, she was oblivious to having an audience then. On the other hand, I supposed demonstrating something before a group of people was far different from making a speech before them. All in all, considering the upcoming book-signing tour, tonight's event would definitely be a practice run.

Spontaneously, Aunt Iris commanded us to take a seat as she prepared to practice on us the speech she would deliver later. At once I was excited all over again for her, and excited to be getting a sneak preview of what to expect later. Prince showed up just before she got started, beaming from ear to ear, his cheekbones bulging like balls, wondering what was going on. Of course, she shushed him and ordered him to sit. Upon taking a seat next to me, I smiled...then whispered to him what was going on to resolve his curiosity.

"Shucks, and I rushed back home," Prince mocked, and I just shook my head as Aunt Iris began speaking.

I was sure she was keeping track of time, but just in case, I noted the time she started. We sat through it quietly, paying close attention as she requested so that we could adequately comment afterward. In precisely twenty-three minutes, she was done and at the top of her game, I thought. If she was nervous at all, it didn't show. We all thought she would do well tonight and saw nothing in the wording that needed to be changed. We even assured her she had the right amount of emotion to touch the audience.

But time wasn't standing still. The time left before the event we spent getting ready. Mom surprised me with a dress she had bought from a gift shop at the hotel where the convention was held. A turquoise dress that flared from a black, elastic waistband was perfect for the occasion. Mom donned one similar, fitting to her good taste. When Regina made last-minute changes to what she was wearing, from slacks and a ruffled top to a ruffled floral frock instead, all women were wearing dresses.

The honoree stood out in a black fitting dress that broadened from the hips. The dazzling earrings and bracelet set off a stunning combination. Tonight was indeed her night in every way.

The men wore proud faces, looking spiffy from head to toe, donning pale-colored shirts that offset their dark suits and perfect ties. Obviously, they had decided to wear suits to make the honoree proud, as we were overly proud of her. I made a point to check their shoes. And of course, each had that just-visited-the-parlor shine.

In the final moments before leaving the house, we all marveled our approval of one another as we anticipated having such a lovely evening.

Chapter Nineteen

New Discovery

Last night's soiree was the main topic at the breakfast table the next morning. Talking about how Aunt Iris had amazed us all by her stellar speech before an audience of at least two hundred people. We couldn't have been prouder of her. Following the speech, how seamlessly gracious the book signing went. She'd signed copies of her book for fans who purchased copies on the spot and for those who brought copies to the affair to have signed.

When the time had come to eat, there was sweet-sounding music from a small band of four with a fiddler. The music added a dulcet seasoning to the delectable buffet of catered food we'd sat around enjoying as we chatted. Aunt Iris's casserole was one of a few dishes not catered, and I made a point not to miss out having a serving. Because she was *so* right, it was the most sought-after dish, which left some people disappointed that it wasn't enough to go around.

"Is the recipe for the casserole in the book?" I'd

asked Regina as we scanned through the cookbook. After that, we got up and frolicked amongst others in a small area making do for the dance floor. Then we showed off how good dancers we were. It was so much fun. At some point, our parents winded up on the dance floor to "strut their stuff," they called it. We gladly stepped aside–took a seat actually–and watched as they put on a hilarious show from the eighties.

But time flew by much too fast last night, as usual when you're having so much fun. Rain and thunder were dwelling over the island when we stepped out into the darkness. We could hear tree frogs singing, and along the way home, clearly beneath the street lamps, we had spotted tiny frogs dancing in the street, being that rain's like music to their ears.

Altogether, Prince, Regina, and I got up from the breakfast table, trying to decide what we would do with the time we had left to spend together. Mom and Dad had hinted at flying back to Florida before dusk, which allowed us plenty of time to scoot around town and have fun without worrying about time rushing us. Or flying by so fast that it felt like it snuck up on us.

We wasted no time getting dressed in bright-colored shorts and T-shirts. We girls put our hair in ponytails so it wouldn't blow all over the place. Prince just ran a hand over his pageboy do, and we were out the door behind his tall, nimble frame full of vitality.

"Tell you what we're going to do," Prince stated as we walked the scooters to the end of the driveway. "We're going to the tennis court for a few games, but along the way we'll make a few short stops."

"Okay, um, where are we stopping first?" I asked as

Regina looked on.

"Just follow me," he said sternly. Regina and I rolled our eyes and took off behind him. Immediately the vigor of the wind whipped moderately against our skin as it ruffled our clothes.

Prince looked over his shoulder, yelling, "Come on, you're too far behind, keep up."

"Whatever you say, Daddy," Regina shot him sarcasm in her Bermudian accent sounding slightly British...like Prince.

We caught up with him and maintained a steady distance behind him as we made our way to South Road, the main road on the south side of the coastline. The scenery along South Road was hilly with curves winding in and out, unfolding elegant views of rolling terrain rich in color. It was so breathtaking I wanted to breathe it all in. But how could my nostrils handle breathing it all in when so much wind already was coming through? I punned humorously, feeling much exhilaration.

And after so many times visiting Bermuda, riding on the left side of the road still felt awkward to me.

In a short while we arrived at our first stop: Astwood Park. Prince got off his moped and invited us to come along, saying that he would only be a minute if we decided to wait. Since we had visited the park many times, or mostly because we weren't up for a steep hike downward, we told him not to have us come looking for him. We watched him wound through a trail of trees and rocks until he disappeared. He would end up at the edge of a cliff, overlooking a beautiful hideaway, a cove/beach setting, where neighboring tropical birds hovered.

However, making it down to the cove wasn't a

smooth and easy task to some. You literally had to hike your way down or descend by parachute or something. That's exactly why we decided to pass it up and just hang around in the park until he got back.

But I was curious what he was going to do, so I asked Regina. She waved a hand in a nonchalant way. "Who knows...maybe he's looking for someone."

Maybe she was right. He returned sooner than we expected and we were back on the road to our next destination, wherever that may be. About three miles or so up the road, Regina and I soon found out. And we were eyeing each other as we turned into another park, this time South Shore, known for its many beach coves. The trails leading to these coves were flat and easy to walk. For that reason, we decided to go with him to see what he was up to.

Of the many trails in the park, we took the one bringing us to a cliff overlooking Chaplin Bay, another beach surrounded by cliffs. Limestone cliffs enclosed this particular spot, and down below was a coral reef dividing a beautiful blanket of pink sand that extended out to the clear blue water. Oh, if I were an artist I would go crazy setting up an easel to capture this spectacular picture.

I gazed off beyond the extended shoreline and spotted a boat. But it was something else out there that really got my attention. *What is that?* I put on a hard stare, watching as the vessel slowly approached it. "What is that out there?" I muttered the words now.

"Huh? Out where?"

I dampened my curiosity by not responding to Prince. I didn't want to spoil the moment with my hang-ups if it wasn't necessary. So in the meantime I zipped my lips, assuming that what was out there was only for my eyes to see.

However, my trying to keep quiet was getting harder by the minute—those people out there were real for Pete's sake. I had to say something now or I would have exploded. Besides, I could always depend on my cousins and talk to them about anything. And right now I desperately needed a reality check.

"Oh hell...I forgot. Come on let's get out of here," Prince said turning his back, assuming we would follow.

"Hey! Hold up. What's the rush?"

Prince turned around, looking annoyingly surprised to my objection.

"I need to know if I'm seeing things," I said pointing a finger toward the water.

He didn't speak up immediately. "You mean...that gigantic rock out there?" He said hesitantly, looking that way. "No, Pia. You're not seeing things. Not this time, it's really there."

Thank goodness, I sighed, pretending to wipe sweat from my forehead. "But..." It suddenly dawned on me one crucial fact: it was impossible for a rock of that magnitude to....

"Look, Pia," Prince interjected, "I know exactly what you are thinking, but it wasn't like it just, poof, popped up." Prince grabbed the top of his head, looking shamefaced, "That didn't come out right."

Immediately I gazed at the peculiar look on his face. A similar look was on Regina's, too.

"Then how did it get there?"

"The...the storm," Prince said cautiously. "We had a huge storm...say about...six months ago. It was the worst storm ever. And it had to of been the thunder that woke me up as I hit the floor. And you know how hard I sleep. That next morning everybody was talking about it and it was all over the news, in the papers, everywhere."

"Well that's funny; I didn't hear anything about it. I don't think Mom and Dad heard about it either."

"Yeah, well...you weren't supposed to know," Prince informed me as Regina nodded, agreeing with big brother.

"What–why not?" I questioned though I already sensed why. "I can't believe this. You of all people should be curious about how a rock of that size, big enough to build a town on, got there in the first place. Here today, maybe gone tomorrow. *Hello!* You see where I'm going with this?"

"Of course. But if I told you that it was an earthquake that night, what would you say to that?" Prince countered.

"An earthquake?"

"An earthquake and a thunderstorm happening at the same time, if you can believe that. I suppose it's possible, but I'd never heard of that happening until that night." He shook his head. "The thought of it sounds scary–and it was. And it was this blast of thunder that sounded like an atomic boom."

Regina's eyes widened, nodding reticently.

Prince went on, "Though it's strange, but it had to of been when it happened–the earthquake I mean. If that's what it was, because I didn't feel anything move, except for when I hit the floor. Me, Regina, Mom and Dad, none of us felt anything resembling an earthquake. But it's not to say that so many other people did. But...I don't know...most people I talked to thought everything about that night was weird. There were no signs of an earthquake anywhere except—when you look out there—how could it have not been an earthquake? I mean, what else could have caused that?"

"He's right you know. Because it certainly didn't sail in here on its own," Regina communicated now.

"Last I heard they're still conducting studies. Maybe that's what they're doing out there now," Prince said looking off in that direction.

"Why, what do you think they're looking for?" I couldn't be more curious.

Prince put a hand on my shoulder. "Come on. Let's walk back this way." We headed toward the entrance as he continued.

"Now, the word is, the earthquake registered a 3.2 magnitude, not enough to have caused that much of a shift in the earth."

"Like an island-size chuck rising above the water, you mean? But there was an earthquake?" I was confused.

"Yeah but...wouldn't it have caused a tsunami? This is what had most people wondering. And since they're not sure how or why the rock rose out of the water, they did whatever studies to find out. They're probably still doing it for all I know."

Regina chimed in, "I know all of this sound crazy, but I'm sure they'll come up with something that'll explain everything."

"And you believe that, after all this time?" I questioned.

She shrugged. "Everybody I've talked to seems to think so."

"Besides, it's been six months. It's ancient news

now," Prince contended.

"It's still news because no one really knows what happened; that's what you're telling me. Is that all you know?" I was hungry for more information.

"Yeah, that's it."

"Well, let's talk to Uncle John, maybe he knows more."

"Let's not."

"Why?" I stared agape at Prince. But Regina's voice resonated softly, so my question went to her.

"Pia, you're not still having those strange visions, are you? It's been a while since we've talked about it."

What does that have to do with anything? I wanted to say. But the deep concern in her eyes, I grew suspicious of, and I assumed my expression showed it. However, before I could answer her, Prince jumped back in, moving us along.

"It's like this, Pia. You weren't supposed to know. We had to promise not to talk to you about this. We just assumed the hush-hush had something to do with...you know." Prince sighed. "I made a big mistake coming here. Had I been thinking, I wouldn't have."

"Now just how long you think you would've pulled that off?" I said as we settled down at a picnic table. "It just doesn't make sense, being that we come here all the time. Now come on...you knew I would have found out eventually." *Six months?* I couldn't believe they managed to keep this from me for as long as they had.

"You think I didn't know that! We tried to explain that to Dad, but you know how he—all of them—can be."

"Yeah, I know. My parents are way too protective and untrusting." That basically summed it up. I looked up at Regina, contemplating me.

"Is it because you still have the visions?" she slithered the question back at me since I didn't get around to answering it before.

"Nah," I lied. "Even if I was, that's no reason to treat me like I'm some kind of Humpty Dumpty. I'm stronger than you think. Don't keep things from me because you think I can't handle it. You have to trust me."

Regina put on a gracious smile, nodding.

"Now, with that said...yes, I do still see things. And yes, I saw that same island I always see on our way here yesterday—and yes, I dreamt about it last night. Now do I appear broken down about it to you? Hmm? No, of course not!" I said my piece and dropped it. I went back to talking about the new addition to Bermuda. That one thing everyone could see, yet had the nerve to try to keep it from me, thinking it's for my own good. I still couldn't believe how long they'd gotten away with it.

"You seem just fine to me. Just promise you won't say anything to our parents about all this because I slipped up big-time bringing you here." Prince simplified his wants.

I exhaled deeply. "You're overreacting. I can't see what the big deal is. Unless...there's something more going on that you're not telling me?"

"No, that's not it," said Regina.

"I've told you everything we know. And you now know that it wasn't our idea to keep it from you in the first place," Prince corrected. "So you *have to* keep quiet about this—promise?

"Okay, fine then. I won't say anything," I surrendered with agitation. How could they be so calm about something so significant anyway? I thought. True, I was into islands, no question about it...because being wired to things out of the ordinary had become a way of life for me. But there was nothing I could do about it. Nothing.

Just as an influx of people unloaded off a bus, we were leaving the park. Our next stop was at a tennis court. After the new discovery on our last stop, I had to get worked up to ensure a lasting match of tennis. Without a doubt, Prince was gunning for one. Anyway, it was good focusing on something else for a while.

Prince was a great competitor, and he always looked forward to battling with me every chance he got. And with Regina off on the sideline watching, he joked about having a worthy contender in the family. Tennis wasn't Regina's strong suit, but she loved playing regardless, and really loved watching us in a head-to-head battle.

We played a few games, taking in-between breaks. Later we were totally spent and satisfied, and ready to hop back on the scooters to hang ourselves out to dry. However, Regina had answered a call from Aunt Iris urging us to head back; Mom and Dad were ready to leave for Florida. We were so disappointed: Once again time was cutting into our playtime.

Heading back as instructed, we clearly saw daunting thunderheads approaching the area. As it turned out, the storm was the reason for the change of plans. Dad definitely did not want to meet with a storm.

Our good-byes lasted the whole trip to the airport as

everyone went along for the ride. Prince made me promise again that I wouldn't say anything about the island, and I assured he had no reason to worry though I knew it wasn't right. My suspicion was growing and growing. Something about that island being there was way off for sure.

Soon we were flying over Bermuda through pounding rain that we quickly left behind. About the white rooftops: Mom had told me that every three years they were painted, or lime washed, the reason why they kept a pristine look. She insisted she had told me before. Apparently I must have lost that piece of information somewhere. Still, I couldn't see the paint alone doing the trick, with the sun beating down on the roofing all day long, not to mention storms dropping by for a short or extended visit. "Oh well." I accepted that as fact just the same. The mild anxiety attack was letting up, so I accepted relaxation, too.

As time went by, I caught myself a few times in a daze and had to remind my eyes to blink. I was so fixated on today's discovery and everything else that had transpired in days past that lead up to this one. And in a matter of time, Cameron and I would come together, picking up where we'd left off. If only I could close my eyes and go into an image-free nap until we got there.

The Richter scale—as I said, if only I could take a nap—there was the possibility that it wasn't working right. But surely they would have figured that out by now. In that case, the public should have been informed. All aspects of it were strange: the whole incident not going viral. So hush-hush it was; right down to family wanting to brush it under the rug never to be discussed again—or discussed with me.

Maybe it was top-secret, I thought suddenly. You never know about the government. Once in political science, we got into a heated discussion about top-secret stuff. What interested me most in the debate was the sightings of unidentified flying objects (UFOs) and the belief that the government had met with aliens and was keeping it concealed from us—the public. They denied the claim, though. But then a video popped up, telling a different story. Revealed in the video was a hairless creature—an ET-looking creature with a triangular-shaped head and deep-set dark eyes, spread way apart—being interrogated. They got nothing but gibberish from the creature. Still, government officials called it nonsense, insisting it was a concocted footage.

However, what I was itching to know was why the government would ignore sightings of UFOs. So I had asked the teacher, and another student sounded after me, "Yeah, why would they? It's definitely a threat to national security." Then the teacher said, "That's just it; the government wouldn't ignore something like this, even though they may appear to be."

The discussion heated up and went on and on. That had been one interesting hour.

The part about the aliens stood out then and was at the forefront now...for obvious reasons. If it was true that something from beyond has visited us and been caught, likely it was under tight security while government officials conducted their studies because society would wreak havoc if we knew. Perhaps that's what the government is thinking. The teacher thought so anyway.

Chaos, yeah, I could see that.

As for that island, there should be more noise about it, I thought. I lay my head against the window, closed my eyes, and imagined being an exotic specimen, a guinea pig type specimen, under a universal microscope that the entire world was glued to watching, told to *shush* to not disturb the study in any way. A study...on me...the weirdo...whole world watching....

I stifled a breath as a bump jarred me out of a catnap.

A study...on me the weird alien... With a hand covering a yawn, I instantly recalled where my mind was before dozing off. Too bizarre, being an alien and all, I had to admit for the record.

I looked out the window, thinking I couldn't have been asleep for long. But when I saw what we were approaching, I had an idea how long I'd been asleep. And that I woke up when I did was incredible timing, like clockwork.

Like clockwork, I whispered. *Can you hear me?* Telepathically, how otherwise can you communicate with the unknown? I peered down below, trancelike, testing it as if my pupils had a zooming mechanism to transmit my thoughts to another. It was time to find the underlying cause of my hang-ups if telepathically was at all the way to go about it. My eyes blinked though I maintained a steady gaze, powered by all five senses and an overcharged brain. I was desperate to succeed in connecting on this level. Closer, closer to the island, the plane approached. *I see you, I believe you're there...speak to me.*

I cleared my head then, waiting, waiting to receive

the first sign of communication, regardless of how silly I was starting to feel. Captivated by tension, my fingertips drummed the armrest, becoming still moments later. Maybe closing my eyes would help, so I tried it, waited. Almost to the island now, disappointment flushed through me. I wailed silently, *Are you there? What do you want? Why me?*

Directly overhead now, a remote chance of connecting was passing by. If not now, then when? At this point, I was shutting off this absurdity until a dim humming in my ears started. *Yeah right, perfect, just perfect.* I was really pissed by now. But then something different began to happen. My brain—I don't know—felt like neurons popping neurotically in my entire head. The humming was phasing out, and the sensation of it seemed to spread through my veins by way of a sizeable IV.

Could this be...?

It is, these words charmed softly and I froze, goose bumps plaguing my arms. And like a liniment to heal my sudden fright, every muscle, every nerve, even my heartbeats, were wiped out completely, morphed into what felt like total calmness of body and spirit—no, just spirit. My body, I couldn't feel. Scared, this had become much more than what I'd bargained for, and I wanted to take it all back, put what was happening in reverse.

Too late. I was at peace, a kind of suspended animation with such stillness and quietness all around me. No sound. Where did it all go? The sound of the engines. Gone. The air friction. Gone. I couldn't hear a thing. In this noetic state, nothing appeared alive or real. I imagined this resembling the process of death, the first stage of moving on—I pushed it out, wouldn't give it a chance to latch on, plant roots. There was a time for everything, and this wasn't the time to be thinking...about death.

Ferret.

Ferret? I wondered about this beau geste, at the same time, pressing for clarity. *Ferret, a name? An animal? What?*

Ferret...Ferret...Ferret. It seemed to sing to me, penetrating me with the word, or name, that meant nothing to me.

Before I knew it, I was back to normal, peering eagerly out the window, knowing I would find the island nowhere in sight. Mom was looking away as I straightened my head. Then I released a breath I didn't know I was holding.

I relaxed, took a minute to form a conclusion, mostly wondering what an ESP experience was really like. Poignant and simple was how I imagined it to be. The way I've seen it in movies–not so much how a medium would communicate with the dead, however...but kind of...like that.

Ferret. It had to come from somewhere...had to have significant meaning. And I couldn't help wondering what it meant to me, certain that it did mean something.

As we were coming in for a landing, I reached for my cell phone and powered it up. The roaming sign was gone, and it was connected to the max, showing five bars and a fully charged battery. Great! I was back in business.

There were messages waiting, text and voice. First, I

checked the voice message, suspecting it was from Cameron. Just what I thought: no curiosity whatsoever in his message, letting me know the part where I confessed didn't record. His only concern was that he missed my call. Next, I checked text messages—two. One from a friend, the other from *Cameron*, making sure I got his voice message. He also insisted I call the first chance I got.

I did just that—not immediately, however—but much later. First things first: I was starving for information, so my first priority was a little fact-checking of my own. (I wouldn't rest until I did.) And to do that, I needed access to the Internet. The sooner, the better. I couldn't get home fast enough. But when we got there, I was faced with a disappointing setback due to a power outage in the area. We got word that it had been out approximately two hours already. After unloading our stuff from the car, Dad decided that we would go check out a new seafood restaurant called *Ocean Blue.*

Soon we were back in the car, going to check out the new place, and I was antsy about getting online to do some research. The outage couldn't have come at a worse time.

In spite of the inconvenience of the outage, and the peculiar discovery back in Bermuda, I would say "perfect timing" was the essence of this day. We'd left in time to dodge the storm back in Bermuda. We'd missed a massive backup due to an overturned vehicle, and there'd been no waiting at the fabulous new seafood restaurant. Even more, the power was restored the second we walked into the house, just as a storm rolled in.

One other thing, *Ferret*, perhaps it was perfect timing as well, though I had yet to learn how.

Chapter Twenty

The Confession

"Mom, Dad? I'm going for a walk...beach," I announced headed for the back door.

"Okay." Mom waved absentmindedly. They both were out front, preoccupied with neighbors. As I made my exit, I thought, one thing good about living on the beach, it was an avenue for a quick escape. Literally.

Last night when I finally got around to calling Cameron, we talked long enough to agree on a time to meet, around ten, at the café. And in the time it took me to arrive, here he was, standing outside the entrance, looking cool and collective.

"Hey," I said.

"Hey yourself," he replied with a radiant smile. "So what do you want to do? Hang out here? Take a walk?"

"Yeah, let's walk." The morning was cool, and the setting was mellow with a slight gathering of people here and there. It was indeed perfect for taking a stroll so I led the way.

"So, how was your trip?"

"It was nice. Bermuda is always nice. It's an interesting place to visit. I didn't get around to telling you, but I have relatives there. Cousins. An aunt, uncle. And they love it there, wouldn't dream of living anywhere else. I bet you would love it there. It's a small place, big on history and mystery—pink beaches. You have to go someday to see it with your own eyes." I stop to check myself; maybe I was rambling a bit too much.

"Mmm...maybe someday I will." He smiled and so did I.

I looked straight ahead, taking a deep breath of the scented ocean. We both turned speechless, with the exact same thing on our minds, one looking for the other to broach the subject. As it turned out, Cameron did.

"Look, Pia. I'm going to cut to the chase."

"Okay," I said, gazing up at him.

"I was really surprised to see that you had called and then took the time to leave a message. It let me know you really gave it some thought. And as to *feeling better,* I really do. A tremendous load has been lifted...even more so now that you're here." He fixed an honest expression on his face. "But...I wonder about the message you intended to leave. On my end, it cut off before you finished."

"How much of it did you get?"

"Well, it cut off right where you were saying how I might feel better about something. What exactly?"

"Well...about what you said you saw and...how it could be connected...to me."

"Yeah. Go on."

"How you were able to see things like that, it's awfully hard to believe. It's as though you have a unique ability you're not even aware of. Like you're part man and...part something else."

"Yeah, it's strange alright, and I know what you mean. Except for one thing, I seem to only have that ability when you're around. The dreams, on the other hand, that's a different story."

"What do you mean?"

"I had another one about you that night."

My inquisitive gaze beckoned him to go on.

"About you in a plane crash," he enlightened.

"Really? That's strange because I dreamed of a plane crashing that night, too..." I trailed off in thought.

"Good thing it was just a dream, no need to dwell on it, right?" he remarked, and I agreed without question.

"What are we going to do, Pia?" His tone changed along with the subject.

"I'm not sure what you mean."

"I mean...I haven't been doing anything but thinking about the last time we were together—and everything we discussed. I would like to know how you stand on the subject now. Don't get me wrong; I don't want you to think I'm trying to pressure you or anything like that. But...I'd like to know why we are here. What changed your mind about seeing me again?"

"You must have some idea, don't you?"

"I think I need to hear it from you. I wasn't sure I would see you again, but here we are."

"I know. After I thought about it, I realized I wasn't being fair," I admitted as we advanced up the white walkway. "It was wrong to leave you wondering when you obviously needed someone to talk to and help figure this thing out."

That was my way of confessing without confessing, my way of saying sorry for lying and leaving him thinking the problem was all his and only his. But I was skeptical, not understanding any of it myself. And I still couldn't shake the feeling that he was part of some grand scheme.

"I just want you to know that you matter. Really. That's why I tried reaching you before I left."

"And getting that message meant the world to me. *The world to me, Pia.* Do you hear me?"

"Cameron? There was more I intended to tell you." I started faithfully then stopped. Creeping in was the moment of truth, a reminder that once I tell him there was no taking it back.

"More? Okay, let's hear it." He hugged my shoulders and guided me to an empty bench facing the ocean.

I settled down on the cement bench next to him and gazed off into the ocean. "The beauty is endless," I said softly.

"What's that?" he said, clutching my hand.

"The ocean. Do you ever stare out and just let your imagination run wild?" I was stalling, getting cold feet.

"Sometimes. But I can only imagine what you're about to tell me right now. Seriously."

"Yeah, right," I snorted. "I don't know, Cameron. Maybe...maybe this is a mistake, you know?"

"No, I don't. I know the chemistry between us is"—he broke, searching for the right words—"is so confrontational and even compromising at times, like how I feel it is now. I don't know if it's just with me, but you shut down when it comes to really getting to the heart of what's going on with us. I know I said that I won't pressure you, and believe me I'm not but—"

"Nothing's going on with us," I jumped up and so did he.

"Dang, Pia, come on, don't be like that," he pleaded. "What did I say wrong? You can't keep running away. You have to talk to someone about this, and it might as well be me. How can you not know that? Trust me, Pia. I'm the one person you can trust..."

I drifted farther away, his voice catching up to me, inundating me as I resisted, "Don't...just leave me alone, stay away..." But I was embarrassed and confused too, knowing that he deserved better and screaming to tell him already.

Synchronically, there was that part of me that had to fight every minute, down to every second before reaching that pivotal point of giving him what he deserved. Cameron was right: because the most vulnerable part of me, I kept hidden, confidential. It had become a habit to say the least and as usual, old habits die hard.

"Pia...Pia," he kept calling out to me.

I stood still now, wishing for the wind to carry me like a leaf far, far away. If only it had the strength to do so, leaving all my troubles behind, especially the truth I couldn't bear facing but had to. Slowly, to face his lopsided carriage with hands tightly tucked in back pockets, I turned and moved toward him, being I couldn't resist the gentleness adorning his eyes and good looks.

"Come on." He held out his hand. I gradually moved toward him, took it and we walked back over to the bench.

"It's like this, Pia," he said kindly as we settled down.

"I wasn't saying I don't like it or *you.* Because I'm hooked, I find everything about you attractive, extremely fascinating, and we have fun together in spite of everything. It's as though I've known you...since forever. Don't you feel the same way?"

"No, you gotta be kidding. It's more like I've been trying to avoid you my whole life." I put on a joking smile to his now-wide eyes.

"Well just be thankful that it's only been a week then."

"It's the visions, Cameron. That's why you feel that way about me. *The visions,*" I stressed. "You can't admit it even now."

He slumped forward, sighed, and folded his hands. "All I'm trying to say is that I'm here, Pia, here for *you* for as long as you will have me. I don't want you feeling threatened by me in any way. I want you to trust me, believe that I'm truly your friend." He looked down to the ground, lightly nodding his head. "Is that too much for you still?"

I shied away from his hypnotic plea. It wasn't exactly what I needed this moment. What I needed—what I needed for a while now—was for someone to understand me through and through, without me having to use words, my voice, to make myself clear. That way I wouldn't have to break the oath I made to myself.

"O...kay..." I said. My thoughts tongue-tied because there was a lot riding on what I was about to say. "I know—" In an instant my thought process shifted, back to yesterday.

Yesterday, when we got back from eating out, I went online and did a search on Bermuda dating back six months, looking for more info on what happened there. Prince was right: The Richter scale registered about 3.9, which was high enough to trigger a tsunami, according to several articles I'd read. Then I came across the article *Don't Exist,* which lead my search to Google Satellite.

How could that be? Just yesterday, we all saw the formation though no one was sure how it got there. I zoomed in on the precise location it should be but...nothing was there. Did it really disappear? No. I wasn't ready to believe that. Immediately I checked the date of the article; if not published since we left Bermuda then I knew better. But I had ended my search believing there was a glitch in Google maps, or the problem was with the space satellite itself.

"The space satellite," I said after a short pause, "shouldn't it pick up all images on earth, images at least the size of a car? And if it didn't, what do you think it means?"

"Uh..." Cameron hesitated, wearing a "where is this coming from" expression. "Whoa, you really got my imagination going there for a minute. But to answer your first question: Yeah, it should. It would have to be broken if it didn't. The purpose of the satellite is to show what's happening in real time, like the weather. And if it didn't, then Houston we got a problem."

I was afraid he would say something like that.

"Pia?" He gazed into my eyes as his fingers gently ran over my nape. He said nothing more. Had decided not to pressure me, I supposed. Not even a curious remark to my concern about the satellite; he remained quiet.

I averted my eyes. *Just finish the voice message. Get it*

out of the way. Right then I decided that now was the time.

"You wonder about the rest of the message. Well, if you'd gotten the whole message, you would know that you were right all along. That yeah, I do see things. Apparitions. Images. Reflections. Visual projections. Ghosts. Whatever you want to call 'em."

I faced him then, expecting to see a shock-clad face. "You don't seem surprised. Are you disappointed?" Feeling timider, I averted my eyes again, waiting for him to say something.

"No...not surprised. And why would I be disappointed? Deep down I already knew. Because...it just didn't make sense...*me hallucinating*—and I know, nothing about all this makes sense."

"I can't explain why I didn't see the first one you falling off the skateboard, or even the last one of you rescuing me out of the water. But the other one...the foggy one, I did see."

"How long, Pia, have you been seeing these things?"

"For about four years now. Started around the time your parents disappeared." He gave a curious stare. Suddenly I realized my thoughts just spilled on sensitive ears. "I'm sorry. I didn't mean to say that."

"I don't understand. Are you thinking some way this is tied to my parents?"

I signified uncertainty, fidgeting a bit, not wanting to admit readily what I thought.

"Why?" he urged.

My head motioned slightly. "I don't know. Maybe it's because of how they disappeared...the whole mystery behind it."

"I still don't understand. Is there something else

you're not telling me?"

I nodded. "Around that same time, I went missing. In the middle of the night. For hours, it was as if I'd disappeared off the face of the earth. When I finally turned up the next day, I had no clue what had happened, and where I'd been all that time. Then later the visions started."

He took my hand, locked my fingers with his. "All that time...you haven't remembered anything?"

"All that time...no. All I remember about that night was going to bed, closing my eyes. I don't know...after that, it was as if I woke up on the beach. How I ended up there is one big mystery."

"Wow. I don't know what to say. It's incredible. What do you think happened? Kidnapping? Sleepwalking?"

"No. As for sleepwalking, that would mean I had a key, which I didn't have." I chuckled. "You know, trying to figure out what happened, how it happened, had everybody on edge, going crazy if you ask me. The crazier it sounded, the harder it was to believe me. And no one could fathom kidnapping, not even my parents. It was the most insane period of my life, and just when I thought it couldn't get worse, the visions started."

Cameron remained quiet for a moment, digesting it all. "And the visions started after that?" he remarked, mostly to himself.

"Mmm, what are you thinking?" I asked.

"I don't know actually. Ah...you saw a doctor, right? What did he have to say?" he mustered up something.

"My doctor calls it depersonalization disorder. But he says my case is rare with the anxiety attacks and out-of-body sensation, and, the hallucinations. Sound familiar?" My eyes examined his now.

"Anxiety, hallucination, yeah, it does. But look, I still don't see what any of this has to do with my parents."

"And you wouldn't–hell–I don't even know. It's just the mystery and the timing...both incidents occurring around the same time. You see?"

"Yeah...I see," he said drawing me into the tender rhythm of his body where I started melting away. "Fate, Pia. I still believe that's what brought us together. And if it were in my power, I would turn back the hands of time. Things would be different," he whispered. My eyes widened, but I kept my curiosity to myself and let silence rule the moment, if only for a little while.

I winced as I trained my ears on a faint sound. I lay still against him, intently waiting to hear it again. Then I heard it again; growling it sounded like, ferociously brewing and varying in tempo. I smiled up at Cameron when it was obvious that the growls lurked from within him. He stared back with a broad smile.

"You want to go grab a burger or something. To tame that beast inside you," I teased.

"Nah. I'm okay."

"Really? How can you stand it? It's so annoying."

"All right, all right." He then got up, pulled me up, too. "I better before it jumps out and starts nibbling at your cheek," he growled, his breath fanlike at my cheek. "See how good we are together?"

I didn't answer him. This thing called *us* was too fresh to be sure about anything, regardless of how good we seemed together and–

Suddenly something else popped in my mind,

strange because it was like I was trying to remember something other than what I was thinking. Whatever it was, it was right there on the tip of my tongue. And then, in a surprisingly weird way, like how *Ferret* entered my mind, it came to me.

All the power I would ever need was in Cameron's hands now.

Chapter Twenty-One

Eye on Fate

A brainstorm. That's what I was having as we sat in a booth devouring burgers and fries. Not sure if I would weigh him down with too much information too soon, I was reluctant to share with him the idea parading around in my head.

Then how should I move forward with my idea? Having so many questions I needed answers to, I had to go forward one way or another. And since he knew so much about me already, it was worth testing my idea out on him, and in turn, testing the fate he firmly believed in. Because fate had power; that's what I was thinking now.

"You think you got room for some of that chocolate cake?" Cameron asked.

"Nah. I'll pass. But you go 'head if you like."

"The slices are too big for me to eat by myself."

"Just take the rest home with you."

"Nope," he said, shaking his head, "I'll just leave it."

Since he'd treated me with a burger and fries, I got the waiter's attention and ordered a slice. "Don't even think about," I charged at the rejection I knew was coming.

"If you're doing it for me...I've changed my mind...don't want it anymore," he said, but I wasn't buying it.

"It's okay, Cameron. Let me do this for you. If you haven't noticed, I insist."

A male waiter, stocky, placed the cake on the table, and Cameron folded his arms, posing a sulky look. "I told you. I'm not going to eat it."

"You mean to tell me you'd let my money go to waste like that? You should be obliged, and indulge. Look–look at my plate...almost gone."

He chuckled. "Tell you what. Eat a little of it, then I'll oblige you by eating the rest."

I thought a moment, feeling trapped in this little fight I started, and now I had to compromise to get out of it. Oh what the heck, fair is fair, I thought as I picked up a fork, right away cut off a chunk. "Umm, moist." I smiled as it melted in my mouth. Then I slid the plate over to him.

"A deal is a deal." He stabbed off a piece, and it disappeared in his mouth. "Good, thanks."

"Not at all," I said as the idea from the brainstorm continued dancing around in my head, wanting to be unleashed. Still I wasn't sure how or even if I should approach him about it.

He slid the cake back to me. "What's on your mind?" he asked.

Gosh, was it that obvious? "Eh, nothing," I said, forking off another piece. The cake really was good.

"About the disappearances," Cameron said, "the

images and anything else, I was thinking how much of a burden it must be for any one person to take on alone. How do you do it? Other than that, you seem perfectly normal. No one would think otherwise. How do you keep from losing it?"

"I don't know. When I look back on it all, I wonder myself. At the beginning, though, it wasn't easy at all trying to deal with it and be normal at the same time...almost impossible; it was that bad. But over time, and with therapy, I was able to get a stronghold on the condition and nip it in the butt." I chuckled. "That's what my therapist used to say.

"But I didn't start getting better until I was off the meds. They never really worked anyway—not entirely. And after a while, they started making me worse.

"I used to have atrocious anxiety attacks. So bad I would curl up in a ball. Can you imagine that? During the attacks is when I usually have the visions. But the attacks aren't as severe as they once were. They're much milder and controllable now." I smiled. "I nipped them in the butt."

"Maybe in time the attacks, the visions, will all stop. It did for me—the hallucinations, that is."

"Yeah." A pause. "Uh. Remember that story you showed me on the Internet about that mysterious island?" I asked, easing my nagging idea into the conversation.

"Yeah. What about it?"

"Well. Do you *really* believe it?"

His lips puckered as he gathered his thoughts. "There's no proof that it actually happened, but that doesn't mean anything. I mean, it's possible. I looked beyond that particular story and found another one about a scientist doing some kind of test around the same time that may have caused it to appear. Of course, there are still unanswered questions in that theory, too."

"But you believe. That's what matters."

"Why? What got you so worked up over this?"

"Um...I guess you can say I have a thing for islands. Or I should say, they have a thing for me."

He rolled his eyes in surprise and chuckled. "And I'm dying to hear all about it."

I couldn't much blame him for not taking me seriously; my wording was quirky and unpredictable. But that didn't stop me from going on.

"How 'bout we fly out to investigate one?"

He distorted his face, knocked the table with knuckles. "Come again."

"I'm talking about fate. Our fate. Remember? You still believe in it, don't you?"

"Yeah, I do. But what in the devil are you talking about? You got me in suspense over here. Tell me what's going on in that lovely head of yours."

"I don't know. Maybe this is all wrong," I said.

"You have to tell me if you really want my opinion, you know that."

I then looked at him; the urge to tell him was nearly slipping off my tongue. "There's something else I need to tell you. About this place I see whenever we fly to Bermuda."

His cell phone rang. "Hold that thought."

Right then my cellphone rang. It was Mom. I held up a finger, letting him know that I was stepping outside to take the call. The conversation didn't last long; Mom was just checking up on me. Dad was out, and she was about to visit with the neighbor next door.

Moments later, Cameron stepped outside. "That was my uncle, asking me to do that house call we'd talked about earlier. That's what he calls it when people need immediate service on their computers. Well anyway, I said that I'll be there in about thirty minutes. I'm not sure how long it'd be, but you can come along for the ride if you like. That'll give us time to finish talking."

"No, I can't. I need to get back."

"Well, I still have a little time before I take off. So tell me more about this place."

"It's nothing, really. Just another one of those illusions. I probably shouldn't have brought it up."

"I know better than that, I can tell. It's written all over your face," he said, caressing my chin. "I honestly believe we were brought together for reasons that can't be explained now. So if you want to say something, don't be afraid to try it out on me. I may surprise you. You must feel by now that I'm here for a reason."

At those words, I gazed at him. There was a credible visage about him, and how our hands came together, swaying, was magnetic. "Tell you what, you go 'head, and we'll just talk later."

He nodded. "Okay...later then. By the way, how much time do I have?"

My expression oblique, I asked, "Excuse me?"

"Any day now you'll be going back to Texas. When?"

"Oh...not until Sunday. Enough time?"

"Not really, but I'd like to make the best of the little time I, we, have left. So, um, can I drop you off?"

"No, I'll be okay. I'll just go back the way I came."

"All right then. Be expecting a call from me, say, in two to three hours."

"Okay. Hey?" I grabbed him before he took off. "About the house call, you don't think the patient is delusional, do you?"

He gazed at me, showing no sign of being confused. "A little bit, but it'll be okay." His voice was caring; his words, honest; and his expression, legitimately pure.

"And you won't say anything to—"

"Don't worry, I won't. I have as much reason to keep this between us as you do."

"Okay, well, you better get going." I smiled.

He landed a kiss on my cheek, "Talk to you later," and he was off.

"Hey. Look at you, come on in here." I was glad when I looked out and saw Stephanie standing on the front porch, looking so radiant in the shade. She had on a sneaky little smile, a white top, and green skirt.

"Hey back to ya," she said, entering. "Did you forget to call to let me know you were back?"

"Uh...no. I didn't forget you. How can I forget you? I've just been doing this and that since we got back yesterday. I didn't miss anything while I was gone, did I?" I simpered as I emptied Kool-Aid in a pitcher and began stirring.

"Are you kidding? Nothing at all."

"Honestly, I thought you may have heard something about those guys that nearly killed me. Especially that lunatic driving the boat."

"Nope. Not yet. They're probably long gone by now, I hate to say. What did your folks think about what happened?"

I balled my lips. "About that. I didn't tell them."

"What? Why?"

"Forgot about it...had other things on my mind. Hadn't thought about it until now."

"Oh well. I kinda understand, I guess."

"Yep," I sighed, reaching in the fridge for a bottle of lemon juice. "Besides, it wasn't the skier's fault. I saw that gruesome look on his face as he came at me. And he was trying to get that other guy to slow down." I opened the lemon juice and poured some into the pitcher.

"But he took off. Don't forget that."

"That...he did." I got quiet. "Hey, get you a cup if you want some," I offered as I mixed in the lemon juice.

We added ice and filled our tall plastic cups to the rim almost and went out on the back porch. Knowing Stephanie, I knew our first heated discussion would be about Cameron. So when she asked, I got that out of the way fast by telling her that I had met with him earlier. And my candidness surprised her. What was the point of pretending for the sake of pleasing her? It was only fogging things up for me, although I was perfectly capable of handling things on my own. And time had come for her to do nothing but accept that.

But when I also mentioned that we "might be soul mates," she was on the verge of freaking out until I said, "Just kidding" and laughed it off. I had to bring the conversation under wraps because her tone was excitable and would've attracted eavesdroppers and suspicion. My parents were around here somewhere, after all.

Once getting Cameron out in the air, I filled her in about my family in Bermuda, in particular about Aunt Iris and her new cookbook, and the party we went to in her honor. She'd never been to Bermuda either, and I thought it would be nice if she went with us sometime. I even told her as much, and from there, our chatting went on and on as always, nonstop. It became more entertaining and fun talking about any and everything. We carried on the tempo from chatting quietly to laughing up a storm, back to quiet and laughing up a storm some more. Like two peas in a pod.

Chapter Twenty-Two

The Promise

It was four o'clock when Cameron finally called. Way past the three hours he'd first expected.

"You were busy, I understand," I said to his apology.

"Can you meet with me now? I really would like to hear more about your 'thing for islands.'"

"Maybe–"

"Don't, Pia. Really, we have to pick up where we left off. I know how important all this is to you. I know you know that."

"Yeah...I do," I murmured. It was happening again, that eerie feeling of communicating with–what? If only I knew. But not only that, Cameron's tone and choice of words touched me.

"What was that?"

"Nothing."

"I only have until Sunday, remember?"

"Yeah, not much time left. Okay," I said, realizing this was a perfect time to get away. My parents were in the front room with the next-door neighbors, the Jenkins. Dad and Mr. Jenkins had spent most of the day together out. Now my parents were entertaining him and his wife if you would call it entertaining. They were all watching a program on television. I figured they wouldn't miss me. Besides, I couldn't ignore the odd feeling of having to see this through. "I'll be coming up the beach. Meet me."

Not a cloud in the sky. I traversed not too far up the beach before spotting him in the distance. His colors, black Bermuda shorts and yellow T-shirt, stood out. As did his slim legs, and his sure-footed walk. It was Cameron all right.

I wandered closer to the water, and the rippling waves running up my legs stalled me. (I loved doing this so much.) As the water receded, I kicked off my flip-flops to make romping about the waves easier. (It always seemed an afterthought to do that.) Then I gradually moved along the shoreline, slowly but surely to Cameron.

I waved when he was close enough for me to really identify him. At the same time, I became aware of the same calmness I felt yesterday coming back from Bermuda. And taking center stage in my noggin was that magical word: *Ferret.* Still I had no idea what it meant or where it came from, except my delusional contact with the unknown (the island). It couldn't have come from anywhere else. Earlier, I researched the word. It had to mean something other than its allusion to a hairy animal. I was right. It had been the name of a great philosopher, theorist of the fifteenth century, who advocated that the end justified the means. However, when I read the meaning in the dictionary, an eerie feeling came over me again, leaving me with intrigue, as if the meaning had a secret code I desired to crack. I pondered it so hard trying to import something significant, knowing it had to be something related to the changes I went through. And at that moment, I was totally convinced *something* was trying to communicate with me. I had become emotionally frantic and desperate just thinking about it. My palms dampened. My face was tingling—I was hyperventilating.

Then later it came to me that Cameron had a sort of power, and it was then I put it all together, cracked the code, I should say.

Now, as we inched closer, narrowing the gap of finding out our fate, I wondered how he would react once I've told him exactly what's on my mind. How much could he actually stand without freaking out on me? Or would any of this surprise him at all?

I would soon find out.

He approached, holding out his hand. "Come on. We're going to do a little trespassing."

I flung my hands behind me. "Trespassing?"

"Yep, come on. It'll be fine."

"I don't get it."

He held his hands prayerfully as he bent forward and then deftly snatched mine.

"Where are we going?" I grumbled.

"See up there?" He pointed at the resort over the hill. "There's a lovely atrium in the back with a nice lounging area. We're going there to talk."

"It's open to anyone? Anyone like us?"

He shook his head. "Not exactly, but I know the code. It'll be all right. You'll see."

"But why can't we talk here?" I wondered.

He stopped. "We can. But I thought it'd be nice to change the scenery." His handsome smile silenced me, and he continued to lead the way up the sandy slope and through an iron gate. It didn't take long to enter private property with thief-like hands.

I had to admit, though, he was right. I liked it, and no one seemed to notice us. Circling, I looked the place over. There was a fountain flanked by shrubs. A few trees of various shades of green and some flowery. Patio-style furnishing filled in most gaps. Above was the blue sky and really tall trees in the wing. The setting was charmingly cozy.

"How do you know about this place?" I had to ask.

"Just by meeting people," he said blasé-like.

"Oh, I see."

"It's the truth," he assured as we sat on vinyl cushions, keeping quiet until a couple went by.

"Now tell me before time runs out on us again." His tone was low.

In a lean, I crossed my legs. "Promise me you won't freak out."

"You know you're good at building suspense—yeah, I promise."

I grimaced, trying to find the right way to approach the matter, taking longer than he liked apparently.

"You can't just come out and tell me, can you?"

"No, but I'm trying. It's more complicated than I thought."

"It was easy for you to tell me about the illusions.

How hard can it be?"

"Remind you, I had a difficult time with that too. But...I don't know." Maybe it was due to my secret agenda I thought he would flat out reject. Yes, that was different all right.

Regardless, I had to get my point across because I was running out of time. Come Sunday I'd be back home in Texas, which would place my hunch at a disadvantage because timing was everything. And this was the time. Somehow, I just knew. And if I didn't move fast, the opportunity would go down the drain forever. Somehow I knew that too.

Then, in a blink, focusing on a setting, I knew the best place to start; and without further delay, I began.

"While in Bermuda, I heard about this storm that hit the island about six months ago. Lightning, earth-moving thunders, and lots and lots of rain. The thunder was so loud some say it felt like the ground really moved. Whether it did or not is still not known. From my understanding, they're still investigating what went on that night."

"Why? Why would they investigate a thunderstorm?"

Good question. "Because it seems there was an earthquake. They say measured 3.7 on the Richter scale."

"Wait a minute. I seem to recall hearing something about it. A rock, about a quarter mile in diameter, rose above sea level."

"Yes. So you know about it?"

"Not really...that's all I know. I haven't heard anything more about it."

"And I hadn't heard anything until yesterday.

They're still researching because it's not clear what caused the rock to surface. I was on the Internet yesterday, doing a little research on my own. Don't you know it would have taken a huge earthquake to cause any damage or even cause that much movement on the earth? Not only that but a tsunami?"

"That is something to think about. But there has to be a logical explanation."

"That's what I thought. But how that rock came about is one big mystery. A 3.7 reading wouldn't have moved the earth like that. You hear me?"

"Yeah," he muttered. "It makes you wonder what really happened."

"Exactly." I nodded.

"Interesting. But now I'm more confused than ever. Does that have anything to do with the here and now?"

"I'm wondering." I paused then, carefully collecting my words. "I have reasons to believe that I'm...a little psychic." *Yes, that's it,* I thought as I observed the deep grooves now in Cameron's forehead. "I know how that must sound, but with all of the weird stuff that's happened—this is more of it."

"Wait...okay, okay, psychic...I mean, that could be a good thing. Is it because of the illusions you think you're psychic?"

"Yes—no. I mean, it's hard to say. Before now, I haven't given it much thought. I always thought the dreams, the images, were signs of the future—yes. But hardly any of the visions happened for real, not like the way we know they have. But never have I—not like I do now—felt so strongly about this."

"Then what's changed?"

Together, we glanced across the way when other people appeared, a middle-aged couple. They seemed to be lingering. Albeit we were keeping a low tone, it was time to move to a different setting, I thought.

Cameron stood up. "I can use something to drink. What about you?"

"Yeah." We walked over to a soda machine. "We probably should go, so we can have more privacy," I suggested.

"I was thinking that."

After getting the sodas, we headed back toward the beach. "It was a nice getaway, however short." I decided to lend a compliment.

"Thanks." He clasped my hand in his and quested eye contact. "Go 'head, tell me what's different now."

"Well, I had a telepathic, or should I say, *psychic experience* yesterday. With something I've been seeing for a long time now. As of yesterday, I call it Ferret." I looked up at him and, as psychic as I was, read the strange look in his eyes. "It, believe it or not, is an island."

"Ferret? An island? This keeps getting good. Look...how 'bout I don't say another word. It's clear you have a lot of explaining to do, so I'll shut up and listen. Because right now I don't know what to think until I've heard it all...and maybe even then I won't know what to think. Just go ahead, take your time, and just know I'm listening. No interruptions, okay?"

I started again with *Ferret.* True to his word, he did...heard me out with no interruptions till I ran dry of my fantasies, though in my heart, they weren't fantasies but very much real. Yes, they were very real. Even though I clammed up at times trying to get all that I had to say out, thinking it was ridiculous and I, a total lunatic for exposing myself like that. But Cameron kept encouraging me to go on by squeezing my hand and gazing at me with loving eyes, remaining silent to the end.

When I stopped, he had heard it all, about my dreams, about the strange new things that happened since being back here in Florida, about my sightings of the island—everything. He also knew how I came to call it *Ferret*. Though I was in tell-all mode, I held back telling him the monster I thought he was. Aside from jeopardizing our relationship, I couldn't risk a chance of a lifetime that wouldn't be possible, at this time, without him.

Bottom line: I needed Cameron.

For now, I had said all I needed to say. Our hands still joined as we strolled in reticence. He gave mine a gentle squeeze, gazing into my eyes, his twinkling.

"What can I say? That's incredible," he finally said.

"Yeah...out-of-this-world incredible," I responded.

"I don't know why, but I feel this has been a long time coming."

"Why? Because of fate?"

He nodded. "It's the only logical reason. Because...how can you imagine something like that? We're on earth—not out of this world—where anything is fair game or possible." He took a moment. "How are we supposed to deal with something so bizarre? I wish I had the power to erase this fantasy out of your head. But how can I? Seeing what you've been going through, I feel a sense of rage. It's maddening trying to imagine what it's been like not having anyone understand what you've been going through. And I can see why you couldn't talk about it."

"Looks like you're the lucky one," I said.

He drew me closer to him as we continued along the shoreline dodging waves. "Like I said before, I'm here for you. For what it's worth, I would do anything in my power to help see you through all this..."

I was hearing my opportunity, my cue, to let him in on my plan. He deserved to know fully why I spilled my guts to him, and I prayed he wouldn't hate me for it. That he would come to understand the necessity of my bizarre idea, though more surprises appeared to be the furthest thing from his mind now, having had so much dumped on him already. However, I had to finish telling him, to make clear my purpose. Otherwise, it would all be for nothing.

So I went straight to the point.

"I want you to help me get to Ferret."

He pushed me away, revealing a shocking look of disbelief. "You want me to do what! How...just how am I supposed to do that?" he roared.

"Your cousin, Brian."

"Brian?" Pawing at his forehead, he stared bewilderingly. "Why, Pia...why even go there? You can't be serious."

"But I am and I have to go there. Going there could be the only way to be cured of this miserable sickness finally and forever. The dreams, Cameron...they must mean something. Just maybe we were destined to meet so that I—we—would have this opportunity to find out."

"What? Find out what?"

I dropped my head momentarily. "About the visions. Aren't you curious about them? How we were able to share the same hallucination? How weird is that? You said yourself that we were brought together by fate. I know thinking of this based on fate alone isn't enough. But maybe this is the very thing you were trying to say when you said you felt 'this has been a long time coming'—just now. Remember? And remember the maze. Some analogy that was, wouldn't you say? Sounds like fate to me." As I spoke, I realized he had built my case for me.

He grunted. "It's just that I don't believe in this thing you call Ferret. It's all in your head! It's not real."

Abruptly, I turned my back on him, walking away as I yelled, "Thanks for believing in me."

"Okay, what if I do see this island, then what?" he asked.

"*What if?* I don't know. All I know is that we have to go out there and see what happens. We have to investigate. It's what Ferret means, to investigate after all." I cringed as I faced him. "I just know it's meant for me to go there. I feel it in my bones."

He gave me a solemn look as he fondled my nape. "I'm sorry, Pia, but I can't. I don't feel it in my bones."

I pulled loose of his hold as my tears welled. Then my fuming steps distanced us as tears began streaming down my face. "How can you not! You saw the visions. We're in this together," I said, pushing forward.

"Ask me, Pia. Ask if I've seen one today."

"You said that you were here for me and that you will do anything for me," I retorted as he trailed behind me.

"And I meant that, just not this way. Come on, slow down," he begged, but I didn't—no way. "Maybe I will accommodate you but not now. We have time to think about this."

"We're running out of time. I'm leaving Sunday." Suddenly I stopped, realizing I was too mad to see that I was walking in the wrong direction home.

"Then next time." He stopped, too. "Why can't you see how irrational this is?"

"Trust me. I'm asking you now. Why can't you trust that I need you to do this for me? Why? Why? Can't you hear it, over and over again? You worry about me going insane, that'd do it."

He wiped away my tears, appearing to be in deep thought as he said, "You look so pure, so modest, so irresistible." Then, he hugged my neck, and we began with baby steps, walking in the direction of the house. "It's not fair, Pia, to ask me to get involve like this. Why can't you see that?"

"But it's in your power..." I just closed my eyes and buried my head in his chest, thinking about what he just said. He was right. Deep down, I knew that. That's why I had a hard time telling him in the first place.

"B-but...but what is fair? It's not fair that I have to go on suffering from this while, in my heart, I know I have to do this. It can't be explained. Not everything can be, you know. How was it we saw the same things? Can you explain it—can I? How I see it, nothing about this is fair. Please, I'm not insane."

"Look...you're wrong. I don't think you're crazy. Because...if you were, then I would be too." He drew a deep breath and then exhaled. "I promise. I promise that I'll get with Brian on this."

"Will you really? We don't have much time you

know."

"I know. I'll get back to you later after speaking with him. If all goes well, we'll get this out of the way tomorrow, since it's the only day we got. Right?" he said and I nodded. "He has access to practically any plane I would think, so that shouldn't be a problem. There's the weather to consider, though."

"It'll be perfect, I just know it."

"Right...in your bones kind of thing," he remarked in a dejected tone.

My cell phone sounded. I knew at once that it was my parents. I'd skipped away without telling them so I couldn't ignore it. They would only be worried.

"Hey, sweetie, where did you run off to? Are you with Stephanie?"

"No, Mom, Stephanie had something to do, and I ended up walking the beach. You know me."

"Well, head back. We're going for an evening cruise and dinner downtown in Fort Lauderdale."

"Okay...be right there," I said and hung up.

"Well, that's that," I said to Cameron. "My parents want to do dinner and a cruise this evening. So how...what will you tell him exactly?" I wondered aloud.

"Ooh, uh, the truth. I would say you saw something out of the ordinary about forty-five minutes off the coast toward Bermuda, and we want to go out and get a closer look to see exactly what it is—if it's still there. I think that alone would get him interested. He's a sci-fi, mystery-type person. And he is adventurous, and would find this hunt adventurous. He's like Will Smith in *Independence Day. Let's kick some ass.*" He grimaced a little, studying me somewhat.

"Cameron, you have to assure him how important this is to me. He may surprise you and find this ordeal not appealing at all."

He puckered his lips and nodded. "That's right, as long as you know that."

"All the more reason to convince him. I know it sounds like a long shot but—"

"You know you can't get your hopes up. He could flat-out *reject it,* not knowing what he's in for."

"This is too important. You have to convince him." He just stared at me, and my begging spirit staring back at him came through quietly it seemed.

Softly he spoke, "If nothing gets in the way, I think I can get him to do it for me. I've got a pile this high"—he raised a hand to his head—" of favors I could collect on."

My lips spread as I looked into his eyes. "Then it shouldn't be a problem. We have to do this. I can't say it enough. And you know how much this means, Cameron. Not just to me, but to you too, though you may not feel it now. Call me as soon as you hear something. I'll be waiting. Well...I better get going."

"Wait a minute." He tugged at my arm. "Since you'll be out with your folks, maybe I should send you a text instead of calling?"

"Right, a text," I agreed as he squeezed my arm. But something else was on his mind. Not only did I sense it, but I could also see it in his eyes. A deep longing. Of which I was willing to submit to.

I stepped closer, curled my neck, and pressed my lips to his cheek. Slowly, my lips brushed his cheek as he turned, his lips meeting mine. Gently, his tongue parted my lips, instantly pouring inside me an arousal that came to possess me like never before. How could a kiss be so powerful? Could it be explained? Never had I felt this way before. His grip on my arm then relaxed as we parted, and I slowly backed away.

“I’ll be waiting to hear from you,” I said, and he nodded, “Okay.”

I waved as the gap widened between us. He just stood there, peacefully, the breeze rippling at his fibers.

Chapter Twenty-Three

Shattered Dilemma

"This is an excellent day for fly-fishing, Isaac. I just found out they're schooling, so fish are all over the place." Mr. Jenkins, an average-built man with specks of gray hair, told Dad. They were out in the driveway loading fishing stuff on the truck, while I stood looking out the door eavesdropping, though not intentionally.

I completely agreed with him on grounds that there was nothing in the sky or in the forecast to threaten this picture-perfect day. A gorgeous blue sky with light clouds brushing through it. The temperature was about seventy-eight degrees. Much like it was yesterday. It was indeed a great day all the way around for outdoor activities.

My parents had expressed interest in fly-fishing but never had gotten around to doing it. So when Mr. Jenkins invited them to join him and his new wife, they thought the timing was impeccable, especially since their timetable for today was wide open. Though they weren't prepared for fishing per se, everything they needed either Mr.

Jenkins had, or they could get once they got to the place. It's so easy to do things on the spur of the moment down here, given to tourism.

This day their all-day time slot was no longer blank. It had been quite different at the start of the week since it was all about the convention. When that was over, it was off to Bermuda. Yesterday was the first real day of relaxation. And today, well, was perfect for challenges and exploring something new.

Hopefully for me, today would be for solving the riddle in my life.

"Are you sure you don't want to go?" said Mom.

"A day at the Everglades. Nah, ah-ah," I rebuffed a second time. "You two just go and have fun with the Jenkins. You don't need me tagging behind you today too," I said, referring to a lovely evening we had cruising along the river after a superb dinner yesterday. "And besides, I don't want to mess up my clothes. I'll be okay here by myself."

Dad overheard. "Make sure you keep behaving yourself." He winked, walking back outside wearing much anticipation.

"Fly-fishing doesn't sound like a luxurious way to spend the day...I understand," Mom said, grabbing an old long-sleeved cardigan off the back of the chair and draping it over her arm. Her hair drawn back in a ponytail and lips glossed up, Mom always looked good for any occasion. But looking at her from the neck up (the chic necklace, light makeup), she didn't look like she was about to go fishing. Whereas the quasi-shabby attire she mustered up—old jeans and spotted T-shirt—fit the bill.

"Come...give me some sugar." She stepped toward me.

"Mom," I heaved, and she just smacked her lips on my forehead. Quickly, she laid down the same rules for me to abide by and then left to pile in the truck with everyone else.

As they drove away, it crossed my mind how unusually convenient and easy it was for them to be on their way to do something they had meant to do for a while now. It had somewhat of a supernatural feel to it, having the entire day opened up just for me to venture out and do the unthinkable. Oh, if only they knew what I had planned today, I would be dead meat. It really was too perfect, too mysterious to think how everything just fell into place, and with no effort whatsoever on my part. No using the beach for a quick getaway. No little white lies. No nothing.

I glanced at the clock on the wall: 7:20 a.m. Cameron was standing by to hear from me. I surely hoped he was up. Promptly, I veered through the house to reach my cell phone in my room. Cameron assured me that he'd convinced Brian and that he was just waiting for him to call back with a time to work around. That was last night, though. My God, I hoped nothing had changed to screw this up for me. The opportunity for fly-fishing couldn't have come at a better time. How lucky was that? So far so good.

"Are you ready now?" were the first words out of his mouth.

"I will be. Cameron, promise me nothing will go wrong."

"Just calm down, there's no problem. But we need

to get there as soon as possible so we'll be there when the plane's ready. 'Any time before nine,' Brian said. Can you be ready in...say twenty minutes? That'd give us plenty of time to get through any traffic."

"No problem. I'll meet you in the same place, the bank parking lot."

"You bet. I'll see you then."

I got ready in a jiffy and locked up the house behind me. As I was walking up the street, I heard indistinct voices coming from in or around a house. Unexpectedly, one called out my name.

"Damn it," I squawked to myself and whirled around, saw her coming from the porch of a white-brick house. "Stephanie, hey, you're up awfully early. What's up?"

"This." She fanned a thick white envelope, walking up to me. "For Mom. Where are you off to so early? Wait. Let me guess. Cameron?"

"Ah, yeah...we're going to see a movie or something." *Maybe too early for a movie.* I hiked my eyebrows, thinking, oh what the heck. "I would ask you to go, but we both know how you feel about him. So how 'bout I catch up with you later."

"Yeah, okay. But a movie, this early? Just tell me in my ear where you're going for real, Pia. You have to be careful with him."

"No need to whisper because we are going to a movie. Breakfast first, then a movie. Okay?"

"What movie are you going to see?"

"I'm not sure. We'll decide over breakfast. Okay, see ya later?" I pleaded a little. "I really have to go."

She turned sideways as though she was about to go

but then hesitated. "I don't know. I don't have a good feeling about this. Maybe I should go with you."

She got to be kidding me. I was starting to get edgy, trying not to show it. Consequently, I was hoping I could talk her out of it and fast; I didn't have time to waste.

"Ah." She waved a hand. "You go 'head. On second thought, it'd be absolute torture being in his space, breathing his air. It'd be like suffocating myself."

Boy was she being dramatic. If only I had time to set her straight.

"Besides, I can't get away now if I wanted to." She grimaced.

Whew, that's a relief. Really saved me the trouble of being rude, telling her she couldn't go anyway.

She went on. "But I promise he'd have to answer to me if he gets out of line or hurt a hair on your head," she said, stabbing the air, which she did so well. A sure sign that she was getting worked up.

"You know...have it your way. Go, be busy, I gotta go." I faked a smile, waved, and started walking.

"Wait, hold up."

"What now?"

"You're not mad at me, are you?" was her response to my agitated look.

"What do you think?" I was so pissed I couldn't look at her. I just stared past her, pretending that something or someone was behind her. She whipped her head around, saw that nothing was there, and quickly turned back, like snapping the neck back into place.

"What!"

I hunched my shoulders. "Nothing. You need to check yourself."

"Me? I don't think so," she retorted with emphasis.

"So what are you planning to do? Tell on me?" By now, I wasn't sure if I could trust her. The vendetta she had for Cameron, you would think he personally assaulted her.

"No. You know I wouldn't do that." She exhaled. "All right...go. I'll catch up with you later."

That's my girl.

"Just be careful and call if you need me."

"Don't worry, I'll be fine." Backing off, I blew her a kiss, then turned and got moving. Cameron was waiting.

Brian was outside talking with a mechanic when we pulled up, and he held up a finger to acknowledge us.

"You think the plane's ready?" I asked Cameron.

"I don't know, but we'll soon find out."

We sat in the truck waiting. When Brian finally came over, he stuck his head in the window. "The plane is almost ready. You can wait here or inside. Either way, I'll be back in a bit." Then he rushed off, but not before saying, "I hope you guys know what you're doing."

"What do you think he means by that?" I asked even though I thought I already knew.

"He wasn't too thrilled about the idea at first. But no need to worry now."

I'll try not to. "Cameron, thanks. Thanks for going out of your way to convince him how important this is to me. But—"

"But you're welcome." He bent over and fingered my nose. "And don't worry. Believe me when I say there's nothing I won't do for you."

I smiled as a warm feeling came over me. Nothing can go wrong with him behind me; I wanted to believe nothing other than that. But Brian was back with a shattering effect. He leaned slightly on the door and announced, "I'm sorry, but I can't go through with this without knowing what we're in for. I tried to get it out of Cuz here, with no luck, so that leaves you. I can't trust you to steer me blindfolded. What do you expect to find out there when there's nothing to be found?"

As his stern, demanding look hit me like a lion's growl, my insides tanked hard, and my throat knotted up. All the hope I had left was dying this very moment.

"Probably nothing, Brian, just lay off. You gave me your word. And you said you wouldn't bring this up."

But Brian wouldn't budge and continued driving at me like a determined drill sergeant. At least that's how I felt as tension began mounting through his urgency to know. "Why can't you give a hint to what's going on?" His tone was like a ranting chorus. "Don't you know that there's nothing but ocean out there. Nothing but ocean between here and Bermuda. That's the course, isn't it?"

I felt so overpowered because I had no supporting arguments. Feeling shamed and humiliated, all I could do was drop my head in my palms and try to prevent myself from weeping.

"Stop, Brian! You bastard."

"I'm sorry, man. I know I promised, but the more I thought about it, it just doesn't seem right, not to mention a waste of time."

Oh no. It was really happening. All that I hoped for was falling to pieces, and I couldn't hold back the sorrow starting to spill into the palm of my hands. How...how could this be happening? How could he have changed his mind without warning, without as much as compassion? How could Cameron not see it coming? He had assured me that it wouldn't be a problem. That Brian was more than willing to repay a favor. And how could he dare do this after we'd come all this way? All this way for nothing.

The door flew open. Cameron got out and rushed Brian against the truck. Gradually they distanced themselves from the truck as they carried on the fencing back and forth. With tears drenching my face, I watched as these people, who out of nowhere landed in my lap and now whom I depended on, go head-to-head in a verbal scuffle over me. And I felt helpless, useless. All the while, the conflict between them was entirely my fault. I was hoping, just hoping that it'd work out in my favor.

I was pitifully useless.

Maybe not. I wiped away the tears and forced the door open. "I didn't come this close for nothing," I slurred. Padding across the pavement, I was determined to settle this.

But how? I wasn't about to tell him that I had a conversation with this island I called Ferret, which by the way, invited me for a visit. Oh no, not on my life! He was showing already that an act of craziness was hopeless in his book. And judging from his reaction, Cameron obviously hadn't told him a thing, and that simply wasn't going to fly. It simply wasn't enough for him to go out on the limb even if he owed Cameron tons of favors.

Just what would be his reaction if I gave in and told him everything? Would he be more inclined to do it? I almost knew the answer. But was it worth the chance?

How could I convince myself in the few steps I had left before reaching them? Darn. He would declare not only me but also Cameron certifiable and would certainly flush this grand opportunity down the toilet and toss the plunger to another stratosphere. The chance of him giving it a second thought; I didn't think so even if my life depended on it. Just the same, I had to keep my hope alive.

"Didn't I tell you it was hard to explain," Cameron was saying as I approached. He held up his hand for me to back off when he saw me coming. But I lowered it when I got up to him.

"I think I know what's going on with you, Brian, and I can't much blame you. You're concerned that I may be involving your cousin here in some kind of danger. But I promise you, there's no danger in what I'm asking you to do. We fly over that area all the time. Going back and forth to Bermuda." For all it was worth—and it was worth everything—I was giving it my best shot.

"You're right. But I'm not only concerned about Cameron's safety, but your safety as well. I am liable for your safety, and the best way to keep you safe is to know what I'm up against. Why can't you tell me what this is you think you saw?"

"Because I can't say for sure. What I can do is point it out to you when I see it. And there's a chance it won't even be there. So we all can chalk it up as a nice day sightseeing or as a lesson of some sort," I tried rationalizing, not believing a word, but my heart said so anyway. Because I knew better, I knew Ferret would be there. And chances were I would be the only one to see it. Just like always. Yet there was a small chance that

Cameron would see it. A very good one. He was the only one ever to see my illusions. "And believe me, the worst thing that can come out of this trip is that you see nothing."

"See nothing, the worst thing? How 'bout the worst thing is that the plane disappears," Brian said, squaring me through shifty eyes. And I felt faced with a tough move by my opponent in a game of chess.

"No. You don't really think that, do you?" I looked at both of them, focusing more on Cameron. "Cameron?"

"You know that's the furthest thing from my mind right now," Cameron assured. "Drop it right now because that excuse won't fly with me, Brian. I won't let you use me as your scapegoat."

"I'm just being realistic. Anything is possible. Right?" Then, he sighed. "What about the time? Not to mention money."

"Then don't mention it," Cameron fired a rebuttal loaded with tension. He got into Brian's face. "This is a fine time to show your ass and I–"

I jumped in. "Please, I understand your position in all of this, but just do this one thing for me–us. Look, I don't want you to go out there expecting to see something I can't explain. But once I point it out to you and you do see it–and a part of me hope you do–then maybe we all will be asking same questions: What is that? How could it possibly be there? Believe me...you have to see it to believe it." I looked down at the pavement now. "As strange as that may sound."

Our eyes scrounged at one another, ready or expecting to hear more lingering or rash thoughts. Then

Brian nodded slightly. “And you have flown over this area many times before and lived to tell about it?”

I nodded in response, regardless that he’d just mocked me. “That’s right. I’m living proof.”

“What are you going to do, man?” Cameron jabbed.

Brian’s arms flung sidelong. “What am I going to do, eh?” He then turned and marched away like a ranking officer. We stared after him in disbelief.

What! I looked at Cameron, words stuck in my clamoring head. I couldn’t speak, not yell even.

“I’ve failed,” I murmured finally. “Look at him. I can’t believe he’s really not going to...”

Cameron spoke bitterly, “Sorry, Pia. I forgot that he can be an real ass at times.”

Suddenly Brian stopped in mid-stride. “Now who’s holding who up?” Hearing those words was a heavenly sound to my ears. I beamed. So did Cameron. We were beaming at each other.

Brian twitched his head. “Come on. I’m dying to find out what the mystery is all about.”

“You and me both,” I think I heard Cameron say as we moved almost in single file, briskly.

Chapter Twenty-Four

Onboard a Search

Before long, we were aboard the plane, climbing to cruising altitude. My usual anxiety attack happened without notice. And neither of us could hold a steady conversation of sorts for being a little unsettled about what lay ahead of us. However, we gave it our best shot.

"Whatever this is, I'm assuming your parents didn't see it," Brian decided to ask after a while. The notion must have just come to him; otherwise, he would have asked before now, I thought. He posed in a nonchalant manner, giving me the impression that he already knew the answer, but had to hear me say it to clear his conscience.

"Not quite," I answered and was glad he didn't upset the environment like before. We were on our way now, and I wanted to avoid another heated discussion until reaching our destination.

"This is a nice plane. It looks new." I was admiring the pristine interior.

"It's practically a newborn," Brian said.

Cameron sat next to me across a narrow aisle, and began signaling his approval of the plane by nodding, as if he was listening to music. He slouched in the leather seat and then posed a question to Brian about the refrigerator. Brian told him that he was welcomed to whatever's in it. Cameron got up immediately, I thought to check what was in the fridge, but instead, he approached Brian. I couldn't make out what he said but assumed he wanted to get a feel of what it's like being a pilot because he easily positioned himself in the copilot seat.

Somewhat content, I rested my spine and observed the two people I treasured more than anything this very moment. They were fluently engaged in chitchat about the plane—a crash course was what Cameron was getting. Then the conversation went on to sports…happenings around town…work issues…plans for later…They seemed to be covering everything, but who was listening.

As more time elapsed, I found myself remembering the first day I saw the island. How fascinated I was with the rays of lights spurting from it. It looked like a light show. A rare show of its kind. One I had never seen before. I thought I had some imagination to have imagined something so spectacular. There must have been at least ten rays sprouting from the island. In festive unison, the lights merged, becoming one magnificent beam dead center of the terra firma.

"Wow, look, you see that?" I'd say, so excited I wanted my parents to see so they wouldn't miss out. "Right down there, don't you see the lights?" As clear as it was to me, neither of them could see it. And on the spot, reality sank fast and settled to an ugly disappointment.

Not from a rude awakening of it being another one of my illusions...not entirely. It was those spectacular lights turning on the island in a brazen attack, as it became an electrical web frying the place. Smoke puffed out in synchronized pattern, then shortly the whole scene transfigured to a shadowy gloom under the sunset. My problem was how something like that could come out of my head. I wondered that then and now.

And I wondered would anyone other than myself would see it today.

Soon I'd find out.

"We should be coming up on it soon," Brian announced just before hitting a heart-stopping bump.

"Whoa, what was that?" Cameron sounded. He then glanced back to check my reaction. To reveal that everything was fine, I put on a thin smile to cover my jitters.

Brian was saying, "Nothing to worry about, just turbulence," as pilots normally do, making sure we were buckled up.

I then closed my eyes, collecting words for a short prayer. We were nearly there; I could feel it. The turbulence, mostly, setting off the feeling, I believed. And as much as I wanted this, it was just as important nothing go wrong. So I said a little prayer for us to return home safely. But I was compelled to go a step further.

*Please, Lord. I want so much for...*I paused in the prayer. What was it I really wanted? I took a moment to think about it. Yes, of course I wanted them to see the island. The whole purpose of this trip was to put Cameron to the test. If he saw the island, that would be huge.

Then what? It dawned on me that that was the bottom line of Brian's argument. *Then what?* I repeated, realizing the question was loaded.

First of all, I started the prayer over, wishing again for a safe return home. Then I asked for some resolution to this madness so that I'd have my life back. Meanwhile, I sensed a peculiar undercurrent in each word I prayed, like another soul present, saying the words of the prayer. Another one of those feelings I couldn't explain. When I ended the prayer, I just shook it off, or it left on its own.

We're here. Right then I looked out the window. And as always in its timeless proximity, just as enchanting and as tangible as ever through my eyes, there it was.

Quickly I turned to Cameron, whom I sensed eyeing me. Releasing my seat belt, I nodded, "It's there." I anxiously leaped out of my seat and leaned over them, pointing at the sighting. "Right there. Can you see it?"

I looked back and forth between the two of them. They both looked in the direction I pointed, bending forward straining to spot anything. As neither one voiced the immediate words I longed to hear, I endured an emotional shift from eagerness to critical frustration.

"I don't see anything," Cameron said first. "I mean, it might be something there, but it's not clear to me. Maybe if we got closer."

"Yeah...that could be it," said Brian, looking up at me. There was a hint of uncertainty in his voice and all over his face.

"I want you to see it. Just get closer, please," I urged and managed to stop him from asking what I considered the magic question: What is it you see? Still, I wasn't ready to kill the suspense.

He descended the plane, bringing me closer than I had ever been to this place. The closer we got, the more real it appeared–so much that it had to be there; we could even land on it. Staring intently, I waited for it to vanish right before my eyes. If it did, maybe the fantasy would finally be gone from my psyche forever. As yet, that wasn't happening. Admittedly, this image was never like others I'd seen because...it never performed a disappearing act.

The closer we got, it seemed obvious I was in this fantasy alone. Both of them glanced at me, and I couldn't help but ask again even though I already knew the answer. "What do you think that is?"

Again, they made an effort to see, scanning the wide-open ocean out of courtesy and sympathy, and I was hurt, crying inside.

"Nothing," Brian practically whispered. "We probably should turn back now." He looked at me, searching for an objection. But how could I? I didn't have the nerve.

The nose of the plane was slowly turning until suddenly, out of nowhere, a blinding glare struck the plane, and it seemed that we were under attack as it began shaking violently. I crashed to the floor, bumping my head on the way down.

"What the hell you think that was," I heard Cameron say. His voice sounded far away, but I could see the horror in his eyes when his head whirled around.

"Oh my God, is he okay?" I said as Brian slumped over, the unsteadiness of the plane swaying him.

"Oh no! Brian! Brian..." Cameron's voice still sounded distant, and I could see him hurrying to be free of the seat belt. He lifted Brian upright, smacking his face lightly. "Brian! Brian! Wake up..." Then he quickly opened a bottle of water and poured it over his face, trying to bring him back to consciousness.

While he worked on Brian, I was trying with all my might to get up. But the unsteadiness of the plane, the pounding headache, and the dizziness, all were making the simplest task very difficult. But there was more than that going on, I suddenly realized. My coordination was off because I was having a ruthless anxiety attack, the kind I hadn't had in eons. My breathing was labored, and every muscle in my body felt like knots contracting, like a pulled muscle. My heart rate was escalating and the thumping in my ears grew louder.

In the middle of chaos? A fine time for this to be happening. Through barely opened eyes, I looked up at Cameron over me, terror imprinted on his face. His lips were moving, though I couldn't make out what he was saying. At this point, I would have to read lips. The emotional turmoil going on inside me deafened me from the sounds outside of my body. I tried to speak, but all I could do was curl up, shut him out until this hybrid condition of mine ran its course, hoping and praying for a miracle we obviously needed.

Then I felt gentle smacks on my cheeks. "Pia, Pia? Are you okay? Pia?" The sound of his voice was dreamy. I must have passed out...had to. I was feeling faint or like I was just waking up. My body limp, yet alive.

I looked up at him. "Cam—" I tried to speak.

"He's out cold, Pia. We're in big, big trouble. I think the radio is out too. Now this is what I'm going to do. Okay, are you with me? I'm going to move Brian back here, and I want you to take control of this plane."

Coming back to reality fast, I fretted, shaking my head. "No, no."

He was on his feet in a heartbeat. "*No"* wasn't an option. He grabbed my arm, bringing me promptly to my feet. He held my face between his nervous hands at the same time blasting me with his frantic look. "Listen to me. You can do this. Remember what your father taught you and the simulations. Pretend that you're flying in the simulation. Okay? You can do this."

"What! You can't be serious. No, no, I can't, I won't. The simulations are just make-believe. I can't–"

Smashing my face between his hands, he yelled, "Then what are we supposed to do?" He entered the cockpit and began moving Brian. "See," he said, fuming, "Brian is in no shape to fly this plane."

"What's wrong with him? He's not–" I couldn't say the word.

"No. I don't know what happened exactly, but he's unconscious." He panted as he struggled forward with Brian. He strapped him in one of the backseats and reclined it. "You have to do this. You're all we've got."

Frantically, I stared at him. "I need a copilot, my dad–somebody. Will you...will you be my copilot?" I asked, nodding, and I couldn't stop nodding. What I asked of him didn't make sense, no more than I was frightened out of my mind of having to do this all alone. Or maybe it was a way of psyching myself into taking on such a daring role.

"Yes, Pia, I will. We're in this together."

He guided me to the cockpit and helped ease me into position. Through blurred vision, I stared out at eternity, the plane roaring through it. To my amazement, we were still on top of the world rather than crashing into it. *Autopilot* crossed my mind. The plane had to be flying itself. Following the thought was a feeling of relief pricking in my gut, and I began taking deep breaths, taking into account that an attack could recur if I didn't calm down.

Cameron positioned next to me. I sniffled softly. "I'm so sorry for putting you in this situation. I'm so sorry for everything..."

"No matter what, I forgive you. But what I need you to do is concentrate on all those lessons you got in the simulation. Look at the panel, focus."

Wiping away tears, I began examining the layout before me: the instrument panel, the flight controls. *Yes, the control panel.*

"Now"—I turned quickly to his voice—"what's the first thing you should do?" he asked.

"Ugh." Still wiping away tears, I focused again on the panel, a layout that was similar to the design in our plane. Then random steps for operating a plane flashed in my mind, along with the idea of getting help. Then I immediately put on the headphone.

"I tried it already. It's not working," Cameron readily uttered.

"I have to at least try again," I said, and then urgently spoke into the speaker. "Is somebody there? Mayday, Mayday, Mayday..." I then set it to an emergency frequency and tried sending the distress call again, in high hopes of a sheer voice coming through to our rescue. "Mayday, Mayday. Can anyone hear me? We're in desperate need of help. Anybody, can anybody hear me?

We need help, Mayday, Mayday...”

But nothing. Nothing but static. An agonizing static that boosted a degree of desperation I never thought possible.

But here we were, our eyes embracing and casting our desperation for survival.

“We’re on our own,” I solemnly spoke as it was starting to sink in that I had no choice but to fly this plane.

Not missing a beat to keeping me focused, Cameron said as a reminder, “Yeah...with me as your copilot. And I will do all I can to help you, us, through this. So...it’s obvious the plane is flying itself. So, um...how can you tell what direction it’s flying?”

I scanned the panel for the compass gauge. “Here.” I pointed. “We are heading north at sixty degrees.”

“North. Okay, okay. The fuel gauge...Seems we have plenty of fuel to make it back. We shouldn’t be too far off course.”

“Right. We shouldn’t be,” I said, thinking how powerful the disturbance was to have knocked us off course as it did. A drastic change, I thought, remembering that the plane was veering a (right) westerly turn. “It’s odd though,”—Cameron gave me a “what” look as I went on—“how the plane got on autopilot. Remember? Brian was in the process of turning back before whatever that was happened. Did you touch anything?”

“No. I wouldn’t have, not knowing a thing about planes. Is there a problem?”

“No, at least I don’t think so. Maybe Brian managed to turn it on just before losing consciousness. He was turning the yoke—the steering wheel—when everything went crazy. Which means he wasn’t using the autopilot.”

"Which also means the autopilot is buying us time. Fast thinking on Brian's part..." Cameron trailed off. "I-I don't want to think about the what-if...especially if there's still a chance..." The rest simply wouldn't come.

"Yeah, I know." I nodded, looking back at Brian. "I just hope he's okay."

"He's breathing, that's good."

Upon locating the autopilot, I drew a stiff breath then a few more. A method I adopted for minimizing the tension. "The autopilot is here." I managed a smile. "And it looks just like the one in the simulation. What I can do is try programming it to fly us back to Miami."

"Sounds good to me. It's that simple?"

"Yeah...that simple. Just give me a moment." I thought for a moment then blurted, "The GPS."

"Right here," he gladly pointed it out.

"Now how did you know that?" I was surprised.

"That's about the only thing I retained from the crash course I got from Brian," he said.

"Look at this; how convenient. It's like using the maps online."

"Yeah, it is. That's cool. Where are we on the map?"

"We're here," I said as I glanced at the heading indicator. "Based on the position we see here, I will set this, the Heading Indicator, to head west at about 240 degrees."

Feeling confident, I did just that with no trouble. I beamed when the change seemed to register. But then, something serious was wrong. All the lights on the panel went haywire, blinking off and on, as though I'd fed it a virus.

"What happened?"

"The hell if I know," I said, waging a new terror.

As I was about to hit the button to shut it off, the lights stopped, just like that. *Weird,* I thought. But I couldn't dwell on it. The heading indicator was my primary concern. Back and forth, my eyes rolled from outside the window to the indicator and gauge, hoping that the plane would respond to the new course I set, regardless of the malfunctioning lights dancing all over the place.

Nothing was happening. I turned it off and on again, biting my lips, tapping the panel, eager for the plane to change direction so that I could breathe a sigh of relief. Still, no positive feedback, just a few more flashes. Reaching to turn it off again, the machine went up in rage, the blinking lights crazier than before. In a sudden rage myself, I pounced upon the dashboard with my fist. "I think it's playing games with me," I heaved, then amazingly the craziness stopped.

"Maybe," Cameron paused. "Or it could be going crazy because it's really malfunctioning, Pia. Just calm down." He covered my fisted hand. "What now?"

"I don't think you understand. We can't rely on the autopilot getting us back."

"I understand," Cameron solemnly said.

Then a light flashed, the autopilot. I then gave Cameron a peculiar look. *See what I mean?* Next, an array of lights began flashing, and then all lights on the entire panel went berserk again, then at once, they all blacked out.

"Aaahh!" Our panic sounded the alarm. I scrambled to strap down—preparing all over again to step in as the official officer whose job was to save lives, to save the day, whether I could do it or not.

The plane was now in a nosedive, quickly I grabbed the wheel. "Aaahh," we sounded the panic alarm again as my handling of the wheel sent the plane charging upward like a rocket.

After straightening the plane, I looked over at Cameron. Fright was back like vengeance, popping out of his eyes. "Just hold on," I imparted to an otherwise not-so-receptive Cameron. I couldn't much blame him; we were in chaos. This wasn't a simulation or a game, whereas the outlook of a cinematic horror just didn't look good. The lessons I'd gotten over the years had to now count for something. Because at this moment, I was being forced to take the final exam, and if I failed then....

I struggled to keep the plane straight. With the plane swerving like crazy, it was like a kid driving it with a remote control in a park, dodging trees, gliding over hoods of cars, missing a few people's heads—all before coming to a crash landing somewhere. Somewhere, in this situation, was way down below where there was nothing but water.

"I know you can do this, Pia. You have to..." Cameron fed me a mouth full of emotions that I choked on when the plane took another dip. "Whoa, whoa," we both bawled.

"Maybe I should take over," Cameron said.

Glowering, I rebuffed, "What do you mean? Fly the plane? I'm the best we've got." I grunted as I continued to struggle, realizing that my best wasn't good enough.

"Then what is it? Why can't you straighten it up?"

"I'm trying, all right!"

And trying I was. It was like having the devil by the horns trying to tame it, a daunting task I didn't bargain for in spite of everything. The fluctuation was a powerful force to reckon with, having the plane veer in all which a way, so horrific that it nearly spun a full 180 degrees at times.

"You're panicking, Pia. Take it easy!" Cameron yelled.

Turbulence. That's what it was. Not panic or my shortage of skills. Perspiration started trickling down my face, and with the back of my hand, I quickly wiped it away, replacing my damp palms immediately back on the wheel. Even that brief deviation made a difference, which prompted Cameron to reach over and grab the wheel.

"No!" I squalled. "You can't be grabbing the wheel like that."

"Then get a grip!" he said. "If you can't, then maybe I can. Like this..." He began demonstrating how gentle I should be handling the wheel without really touching it. While doing so, I could see he was trying with all his might not to lose it.

"It usually isn't this hard to align the plane. It's the turbulence, I tell you."

"That may be, but you're also panicking. How can you get a hold of the plane if you're panicking? Now c'mon, Pia, you can do it. Just calm down."

Panic, panic, panic. He was more convinced of that being the factor than anything else—and he was wrong...dead wrong. Maybe he was so absorbed with shock that he couldn't see it.

"Save the panic until we're back on the ground, okay? You can do this, Pia. You know you can. You have to.

You've done it before..." On and on he went, saying what I did when hadn't. Not really. He just couldn't help himself.

Another jolt. And his voice raised a couple of more decibels. "C'mon, Pia, you can do it. You can, I know you can. You have more experience at this than you realize...So just keep the plane flying until...until we get someone to help us. And we will, you know. This can't be.... "

I wanted to scream for him to shut up. But I knew he needed this more than I could stand. It was his way of dealing with the situation. It was also his way of helping, encouraging me, and how could I deprive him of that?

He gasped deeply to a bumpier motion of the plane, which revved him up some more. "Your father...he was the best darn teacher–right? He taught you right from where I'm sitting. Here in the copilot seat. You said so yourself. All the more reason I believe in you."

"Right. You're right," I nodded. Dad was my one and only great teacher. Deep down, I knew I had enough lessons in me that I should be able to do this. But was it sufficient for a person scared out of her wits? And why did it seem forever to get past the mayhem?

And then, out of the blue, everything was calm. The turbulence stopped. No kind of friction whatsoever; everything about this moment was eerie yet amazingly peaceful and calm. Even fear seemed to have vanished/stepped aside to let me be so that I could do what I was put in position to do. Aside from all that, lights on the panels blinked on. And when I looked over at Cameron, smiling, even my smile felt eerie.

"See? That's what I'm talking about," Cameron said

grinning.

"Yeah, it seems all that talk you did worked magic. Now that things have calmed down, I have to see about getting us back on course so that we can get back home. See, the lights are back on. But you had better cross your fingers because that could change. Change at any moment."

I eased a trembling foot down on the rudder, hoping not to see signs of failure as with the autopilot. I counted, second by second, tapping a finger on the wheel, for the nose of the plane to begin turning. I glanced over at Cameron. *Turn, turn, turn.* I could almost hear the words pulsating, like from the beat of the drum, inside his head.

"Oh look! It's working! My God it's working!" A resurrection of hope rushed through me.

Life, I felt, life still going on.

I checked the gauge and saw that it too was moving. (None of the others seemed to be working, though.) The gauge moved in accordance with the plane's turn, and when it arrived at the 240 degrees mark, I breathed an elated sigh of relief. I scored a crucial point for the team and it felt so darn good.

"We have a huge problem ahead of us still. Here on out we should keep our fingers crossed...pray. Right now it's a breath of fresh air knowing that we are at least headed back home. But...we're not out of the woods yet. If we–"

"Not *if*, Pia, but *when* we make it back. You have to believe we'll get through this."

He was right. We had to stay positive.

"When we make it back, we're going to need help

landing this plane. Remember, we have no radio communication. No nothing! We are flying this plane with blinders on. We have no way of knowing that we're coming up on another plane. Are you hearing me? We could collide with another plane at any moment. All we can do is pray...pray hard."

Cameron nodded reticently.

I rechecked the heading indicator. "We're still on course, thank goodness."

"We'll make it, Pia. We'll make it."

"Yeah. We have to." In spite of the grave feeling, I managed a smile. "I know we wouldn't be in this mess if it wasn't for me. But if there's any consolation, I'm so grateful to have you as my copilot. And...I think I've found *my wings,*" I acclaimed.

"Yeah. And you couldn't have found them at a better time."

Chapter Twenty-Five

No Man's Land

Ahead was the island, proof we hadn't gone too far off course. The blinding glare causing the chaos flashed in my psyche. Where on earth did it come from in the first place? I wondered. And with the control panels half-functioning (or half-dead), it's a wonder the plane was flying at all.

"Okay?" Cameron questioned.

"Yeah," I nodded. "I was just thinking about Brian. Why you think he hasn't come to yet?"

"I don't know." He then released the seat belt. "But I'll go check on him." He got up, examined Brian the best he could. "I can't say for sure what his condition is. There are no bumps and bruises as far as I can see. His breathing seems normal. Body temperature, normal. His pulse"–he took a moment to check–"is good. It's like he's in a deep sleep."

"But why him and not us? No bumps or bruises. What could've knocked him out like that? It just seems strange."

"I'm with you on that. Whatever's going on, I believe he'll pull through...soon hopefully."

"Yeah, me too. Cameron?" I said, avoiding eye contact. "I have to get closer for a better look."

"What? You can't be serious. What we've been through is much more than what we bargained for. To press our luck is insane."

"Maybe it was just a freak accident."

"You really believe that? Look, it doesn't matter because nothing's there, not to mention the huge risk we would be taking. Just look at Brian and the condition of the plane. No more bright ideas, Pia, so get it through your head, this plane is headed back home *nonstop. We're done out here*."

He was right; of course I knew that. But I had the gumption to see this mission through. Was it actually a figment of my imagination? I had to know once and for all.

"I thought you were in this with me all the way."

"Yeah, and what happened to you being *so sorry* for putting us in this position, huh? Now you're telling me you're seriously thinking about driving this plane into the bottom of the ocean. Look, there's nothing down there for me, and I'm not sorry about that. Damn it! Pia"—he looked out—"that's a graveyard down there. You hear me? A graveyard...you have to get that through your head."

"I don't know how," I wailed. "I promise, *Cameron.* I promise not to bury us. You'll see, all right? You have to trust me because it will drive me crazy not knowing. Please, just trust me on this."

Vexation trembled at his lips. "How close, huh? Don't you know how close you would have to get to figure this thing out?"

"Don't, Cameron. I see what you're saying and don't be angry with me. It won't come to that; you have to trust me...." I went on begging for his approval as I moved the yoke forward. As the plane began a gradual descent, I thought about how he wouldn't give up convincing me that I could handle the plane. Maybe I could return the favor by convincing him to trust me on this.

I couldn't believe myself, but I had to try.

"Listen," I spoke softly, "I'm only dropping the plane a few thousand feet. Right now, we're at 32,000 feet." I looked over at him ignoring me and then continued. "I'll go to about 20,000 feet, and if you still don't see it then...then we're out of here, okay? Forever..." Pain finished the thought.

In my peripheral, I saw him now looking at me, though he upheld the silent treatment.

"We're now at 25,000 feet," I updated. From this altitude, I flew over it, observing the features. The jagged edges of mountains. The smooth rolling hills and wondrous vegetation. There were no signs of life or habitation of any kind, as far as I could see. No paved roads. No buildings. Nothing but a picture of raw beauty.

Surprisingly, my cell phone rang. "Cameron, my phone!" I got excited, patting pockets to locate my phone. The surprise in his face revealed he was thinking what I was thinking. I got hold of it, right away noticing it was from an unknown caller.

"Hello, hello." I could only hear static at first.

"Pia...Megan." I thought I heard; the static was awful.

"Megan? Is that you?" Megan was a friend back home.

"Yes, 'ad 'nection."

"Megan, Megan listen to me. I'm flying the plane, and we're–"

She butted in, "Omigod. You got...wings?"

"Yes, yes, I got my wings but listen–"

"That's wonder–" Her voice, the static, went dead.

"Megan, Megan, Megan–dang!" Exasperated, I tried to get her back–anyone, but to no avail. "I can't believe it. Check your phone, it might be working." Anxious, Cameron was already on it.

"Nah. No service." Regardless of our hopes being up, we suspected as much.

I landed my focus on the gauge. It read 21,000 feet now. Nervousness began building inside me. Could be that it was close to 20,000 feet, and I had made a promise to Cameron. I glanced over at him, asking myself: after being this close what was the chance of my coming this close ever again? Probably not ever, was my answer. And how could I be okay with that? As so many thoughts came to me, I hung to the reality that I could very well be at a point of no return.

It was at that exact moment I made the decision to push through 20,000 feet, duly allowing myself more leeway. My eyes bulging as I did because, after all, I was breaching the promise I made to Cameron, praying that he didn't notice.

"Aaahhh!" We bellowed at the top of our lungs. All of a sudden the plane was plunging through some kind of shield that was stretching like plastic as the plane fought its way through. Then there was this unbearable sound, and our hands went up to plug fingers in our ears. But not for long, though. The excruciating sound lasted only seconds—stopped, just as the plane ripped through that thing.

"Whoa. What in the hell was *that?*" Cameron said in a rhetorical fashion, as it appeared he was experiencing jet lag. I thought because that's exactly how I felt. Hesitantly, he went on to say, "It's almost...as if...we crossed over to another dimension." I gave him a moment to think about that.

The plane. It was my concern. After passing through whatever that was, it wasn't running as smooth. Maybe I imagined this, but the engines sounded like it was trying to cough out phlegm. Quickly I scanned the instrument panel. The gauges appeared to be working, all of them actually. As I wondered when that happened, the engines started to sound better.

Another dimension, I reflected on that as I gaze down on the island.

"We have to get out of here and fast." Cameron said. He was looking through the windshield as well. Then he uttered something strange. "Uuggh..." It sounded as if he was having a stroke or something.

"You okay?"

"I-I...um. Is that what I think it is?"

"Cam...you mean you can see it?"

"Yeah, kinda," he stuttered a bit as he faced me. "An illusion. That's all it is. All of a sudden—I just can't believe it. I'm not sure what you expected, but what I see down there isn't real. It's a mirage, transparent. It's like the other ones I saw. No way is that real no matter how you look at it, Pia. Remember, I went through one. I'm sorry. I know this isn't what you were hoping for."

"No," I responded to his honest, sympathetic tenor.

"Now, can we leave this godforsaken place?"

"Okay." I nodded faintly as a pang of longing crept in, and I was also concerned about the plane. "I don't know if we can go back the way we came. And if we do, I don't know if the plane can take it."

"I was just thinking: The only way to get back is the way we came. What if that's the case?" Silence swept by. "But we have to do something. Since we're not sure about anything, maybe we should try going around it."

"It's worth a try. I'm going to plan a southerly detour for about fifty miles, then redirect the course." I checked the gas gauge. "We should have plenty of fuel to make it back."

As I changed course, the phrase "the point of no return" crossed my mind. It left me wondering had I really come to that point, having come all this way. I couldn't help it: I was dying to set foot on the island.

Was I wrong?

Was it merely a figment of my imagination?

The point of no return, where was it really?

"All in my head," my lips moved quietly, answering myself.

Then suddenly, something was wrong: the engines, sputtering like before but only worse this time. The gauges began spinning out of control and the lights flashing off and on and then at once, all stopped. I nudged the throttle to test for speed and quickly realized the power was dropping. And the gauges began spinning like crazy again.

"Not again!" Fear was back with a vengeance in Cameron's face.

"I don't know what's going on," I said. But I knew

better. "It's Ferret, Cam...Ferret," I said not calmly but finally. "I'm telling you it's Ferret, it has to be. And the way things look now, I have no choice but to land this plane." Shaking my head, "I have no choice. Either I go for the island or we're ending up in the water regardless. Brace yourself because–Omigod Cameron this is it!"

"No, no. There has to be something you can do. You can't put this baby down there...in the middle of the Bermuda Triangle." He was thinking of his parents, not so much of the plane being in trouble and needing to go down somewhere. And his dreadful expression, as though he was staring death in the face, I couldn't bear.

Considering I must do the unthinkable, I had to somehow force that dreadful look out of my mind. There was nothing I could do to relieve the paralyzing horror. Nothing. It was simply out of my hands, whether my hands were exclusively on the wheel or not. There was nothing left for me do, but pray that down there wasn't an illusion of death.

Scanning a terrain of luscious trees, hills and mountains, I searched desperately before time ran out, for somewhere to put the plane down. Somewhere–I started to freak out–there had to be somewhere to land the plane. Just trees, huge rocks: a place to land didn't seem to exist. But there had to be. How could it not be? I'd seen a landing strip in my dreams–if that meant anything.

Finally, coming over a dense floret of trees, my soul cheered when a smooth, lengthy welcome mat–my red carpet–appeared for my starring role. That's what it was after all. Because it would soon be my first time ever, landing a plane.

"There it is. All I have to do is get where there's enough runway to land," I muttered. Then my tenor escalated. "It's Ferret," I said as if I spotted a real live person. "This is not death. If only you could see what I see." When Cameron didn't respond, I looked over my shoulder.

"It has a heart. Your Ferret, it has a heart." He sounded foggy, confused in a way. Yet he had me in awe, waiting for an explanation.

"It's coming to view. Like a sketch being filled in with color, coming to life right before my eyes. Never would I imagine it like this. It's...incredible."

Sated by his revelation, I lit up like a bulb. "Hold on!" I deployed the landing gear and began decreasing speed. Aiming for the center of the makeshift runway to avoid clipping trees and possibly losing a wing, I fully extended the flaps. "Here goes," I shrieked.

Roaring, the plane touched down hard, so hard it bounced along the scratchy strip of loose gravel and dust. In a panic, I slammed the brake, and the plane skidded, roaring like thunder, a plume of dust at its tail I imagined, as I had a time keeping it steady.

"Whoa." Cameron reached over me and got a stronghold on the wheel. This time I didn't resist help.

"It's real. I can't believe it, it's real," he clamored joyfully as the plane slowed to a complete stop.

"Yes, we made it."

We made it! We made it!

That was everything.

Chapter Twenty-Six

No More Iceberg

I reclined as my heavy breathing dwindled back to normal. "How are you over there?" I said, turning to Cameron. He'd settled back down.

"Great job landing the plane, and getting us here in one piece...wherever or whatever this place is," he breathed. "This has been one helluva experience. It's incredible, you're incredible."

I was pleased to see him in a state other than hounding me about making the worst mistake of my life. I smiled when he pinched himself, making sure that he was still in the land of the living. As if that wasn't enough, he bit his tongue and lower lip. Maybe that was enough to convince him because he then relaxed wearing a heavenly face.

"We probably should get out and see what it's like out there, test the air. On second thought, it could be some kind of gas in the air that'd knock us dead as soon as we step off this plane," he said.

"You don't really believe that, do you?" I challenged.

"We shall see." He winked.

Getting out to explore a strange newfangled place that was invisible to the rest of the world was irresistible. So many nights this place came to me in dream form, and for so long I saw it on trips to and from Bermuda. Now finally, I was actually here.

"I'm right behind you. Let's go and really stretch our legs," I said, though my spirit leaped off the plane ahead of me.

On our way off the plane, we checked on Brian. Nothing had changed. His body felt cool, so I grabbed a blanket from overhead and covered him. We knew already from opening the door that it was mild and breezy out.

Outside of the plane, we gasped as we rubbernecked to the tip-top of high mountains and then pivoted to take in all angles of everything surrounding us. An environment that felt strange and lifeless seemed to only exist for this moment, because nature was miraculous and could take it away in a breath, just like that. Then too, one could imagine living in a place like this forever and ever. Trees, exotic trees, velvety hills spread across the island, rolling off rocky, jagged mountains were just too beautiful. Skirting the slopes were ponderous rocks situated like decorative pieces. Everywhere was immaculate, as if meticulously cared for by landscaping architects from nowhere but paradise.

We staggered as we started up the path, our heads still held high taking it all in. In the distance was an ancient-looking mountain. Its altitude, non-sloping with fang-like edges, towered like the ruler of the land–the pinnacle of attraction in my eyes. And I wondered if climbing to the top was even possible.

My wondering went on nonstop. How was this place even possible? How was it possible we were here? How long would we be here? The number one question; were we alone? Someone had to be here, I hoped.

I glanced at Cameron. At times he seemed to walk with extreme caution, as though he expected the ground to magically disappear from underneath him at any moment. After all what we'd been through, anything was possible. When he turned to me, I could see that chilling look of death radiating again.

"I don't know." He shook his head slightly. "I can't be comfortable with this. It's too creepy."

"If it disappears, it won't while we're on it. *Don't ask.* I know that sounds strange, but I have this strange vibe I can't explain." I shrugged. "Like everything else I can't explain."

"I'm getting a weird vibe, too. A vibe that we're stuck here...that we'll never get out of here alive." Our eyes locked. "What if we become a statistic, like the other disappearances in the Bermuda Triangle?"

"Disappearing–I can't think like that. And you shouldn't either. But if at all true, I can't believe for a minute that we arrived here only to disappear and never be heard of again." I paused, thinking and looking around some more. "It seems deserted."

"Why you think that?"

"I didn't see anything resembling buildings or any sign of people living on the island. *It looked deserted,*" I repeated. "What about you, did you see anything while we were up in the air?"

"Uh...I don't remember seeing anything, but that

doesn't mean anything. There must be someone. We have to believe there's somebody here to at least help us get off the island," he said, deflecting my notion entirely, and his too, whether he realized it or not. How we would get off this island was how we should be thinking.

"I got an idea," I warned before yelling. "Is anybody here? Hello, hello! Anybody!" My bellowing caught him by surprise. "Help! Help...anybody!" I continued. "Can anyone hear me? Help, help!"

Then to Cameron, I said, "What if a big bad witch is watching us through a crystal ball, you know, like in the Wizard of Oz? Wait, don't you feel them, hear them, the little munchkins? Come out, come out, wherever you are." I smiled at Cameron.

"Yeah. Come out, come out, wherever you are!" he shouted along with me, we escalating to the top of our lungs. Doing this aroused much humor in our trying time. We surely needed something to stimulate us with anything other than dread, and it felt good for as long as it lasted.

Walking up the road a ways, we came upon a path leading into the mountains and stopped. The sound of running water drew us to exploring the depth of this path even before we landed a foot on it.

"It sounds like a waterfall," Cameron said, hiking up the trail behind me.

I slowed down, scanning off into the trees after hearing movement in the overgrowth. "Listen, did you hear that?" There by a tree, standing on its hind legs, was this furry animal so close I could see its dark, marble eyes peering at me. "You see that? What is it?"

"Oh wow. The first living creature we have come

across so far. And we thought we were all alone." He seemed thrilled.

Suddenly, it leaped toward me, and I jumped back. My arms flew up to guard myself against it.

"Don't be afraid. It wouldn't attack you. They're really quite loving."

"What do you know about it?"

"Would you believe I had one as a pet? When I was a little boy living in Europe?"

"A pet, huh?" Still I was not about to take a chance on being friendly with the creature despite hearing how it might be easy to cozy up to.

"Yeah, I did. Not like this one, though. Mine was smaller, younger, and looked, I have to say, friendlier."

"What?"

"That's not what I meant. See, watch." Cameron moved past me, slowly approaching this animal with a skunk's body and raccoon eyes, and wasn't budging an inch, as he got closer. But then as Cameron kneeled, extending his hand gradually, I sensed the mammal's uneasiness. Cameron was close and could have nailed it in a swift motion, but the skunk-like animal was quicker, dropping to all four legs and scramming like the roadrunner, silver streak in all.

Wait...a silver streak...did I just see that? No. I didn't want to believe that I did. *My mind is playing tricks on me again,* I thought, looking around for it. I could still hear it. Not too far, I spotted its glaring eyes in refuge; it was propped against the tree trunk, mischievous and sneaky like. *What a unique characteristic for an animal to possess.*

"So much for a loving personality," I said. "See it

over there? Maybe it wants you to chase after it." Despite our dire circumstance, I joked. Though on second thought, I wasn't so sure if I really meant it as a joke.

"Ah, ha, ha, ha," Cameron sniggered. "It getting away like that brought back memories: the day when Hank got away from me. That's what I called my little friend, by the way. One day I put him in a bag to sneak him out of the house. I think I was too trusting then, didn't think he would ever leave me. But I was wrong. He jumped out, didn't say so long, see ya later–nothing. Suppose he didn't have time, and I never saw him again. I was one sad, miserable kid after losing Hank. But I had no one to blame but myself. It was my bloody fault."

I smiled at the British accent. "Why didn't your parents just get you another one?"

"My parents wouldn't hear of it. You see, that wasn't my first time sneaking it out of the house, and my parents had given me fair warning. So I had to take the punishment like the little man that I was."

"Sorry. So you didn't get around to saying. What kind of pet was it?"

He gave me a questionable look. "Believe it or not, a ferret." My mouth gaped open as he continued. "Yeah. And that out there is a black-footed ferret."

"What? You're kidding me. A Ferret?"

"Not on your life, Pia. Mine and Brian's included. And I know what you're thinking, but this could be nothing more than a coincidence. So don't–and I know it's a lot to ask–but don't dwell on it. We have enough on our plate as it is. Until we have more to go on, it's just a coincidence. A coincidence, okay?" he said, and I nodded.

A ferret, up-close and personal, today? Naturally it wouldn't be easy to ignore ever seeing this animal. And as we moved along the path in silence, I couldn't get over now affixing "Ferret" to a mammal and not the island. In this situation, merely mentioning the word was thought-provoking, eerie, and I clearly understood Cameron wanting me to hold back on the verbiage.

And now that I thought about it, it really looked like the animals that came up when I researched the word "ferret." But I didn't pay them much attention. Because I never would've thought....

Just a coincidence. He probably was right. That's what I wanted to think anyway; it would certainly ease my mind. And it would do me good—convince me even, if I saw more animals roaming around. So far that ferret was the only live thing we came across. And it couldn't be the only thing around here.

The path curved around the hill leading to a mountainous backdrop draped with bushes and trees with water spouting from it into a pool hugging beneath it. As we were moving in for a closer view, the route shifted to loose slabs of limestone, and pool water oozed over it. Odd rock formations also along the passageway made the setting even more interesting.

"What do you think?" I asked.

"Beautiful...but...I don't know. Something's not right."

"Yeah," I muttered, concentrating. "You would think we'd see things like insects, bugs, birds, creepy-looking fish—any living thing other than that animal."

"You're right. But we're bound to run into someone.

I mean, just look at this place. Somebody has to be keeping up the landscaping. That ferret isn't trimming the hedges with its teeth."

"If that's the case, then it would explain why there's no litter, no evidence of humans or even birds having flocked here. Still, you think it would be this neat? It looks picture-perfect."

Cameron thought for a moment. "Maybe we're putting too much into this. We haven't covered much territory. Let's see what's on the other side."

As we continued on the winding path, we came upon an arched opening, in the center was a pool, and far to the other end was another arched entrance. Slowly we entered.

"Aw, look at this," said Cameron, gawking at the ceiling. "Have you ever seen anything so beautiful? Except in a *National Geographic Magazine*."

"A crystal cave. There's one in Bermuda, not quite like this one. Here, the ceiling is higher, wider. It's pretty remarkable." We moved in farther, still in awe by the conical shapes, vastly hanging from the ceiling, resembling chandeliers made of pure crystal.

"It's quite damp in here," he acknowledged.

"And it smells like rotten eggs, as expected," I rejoined.

To move farther into the cave, we carefully descended layered slabs of limestone, making our way for a more spectacular discovery. Standing at the edge of the pool, we looked up and saw a fenestella or a vortex, rising hundreds of feet above us, though it looked like it opened to the top of the world. "Wow," we voiced numerous times, and I got dizzy cocking my head to such wonderment.

Then Cameron began looking around the cave suspiciously, and after intense observation, he said, "Like I said before, something's not right. There's no fungus, moles, not to mention insects and bats–the kind of things you'd expect to see, especially in a cave. And wait a minute." He moved closer to the pool of water then stooped and began waving a hand in the water.

"What do you think about the water?" I wanted to hear more of what was on his mind.

"Nothing," he said. But this didn't sit well with me, and I persuaded him to speak up. Faintly shaking his head, he said, "Just that, at first, I thought I was looking at a mirage or something of that nature. That's all."

Maybe I was overly sensitive when I thought I'd detected a hint of frustration in his tone. The kind of frustration one may feel after someone pulled a fast one on you or played an unpleasant trick.

I began staring into the water, perhaps hypnotized by its glass-smooth stillness, my reflection so vividly crowned by the chandelier ceiling. Waving my hand over the water, I played with my reflection. Then I dipped my hands into the pool. My reflection shimmered, carried off by the ripples across the pool.

"I have this strange feeling of déjà vu," I quietly thought out loud. "Of course I've done this before, waved a hand in the water, played with my reflection," I said, trying to reason and even shake the feeling. "But I can't put a finger on why."

"The feeling of déjà vu is like that. It creeps up on you without an explanation." Cameron's voice traveled a few feet to reach me. He now examined a portion of the cave's walls.

"Yeah...I suppose you're right." Once again, I dipped my hand into the glass-smoothed pool and noticed that it was cooler, but I didn't think anything of it. I rose to my feet, slowly moving toward Cameron. Before I got far, something about the pool caught my attention. Staring at it, I saw a cloudy vapor rising from it. I knelt over it again and dipped a hand into it, and it was now ice-cold.

Suddenly, a thin layer of ice covered the surface. Astounded, I cracked it. "Cameron, get a hold of this."

In a flash, he was kneeling down next to me. "I wonder what's causing the water to freeze so quickly."

"I don't know. I just cracked the ice in this spot, and it's already covered with ice again."

"It's freezing up too fast."

I touched it again, and my fingers nearly stuck to the ice. "You see that?"

"That doesn't make sense. I feel no change in the temperature," said Cameron as the ice started crackling now.

I then looked to the edge. "Whoa, look at this." The ice had crept over the bank and was cresting at our feet.

"What the..." Cameron was saying, as images of places raced across my vision. Was I trying to remember something? Was that the whole purpose of being here? Enthralled by the images, I didn't know what to think, and I certainly lost touch with what was happening around me, until–

"Pia! It's time to go–now." The urgency in his voice and the yanking of my arm snapped me back into the moment. The entire pool was cracking open. We had to move fast, far from the pool, which was now noisy and swelling as it continued to crack open. Moving as fast as we could to the exit, we stumbled our way up the slabs as the horrifying sound of the crackling pool vibrated throughout the cave.

As we were about to pass the arched entrance, a piercing, shattering noise ordered us to freeze in our tracks, because we had to turn and see what was happening.. The solid-iced pool was now large chunks of ice. And like a ferocious virus, it had spread closer to the cave's perimeter. For an undetermined time, the horrifying sight had of us both stupefied, trapped in terror, until another bombing sound of shattering ice jarred us. It was then we realized this thing, which seemed to have a mind of its own, was now within inches of our feet.

Cameron yanked my arm, and we hauled ass back along the same rugged path, gasping for speed to get as far away as we possibly could as fast as we could. And to me, that meant getting back to the plane.

Hoping to garner a logical explanation for what was happening, I looked to the sky. But I knew I wouldn't find anything there. The sky was blue as ever, and the sun was radiant, emitting the warmth of springtime. And below the blue sky was this vicious cold place turning into Antarctica. So what was causing a sudden deep freeze in the cave? Even though there was no clue to what was happening, I only hoped that it stayed inside the cave and we got as far away from it as possible. However, as soon as we made it back to the waterfall, we were struck with a harrowing discovery.

"It's out here too," I squealed. "I think it's after us. How did it get this far so fast?"

"It's almost like it seeped through the mountain's foundation to catch up to us–if that's what it's trying to do," said Cameron.

Whether it had a mind of its own, the mountain over the pool was now becoming a glacier. And the pool, just like the pool inside the cave, was fast becoming no more. And neither would we if we didn't get across the ice-coated slabs–and fast.

"These slabs are uneven, slippery. I'm going to..." I heard him say, but his voice faded, faded completely as an image bewitched me. A shimmering image, resembling liquid, came through a brush of trees. I had seen it before, this young manly figure the day when time stood still. And as it moved past me, a scream rushed to the top of my lungs and stopped cold. I felt I was about to explode until–

"Aaaaaahhhhh!" The scream exploded as I pointed. "See that!" I said finally. I made a swift turn, forgetting that we were on slippery ground, and we both slipped and tumbled flat on our butts.

"Pia, what...what is it?" Cameron clamored as we tried getting back on our feet without slipping again. By then, the ghost was gone. Now in its place was the ferret. "You mean the ferret?" Cameron was puzzled now, and we both were in a snafu state.

There was no time for discussion; we had to get moving and fast to avoid being frozen in time–this time, the old-fashioned way.

"I got you. Now take it slow, easy. We don't have time for another slip-up. Slow and easy...just take it slow and easy," he repeated.

"A good thing we're wearing sneakers," I said. The

rubber soles gave us enough traction, and we sighed when we made it across without another slip-up.

We stormed our way back through the trail, struggling for our lives, hoping that the monster would slow down and not come after us if indeed its passion was to catch us. Then in the distance, we heard something. A rumbling like thunder. Immediately, we looked at each other, lit up with hope. But to be sure, we stopped to listen more closely.

"It sounds like something's running," said Cameron. The first thing that entered my mind was that we weren't alone on the island after all and that help had finally arrived.

"It sure does," I mirrored the smile lines about his lips. We then moved even quicker around the hill, practically racing each other.

We couldn't move fast enough hoping to see someone other than ourselves on this godforsaken island that seemed to exist in a dream world. The closer we got to the main road, the more convinced we were of someone being there. The minute we made it to the main road–level ground finally–we took off running in the direction of what now sounded like an engine, which happened to be toward the plane.

Through our pangs of great urgency was some enthusiasm flinging dust at our heels as we ran, ran as fast as we could to get to the plane. When the plane came into view, I was overwhelmed with enthusiasm to see the plane alive and kicking. Looking face to face, we naturally read each other's mind; that roaring engine up ahead meant one of two things. With that in mind, we picked up speed as our eagerness accelerated with hope and clouded with suspicion.

When we arrived at the plane, we couldn't board it quickly enough. Once inside, fear toppled my joy when I saw Brian was nowhere around.

"This is a good sign," Cameron said calmly, seeing that I was about to panic. "It only means he's out looking for us. Get a hold of yourself."

"Yeah, you're right," I said, slightly shaking my head. "I don't know what I was thinking." But now I thought about the trouble on the other side of the mountain. "Cameron, we have to find him right away."

"Yeah. He shouldn't be that far since he left the plane running," Cameron said as we got off the plane.

We yelled Brian's name as we tracked up the road. Along the way, I just couldn't shake the feeling that something even stranger was about to happen, and of course I couldn't get that ice monster out of my head. We tracked farther up the straight road, calling out Brian's name as we moved, continuously rotating to watch out for him or anything popping up behind us.

"Maybe he went off the road," said Cameron after a while.

"And that's what I'm afraid of. I can't stop thinking about the cave."

"And we shouldn't. We are in jeopardy for as long as we are on this island. We have to find Brian and get out of here."

"Listen," I said, hearing scrunches off in the trees.

"Brian! Brian!" Cameron hollered hopefully. This went on endlessly seemed like. "Brian! Brian!" We kept calling out his name, which tolled in my head as I breathed sweat. And as seconds counted down, I was anticipating something horrible happening if time ran out, because if it did, time wins. My God, I didn't want time to win.

"Here!" Suddenly Brian appeared from the brush of trees, rushing at top speed as if his life depended on it. And it did, of course. "I've been looking everywhere for you guys. Thank goodness I've found you in time." He huffed.

Instinctively, I craned my neck toward the top of the mountain, so did Cameron, and we saw, whatever this thing was, scouring over the top of the mountain now, and I assumed it was closing in from the area Brian was coming.

"We have to hurry," I said to Cameron and then started yelling, "Hurry Brian! Hurry!" He was coming fast but not fast enough, especially after what came out of his mouth next.

"Hell, what's going on around here?"

"It must be closing in from that side, too," Cameron said. "Talk about global warming, huh?" he then yelled to Brian.

"You got that right. I didn't think it could be so vicious," Brian said, huffing.

"Brian! Look up!" Cameron yelled.

"Ah shit!" Brain then picked up speed from somewhere because he was moving like the roadrunner now.

"Hurry! We have to hurry!" I couldn't say that enough.

When Brian reached us he managed a quick smile. "You just don't know how glad I am to see you two. I don't know where the hell we are but we better get the fuck out of here."

"It's good to see you back in tip-top shape," said Cameron as we hauled ass alongside him, we all, running for our lives.

The horrifying sound of shattering ice was back, and the sound of it was growing as the blob of an ice monster advanced over the mountain. It dawned on me that it was the same sound we heard coming through the shield, only not as painful.

Finally, back at the plane, we discovered it was no longer running. "You didn't turn off the plane, did you?" Brian asked anxiously.

"Nah, we left it running," Cameron and I responded.

We boarded the plane and Brian settled down quickly in the pilot seat. *Hurry, hurry; see if the plane will start,* I screamed inside my head. In his first attempt, the engine roared to life; and then for a short while, it sputtered until it went dead again. In his second attempt, it lasted longer, but the result was the same. The anxiety among us would kill us for sure if the plane didn't start, never mind what was lurking outside. "The third time is the charm," said Brian, and for it to be so, we crossed our fingers. On his third try, the engine came to life and then more sputters. But this time the engines spat out the sputtering and sounded as healthy as ever. It was the most miraculous sound I ever heard; as if I had died and the wonderful sound of the engines brought me back to life.

"All right, take your seats," Brian commanded, and we did, gladly. Looking out the window, I could see the growing glacier in moments of its final approach to the plane. I looked down; just below the window was the ferret, standing on its hind legs. All of the sudden, I felt sympathy. The monstrous threat was closing in and what would happen to this ferret? The only live mammal we'd seen thus far.

My mind began racing, seeing the demise of this animal. "Wait, wait! We can't leave the ferret." Compulsion drove the words out of me and I felt emotionally awkward afterward. What was I thinking?

"What are you talking about?" Brian responded at once. Cameron was staring in disbelief.

"Nothing." I turned back to it and muttered, "The ferret..." The plane was moving, yet it was still there, waving. I couldn't take my eyes off it. Not until it did the honors of vanishing. But then, *he* appeared in its place. It was another moment of "I can't believe my eyes." I even blinked, and he was still there. This person with complicated features and a frowsy look from head to toe—something about him and his unkempt presence was familiar.

"The ghost..." My voice caught in my throat as he waved, fading away. All while the plane moved, I continued to stare as if it/he was still there, as though I wanted him to reappear. "....Gone now." I must have sounded aloof, and I could feel Cameron's concern.

"Looks like we're going to beat it," I heard Brian say.

The plane was roaring up the make-do runway, gaining the speed needed to rise above this rare form of "all hell breaking loose." I was in a trance somewhat, but when the plane started climbing to safety, the impact of relief came as a wake-me-up.

Aching to see what the island looked like now, I just couldn't help myself, and when I looked out, I screamed.

"Pia!" Cameron rushed to my side and looked out

the window. "Holy moly," he groaned, hugging me close now as we looked out at this giant ice formation, thousands of feet in the air, right outside the plane. It must have climbed at the same speed as the plane—but how, why?

Brian said something.

"She's okay, just get far from here," Cameron said to him. Moments later, the thing was gone.

My voice was trembling. "Cameron...what did it look like to you?" I sought confirmation to what I saw.

"Like a huge dude...really big...in a slam-dunking position," he added an afterthought.

"Yeah. It kinda did. You think it was trying to snatch the plane out of the sky?"

"Maybe. But don't worry about it. It didn't happen," his voice soothed.

We continued looking out below. My gaping expression remained, and my body half numb as this thing finished glaciating the place with a vengeance. It was unbelievable what was becoming of the island. A massive monument, sculptured like the Admiralty Range, out in the middle of nowhere.

"Oooh, can you believe that?" said Brian. He was circling the island, too fascinated to be getting as far from it as he possibly could.

Cameron responded by telling him what we'd just seen, and then he said to me, "I'm just thankful we got away in time." Gently, he began massaging my shoulders.

"I just don't know what to make of all this," I said matter-of-factly. "For some reason, I believe we were the only ones down there. That ferret, I don't think it was real—I know it wasn't. It also disappeared in thin air..." I frowned, about to tell what appeared in its place but held back. For no particular reason, I kept it to myself for now.

"Look at it now," I said. The island was as clear as crystal. *It's putting on a show,* I thought, recalling the light show it had done once before.

Cameron and Brian began talking about the unbelievable phenomenon. How the ice monster came out of nowhere, transforming the island into a glacier and then into one monumental crystal.

Incredible! That's what it was.

But something else was happening now. It was shrinking–no, it was dissolving, and emitting vapor as it fused into the sea.

"That's crazy. I wonder what's coming next," Brian said. "Imagine how many thousands of years it would have taken for something of that magnitude to form. And now, zilch, like it never existed."

"I don't know, but global warming works fast," Cameron said to be funny. "And just think: who's going to believe this?" His tone changed. "Let's get out of here now, Brian, before we disappear next."

"Yeah, let's go home," I mumbled.

As Brian began turning away, he said, "You did good, Pia. Taking over and landing the plane. And now, after all this, you probably will be better off."

"I sure hope so." For the first time since forever, the island wasn't there for me to see...evaporated completely. But, out of sight doesn't always mean out of mind. Was it gone for good?

Land the plane? How did he–?

"Brian, how do you know I landed the plane? Cameron, you didn't tell him, did you?" Cameron shook his head. "You were unconscious the entire time, weren't you?"

"About that. Yes and no. I was in limbo—a coma-like state if you will. I could hear what was going on around me, but I couldn't move or talk."

"Do you remember what happened?" asked Cameron.

"You mean how I got like that? No...not a thing."

"Being in that condition must've been really scary," I commented.

Before Brian could respond, an unexpected voice interrupted. "Brian, this is Hennessy. Can you read me?" Our faces lit up, and we were practically freaking out over the surprise.

"Yes...I read you. Go 'head, Hennessy, Brian's here," he said, exhilarated.

"Thank God. Boy am I glad to see you."

"You really see us? Where are you?"

"Right behind you. We're the first of the search party to arrive after receiving a message your plane went missing. We've been searching for about thirty minutes or so. Thank goodness everything seems to be okay."

"We did run into problems with the plane, but everything seems to be okay now."

"We'll stick with you back to the mainland. Wouldn't want to lose you again. To be honest, I think I was about to lose hope until you flew out of that unusual dense fog back there."

"Did you say 'dense fog'?"

"That's right. I can't say where it came from. Suddenly it was there, rising as high as outer space, shaped like a cylinder. I've never seen anything like it, but all of a sudden, there you were, flying out of it."

"*Flying out of it?*" Brian said and we all eyed one another.

"That's what I said. *Now listen.* When we arrived, we were sure we had spotted you, around that same location. I would have bet my life on it. But as we got closer, what we thought we saw seemed to have disappeared or wasn't there at all. It could've been the sun reflecting off the water to create something of a mirage. Though it was strange, I have to say. Like I said, I, along with my copilot here, would have bet our lives that the plane was there.

"Now, I'm even more baffled. That cloud back there you just flew out of, maybe you can shed some light on where you were coming from. How or where did you land the plane in the middle of nowhere and get it back in the air? As incredible as that may sound."

We all looked at one another regarding his suspicion. He didn't see the island, let alone see it disappear. And the fog he spoke of, we saw no fog. The whole time, there was nothing but blue skies. Of course, there was the steam the iceberg produced as it disappeared into the water, but that wasn't what he'd described. Just as the island disappeared, perhaps the fog he claimed to have seen disappeared as well. However, none of us saw it.

If there was anything stranger than fiction, that was it. And we knew already that convincing others of our story would be incredibly challenging. I could hear them now, saying, "You all are delusional, but Hollywood would eat it up." Nevertheless, Brian was ready to give it a shot.

"To start, I have to say we are very lucky to even be

here to tell our story," Brian led with this as an introduction.

"I have to second that," said Hennessy.

"I hope what you're about to unload doesn't insult his sense of reality," Cameron whispered jokingly. Or maybe not.

As Brian got into telling what happened, Cameron and I were amazed by his exact details. In areas he lacked in detail, we eagerly helped him along to keep the story straight.

Chapter Twenty-Seven

Serving the Story

Soon after the radio went out again, and a couple of other planes had joined in the escort back to Miami airport and assisted in landing safely. Authorities at the airport awaited our arrival.

I didn't understand right away when we were told not to be alarmed as we received royal treatment directly from the plane by a couple of security officers and another man dressed more business-like. I didn't suspect anything out of the ordinary. Not until one of them said, "Right this way, please," leading us to a private section of the airport. "I promise this won't take up too much of your time," and again, insisting that we not be alarmed.

"They want to question us about what we saw," said Brian.

Right, how silly of me for not thinking that Hennessy would have shared our experience with the world by now. It was obvious he'd done just that. And now, they were determined to hear more.

The reserved area we were lead to seemed to be used by business people, executives or anyone having special privilege. In this case, that included us. It was a privileged area simply because it was quiet, secluded, accommodating–yet cozy. Though we were just passing through, we ended up in a room with a sizable oval table, hardback chairs surrounding it. Perfect for the meeting we were about to have.

Beverages and sandwiches were set before us on a platter, and we were grateful for the offer. Shortly following, a couple of men from the Federal Aviation Authority (FAA) came in and introduced themselves: James Lord and B. Phillips. The FAA? Drawing interest from the FAA was a bit much, I thought. But what did I know? Brian introduced us individually. They then took a seat before us expressing warm sentiments for our safe return, and then they got on with their agenda.

B. Phillips said, "Since I was here at the airport when all this was coming in, I thought I should stick around for an opportunity to talk to you. One of the pilots in the search conveyed what happened out there. But to make sure there's no miscommunication, I would like to hear the story from you. A phenomenon such as you claim is critical. It's just as important to get precise details of what happened, what you saw out there. I'll be taping the whole conversation from here on out." He placed a recorder in front of us.

"Now, from my understanding, the three of you spent some time on some mysterious island?" B. Phillips asked.

"Yes, sir, we did," Brian stated first, and we reiterated. Then we each, one after another, engaged in telling our extraordinary experience in precise details, just as the FAA agent asked. Starting with how a blinding force knocked the plane off course and knocked our only pilot unconscious, leaving someone like me who had never flown a plane to take control, hoping what little training I had had been enough. And about the barrier we went through, which turned out to be what seemed, another dimension. That it was when the engine started acting up, causing us to make an emergency landing on the island, invisible to the rest of the world until today when Cameron and Brian saw it for the first time.

Their attentive posture was unwavering as we covered the horrifying details of our experience to the end. Not leaving out the most telling part, of how we managed to escape before it iced over completely, becoming pure glacier, the total mass of it dissolving into the ocean.

The interviewer got up and began pacing around the room.

Feeling uneasy, I asked, "Are we in trouble?"

Mr. B. Phillips gave a causal shake of the head. "No...not in trouble. An incredible story, I must say."

"Don't you believe us?" I nudged. I needed him to be clear.

He approached the table and pressed his palms upon it. "Tell me why you were miles off the mainland in the first place. Did you go out there expecting to see this island?" B. Phillips's commanding tone nudged back.

I glanced at the other man, James Lord, leaning forward over the table, whom I thought was unusually quiet through this whole process. Patience, a great deal of patience, was the vibe I perceived from him. Yet I also saw his eagerness to snoop all over this like a canine. The exact same trait in B. Phillips, except he was upfront, more pronounced about his determination. As I glanced a long moment at Brian, I was reminded how he had tried from the beginning to drum out of me my motive for the trip. I couldn't bring myself to tell Brian then, and I wasn't sure if I should tell these FAA men now.

"Well..." I said, still not sure.

"It was just a day sightseeing," Cameron chimed in, looking at Brian.

"Now come on. That far off coast?"

"Sir, that's what it would've been if we hadn't run into trouble," Brian concocted nicely.

"Will either of you give me an honest answer? For Pete's sake, why try to hide it?"

"Why do you find sightseeing off the coast odd, when you don't exactly believe what you've heard so far?" I was compelled to ask whether the question was disrespectful or not.

"You see, that's where you're wrong. I do believe you. As bizarre as it all seems, I do."

His phone rang, and he stepped from the table to answer. The three of us glanced at each other, but for the most part, B. Phillips's phone conversation had our attention. We detected something major had happened, and I for one thought it had something to do with us. When the call ended, he brought to our attention a new development.

"Somehow, the incident has leaked to the press. There are groups of reporters outside as we speak. How this got out, I can't say at the moment. I can help you avoid the press by having security escort you off the property. We can even arrange a ride home. Either way, with a story like this, it's only a matter of time for the press to catch up with you. It's your call."

"I suppose that means we can skip the rest of the interview?" asked Cameron as Brian went along with him, nodding.

"I don't know," I intervened. "Maybe finishing the interview isn't such a bad idea. We did nothing wrong and have nothing to be ashamed of. And maybe it's time that everyone knows how all of this came about. Just maybe...maybe it was meant to be...like fate..."

In his wry, not-so-sure expression, Cameron stated, "As long as you're okay with this. But are you sure? Maybe you should talk to your parents first."

I considered his hint pensively, but I knew I was doing the right thing. "I have a good feeling about this. And again, maybe it's *meant* to be. You see? And in the long run—"

I couldn't say for sure. All I knew was that at this time and place, it felt right. And whatever happened, happened. And if people were curious about it, then how could I deny them the truth? Not only that, Cameron and Brian were mixed up in this now, and I didn't want Cameron to feel obligated to keep my secret. So it was only fair that I share my truth...with the world. At least people were more inclined to believe me now. What more could I ask for, when that was all I ever wanted?

For the first time, I felt good about what I was going to do. Because important people were waiting to hear all about my—should I still think of them as illusions, since now it was a reality?

"Mr. Phillips," I began, "what you understand so far

is that we disappeared for a while, and you know this for a fact, right? That's why you're interested, but, you don't understand how that could've happened. Is that why you believe our story?"

He eased down into the chair and looked at me square in the eyes. "I must admit, young lady, that you're absolutely right. From what I hear, the three of you had vanished from the face of the earth, as we all know it. That concerns me deeply." He then moved the recorder in front of me. "Can we now proceed?"

Yeah. I nodded. Then I proceeded to tell my story from the very beginning, from when I went missing for sixteen hours on that dreadful night....

As I told the chilling story, my head moved in lento motion, observing astonishment, concern, sympathy, and uncertainty from my listeners. I fleshed out particulars such as dates and times of incidents–whatever I deemed important. Here and there when uncertainty arose, I eliminated it with instant clarity. I went on and on in pace with time: second by second, minute by minute, and hour by hour. Hours, although it seemed to have gone that long, the interview didn't last that long. It didn't take me that long to tell my story and answer questions. And when I had nothing more to add, I was relieved and ready to be let go.

And we were, as promised, in reasonable timing. Security escorted us through the maze of the airport to an exit where a car was waiting. Finally, we were on our way back to the aviation company just from the airport, back to where Brian worked and where our means of transportation had been parked all day. I felt a sigh of relief after the taxing experience.

During the quiet trip over, I remembered the phone call from Megan and wondered had she talked to anyone that would have alerted my parents of what was going on. If so, I could only imagine what they must be going through now. Not to mention them scolding me endlessly once I was back in their safe hands. But in the end, they would have to come to terms with the new development and face that my illusions were far more than what they could ever imagine. Possibly now what was left of my thought-to-be illusion would be investigated by scientists; if they could. I was just pleased that I wasn't alone in this anymore.

I closed my eyes, feeling free to exhale more than ever before during this extraordinary day.

However, the relief was short-lived. As soon as we arrived, scores of reporters coming from all directions flocked to us like geese, aggressively and stealthily, jabbing microphones in our faces.

"Pia, is it true that you flew the plane without previous experience?" one reporter asked.

"No...yes," I attempted to answer as flashes from cameras exploded around me...us.

"Brian, when the search team first arrived, there was no sight of the plane. Where were you when you were nowhere to be found?" The questions kept coming.

"Just as you may have already heard, on the island," Brian shot back.

"Was this island your destination today?"

"No," Brian answered, seeming to take charge of this ordeal.

"Then what was your destination?" the reporter egged on.

"What happened while you were on the island?"

"Do you think it will return?"

"Why do you think it was there in the first place? And disappeared? And where to?"

The questioning kept coming from all angles, and of course, we didn't have answers for most of them. But they kept charging at us just the same.

"There was fog where you say the island was that you landed on—and yet, no one else could see it." The microphone went precisely to Cameron. "How do you explain this?"

Cameron hunched his shoulders and retorted aggressively, "You must know we don't have a clue how that came to be. I mean, how can *we*? We're no scientists. We are ordinary people just like you. Maybe one of you would do better at explaining. Believe me when I say this thing is way out of our league."

"You managed to escape an incident in the Bermuda Triangle that not many people live to tell about. Will you share your thoughts on this?"

"No comment," Brian first said.

Then, the reporter placed the mike in front of Cameron. "No comment" was his response as well. But they were not giving up yet.

"Four years ago, you went missing and the city engaged an all-out manhunt to find you. Would you say all of this is somehow connected to that incident?"

I gasped, surprised that he knew that much about me, but I managed to respond as we made our way to the truck. "I have reasons to believe that that disappearance is connected" was my only and final comment. Quickly we jumped into the truck and slammed the doors, shielding ourselves from the madness around us.

"Whew." Cameron closed his eyes for a second then looked over at me as he started the engine.

"I'm *so* sorry for putting you through all this," I expelled.

"Are you kidding? Don't be." He was half grinning. "I wouldn't trade the fifteen minutes of fame for anything. Did you hear them? They already knew our names."

"Yeah. I suppose we are what you call 'famous' now," I said.

"What we experienced today is life-changing."

"You don't know how far this could go. You may feel different later, especially if they start calling us aliens." I added a slight grin. "I'm just apologizing in advance in case you feel different later."

"You really know how to be critical. Nah...no need for an apology and no regrets. Like I told you before, I'm with you through thick and thin, no matter where it leads." He looked off. "And I don't think Brian's having any regrets."

I followed his gaze to what looked like Brian gladly entertaining the few reporters left.

"Just look at him. He's eating it up," Cameron added. Slowly driving off, he blew the horn to get Brian's attention, and each of them raised a fisted hand. Then we were on our way.

Before approaching the turn to my house, I'd made up my mind to have Cameron drop me off at the front door. After all what we had been through and the sacrifices he'd made for me, I couldn't go on hiding him from my parents. Why deny them the opportunity of meeting an incredible young man who had become so important to me in my life? Because of the media, we were probably all over the news already. There was no way keeping them from finding out. So hearing it from me would be better all the way around.

"You can turn here. I'm going to have you drop me off at home."

He gave a serious look. "You know, I was kinda hoping you would come to that decision."

"Yeah. But slow down a bit." He slowed alongside the curb and stopped. "I don't know how this is going to turn out or how my parents will react. And they may not even be at home. They went fly-fishing today in the Everglades, and if they're back, there's a chance they haven't heard anything yet. I guess what I'm saying is, are you sure you're ready to deal with them? I've been lying about you the whole time. The other day my father asked if I was seeing, or halfway interested, in someone, and I said no. My dad doesn't take being lied to too lightly."

"Then what do you recommend? You don't think he'd get a shotgun after me? Or is he huge like the incredible hulk?"

I laughed. "Nah...nah...it's not like that, but you'd be surprised. Nah, I can't imagine my father attacking you."

"Me neither...I know he wouldn't. But it's clear that you have some concerns about me meeting your dad. Is there a chance I'd get away with just meeting your mother?" he asked as the car started moving again. "I suppose meeting one parent is better than meeting no parent."

"Uh," I said as we rounded the corner. "I'll introduce you to both. I suppose you're willing to face the consequences?"

"That I am."

"Hmm. I wonder who's at the door."

"You mean the yellow house with the car in the driveway?" Cameron asked, and I affirmed.

He then pulled to the curb, and we waited to see if someone would come to the door. Between knocks, this person wrote something down on a clipboard; it had me wondering if he was a reporter or someone from the *media den.* After being attacked by a pack of them, I knew upfront how sneaky they could be. No one seemed to be coming to the door, though. My parents weren't home. But this person wasn't getting the message. He just knocked and knocked. One reason my suspicion of him being a reporter was growing by the second.

"Well, lookie there. Looks like 'no one's home' has registered. He's leaving now."

"It's about time," I breathed.

We stayed put for a minute, waiting, watching to see what he'd do next. He came out to the sidewalk slowly, as he jotted some more on that board, gradually making his way to the next house. Since my parents weren't home, I assumed the Jenkins wouldn't be either. We continued to wait until he covered a couple more houses at least.

Maybe he wasn't a reporter after all.

"Well, it looks like they're not here," I said as the car coasted to the house. For the first time since being back, I thought about calling my parents, wondering had they tried reaching me. I pulled out my phone to check. There was a message, but from whom? The caller was unknown. The call likely came in while I was out of range.

I was curious about the call from Megan. What was the probability of Megan passing that info to her parents and leaking it back to mine? No...not that fast anyway. I was more inclined to believe it wasn't Megan at all but a deception of her.

"Is something wrong?" Cameron asked due to my changed expression: puckered lips and squinty eyes.

"No. It's just that I think my parents may have tried to reach me. I just hope they're not going out of their minds with worry. I'm about to check my messages."

"It wouldn't hurt to call either. Just to touch bases."

"Yup. After I check the messages."

There were two. One from Mom urging me to call back, and one from Megan. *She actually called.* It was a friendly message, letting me know about the great time she'd had at Discovery Green (wishing I had been there) and how sorry she was for the bad connection. Hearing that was a relief, to say the least.

I immediately let Cameron know.

Next I called Mom, then Dad. Just like with Mom, I got Dad's voice mail. Shaking my head slightly, I went on and left him a not-to-worry, I'm-okay message, too.

Cameron covered my hand, wearing a concerned look. "I don't know if you realize, but all of this isn't going away anytime soon."

"What do you mean?" I thought he meant our relationship, us.

"The publicity...everything you've been going through. They're going to be hungry for more. Mark my words. This sort of thing doesn't just fade away in a matter of days. You are serious stuff. I don't mean to scare you, but you should be prepared. People can be rude, ugly. You think you can handle that?"

"If all I have to do is tell the truth, then yes. That's all I have. I don't know how anyone can expect more but—I just don't know."

"It's just that...after what happened to my parents, I was tricked by a man who turned out to be a reporter. He was wearing glasses hanging from his nose, a baseball cap, jeans. He looked harmless. Well, anyway, he sat next to me at a mall and opened a newspaper. He didn't seem to notice me. All of his attention was in that paper. My uncle had gone inside a men's shop across the way. I wasn't in the mood for shopping.

"Eventually, this person lowered the paper, looking around, and then struck up a conversation with me. It was just casual talk: how busy the mall was, sports—they really know how to hook you talking about sports. Especially since he was referring to a particular game in the paper. To make a long story short, he managed to get on the subject about my parents, pretending he didn't know who I was. He wondered had I heard about the incident and asked what I thought about it. I totally lost it, Pia. I think that was my first time being out of the house in public like that, and I totally lost it. I mean on the inside, I was coming unglued, and I couldn't understand. Couldn't understand how he could have been so cold to not see that? He kept pressing me and pressing me. 'Surely you have an opinion about it,' he said. Thank goodness, Pia, my uncle came out when he did. I think I was about to go off on him."

"But how did you know he was a reporter?"

"The way he was questioning me—I don't know. The

point is, there's a breed of vultures out there that will surprise you. You have to be on guard." Then he changed the subject. "Are you looking forward to getting back to Texas?"

"Yeah...I am...for the sake of normalcy, school, friends. But being back to normal won't be the same, not having you around. You are what's normal to me now, after all we've been through. It just seems so unreal.

"Cameron, I don't know. I'm...so afraid how Dad will react. He probably will get rid of the house—he almost did before. Heck, he may put me on punishment, homeschool me, and homeschool could very well become *closet school* if he got angry enough. He would punish me until I'm old and gray and ban me from ever using the phone. And how would I ever talk to you or see you again? Even worse, what if he put me out of the house to fend for myself. I don't think I could survive without them." I paused as my eyes met his. "You know, what my parents don't know won't hurt them."

Cameron looked shocked, seriocomic in a way. "That's just it, Pia. I don't think what happened today has really sunk in yet, or you've lost sight of reality just that quick."

"How do you mean?"

"Listen to me. What happened today isn't going away overnight, tomorrow, the next day, no time soon. It's news big time. The whole world probably knows by now. I bet if you go inside and turn on the TV, you'll see practically every station talking about it. Ever been on TV? No? You better believe that you are now.

"Look, your parents probably will be furious, but they'll get over it. Look at it like this, your fears or the mystery of it is out in the open now. That has to count for something. It's a fact that it's not all in your head. Brian and I are proof of that. Besides, I don't believe for a minute that your parents are that bad. And just know that I'm here no matter what—however you need me."

"You're so right," I said, really trying to wrap my mind around the most pivotal day of my life. Because that's exactly what it was. "I didn't mean to hint that all that happened between us was a fling. That would be a huge mistake. You would think I know that. And I do. Really, I do. And I'm so going to miss you. If only I could take you back with me."

"Ah huh." He chuckled. "I hate how that sounds. As if this is a final goodbye. As far as I'm concerned, it ain't happening. How 'bout I come back later after I've gotten cleaned up to meet your parents?"

I nodded because eventually that's what I wanted. "Okay...I'll call you after I've had a chance talk to them."

He leaned over and placed a kiss on my cheek. "No matter what, call me. No matter what. Okay?"

I got out and he left. After this most excruciating day, I opened the front door, wondering how I would begin telling my parents. There was no sense fooling myself, no way could I keep this from them, especially after walking into the house and being startled by Mom's presence.

Chapter Twenty-Eight

Unexpected Surprise

I stood looking out a window at the airport, not at anything in particular though, as drizzling rain coated everything in sight and perhaps dampened my already gloomy spirit. I didn't know. But what I did know, this was a somber day, one of the most depressing days of my life. And there would be many more days like this to come.

All the trust my parents had given me was gone now, gone out the window for a very long journey due to the mistake I made. But in my heart I knew going behind my parents' back was worth it, the right thing to do. And if I had it to do all over again, I wouldn't change a thing.

Surely I was stunned, caught off guard when I walked into the house yesterday and saw Mom standing there waiting for me. And oh, the steaming madness all in her face, scared the hell out of me as she stood there pointing at the TV. It was right there on screen, the whole truth. Like never before, I was busted. Right then I broke down with a flash flood of tears gushing down my face.

"That's not going to work! You better straighten up right now and tell me what you've been up to." The shrill fury in her tone slashed me down to my knees with cupped hands filling with tears.

Sobbing, I sputtered, "I had to, Mom. I had to know and I was right. I was right."

Shortly Dad came in, closed the door, shutting us off from the rest of the world. Before he said anything, I envisioned a raging bull gunning for me. Dad surely brought the bull to life when he charged at me with a deafening roar. All I could do was curl up into a ball. I had no way of escaping what was coming to me for taking matters into my own hands and while doing so, breaching my parents' most sacred trust. I'd created the most harrowing situation that if death came as punishment from Dad's claws then—then I suppose I would have deserved it.

"Over here, now." He grabbed me up off the floor and shoved me down on the sofa. More news coming over the television about our crusade came as a brief distraction. Dad peered at the screen, his lips and jaws tensed up. He flopped down next to me; my body trembled.

Mom interrupted after a while by turning down the volume. "Enough of that...let's hear what you have to say." She sat to the right of me.

Sniffling, I complied. "You have every right to be angry. But I had to go out there, Mom, while I had someone who believed *in me* and was willing to take that chance with me." My reasoning gushed out as tears continued to flow like water from a faucet. I went on, stuttering, smothered by tension, in sweat and tears, in regret, and feeling so much hurt, my hurt and the hurt and pain of my parents. I desperately wanted them to see it from my point of view—to simply understand. But they were far from understanding as they pounded me endlessly with *Why? Why?* "Why did you take matters into your own hands?" "Why couldn't you just leave well enough alone?"

I fought through raw, bitter emotions, blurred vision and stingy tears on my cheeks, and then snorted, "Because I had to...and couldn't go on with it eating at me and me not knowing..."

Dad's voice grew louder, penetrating and chastising my now-sensitive eardrums. Poor Mom, drooping with her face in her hands...she was hurt, and I could feel every bit of her pain, their pain, and I wanted so much to ease them of the pain.

"And when you were nowhere to be found—"

"Mom?" I cut her off; I knew where she was going with that. "I promise you I didn't leave the house that night. You have to believe me. I honestly don't know what happened that night. I didn't lie to you then, and I'm not lying to you now about that night."

"But you did this time. Why?" Mom had asked.

Why? Why? Why? It'd been all I could hear ringing in my head after hitting the pillow last night.

Even now, I could still hear the *whys* as I stood staring out the airport window, waiting for Dad to come back from returning the rental car. And I could still feel the pain and medley of mixed emotions released all through the house last night. I could still feel Mom's warm embrace, hear her soothing coos that eventually warded off Dad's never-ending rants.

"You probably regret ever having me. You won't admit it, but you probably do," I'd said to Mom. Of course, she would never admit that. Dad came and stood over us: "Don't you see? Today we could have lost you forever. Those guys put your life and their own lives in jeopardy."

"I'm sorry, Dad; I'm sorry," I had wept.

God help me I had wept.

I allowed the tormenting scene of yesterday to fizzle out, to give my mind a break from the hurtful playbacks. I now needed something to quench a withered taste in my mouth. I walked over to a small bookstore and got a fruit drink from the cooler. As I popped open the can, Mom looked up from the magazine she was flipping through for a moment. Then I ambled back to the same spot at the window, thinking of nothing but Cameron now. How I wanted so much to hear his voice.

Yesterday Dad yanked the cell phone from me. I was officially on punishment "until hell freezes over." Dad might as well have yanked out one of my organs; the phone was a part of me. How could I live without my phone after being used to having it, and when I was dying inside needing to use it to talk to Cameron?

I didn't mean to sound like a brat, but the phone had been their idea in the first place, saying they needed me accessible at all times. Well, I guessed I would be available from here on out because my life was about to change drastically. Talking on my phone and having fun with friends was dead to me for a long time to come. Day after day I would be cooped up in the house, only to leave for school. That in itself should be considered abusive because it would drive me insane. I was thinking like a brat I knew, but I couldn't help it.

A door opened. I could hear the outdoors, the sizzling sound of vehicles moving on wet pavement. Voices from the outside sharpened then dulled when the door closed. I didn't bother to look that way. Not right away, anyway.

Then slowly I looked over my shoulder. I think it was the sensation that lured me to turn, a delayed reaction of wanting to know who entered or left the building. It took me a moment to see, but when I did, I gasped with joy to see him, Cameron, standing there.

As happy I was to see him, the situation was awkward. Mom's eyes seemed to have him pinned to the wall. She recognized Cameron immediately, and it seemed his instincts kicked in, letting him know she was my mother. It had to be why he wasn't moving a muscle. The stance, Mom's eyes pent on him and his unwillingness to move an inch, was lasting too long, making me uneasy. But I wasn't about to make a move.

What is he doing here? How did he know to find me here after telling him that we were leaving last night? I hadn't talked to him since Dad changed his mind. Dad was so furious he didn't know what he wanted to do. He'd decided eventually to rest up and fly back today.

What are you doing? I thought. The standstill in this situation was needling me. Not knowing what would become of it.

Clearly, he was fidgeting now: the constant lowering of his head, however slightly, his feet unsteady. Yet he exuded great determination and urgency as he glanced from me to Mom repeatedly. *He must be out of his mind,* this thought recurred as I attempted to read his body language. *Mrs. Wade, I beg you. Please, please let me talk to Pia. I have to see her, please—it's important.*

No, no, no. Maybe that's a little too wimpy for Cameron. This would sound more like it: *Mrs. Wade, I need a moment with your daughter. It's very important that I speak with her before you leave for Texas.* Yeah, that's probably more like it.

Surely Mom would give him a hard time, not giving him an inch, which was exactly what she was doing now; it was all in the body language. I imagined lividity in her tone: *Don't you dare go near my daughter. You could have gotten her killed. From yesterday on out, you're having nothing more to do with Pia.*

Still, it was all in the body language.

What's he gonna do? I was getting tense now. He couldn't stand there forever. The steady glances from me to Mom, back to me and so on—well, something had to give because Dad would be back soon.

Mom turned to me, sending a long stare that gradually changed to a concerned one, which I found myself sympathizing with. She then turned to Cameron, said something; next she casually fanned a hand in my direction. The beam in Cameron's face said it all. Mom ended the standoff by granting us a reprieve. Quickly, he rushed over to me. Rushed, because there wasn't a minute to spare, Dad would be back soon, and perhaps Mom's verbiage to Cameron was to "make it quick."

Regardless, I was so full of joy that my words wavered, came out too fast. "What do you...boy...you, you got nerve. You could have gotten me into more trouble. You fool. I can't believe you. How did you know?"

"Just lucky I suppose. I didn't expect to see you, not after you told me you were leaving last night."

"Dad changed his mind. But somehow you found out."

"Again I was lucky. You were backing out the driveway as I drove by. And I thought, 'what do I have to lose?' So I followed you here. I knew it would be a long shot to get a chance to talk to you before you left. But look...by some miracle, it worked out," he said with warm eyes.

"I'm so glad you did. I'm going to miss you so much. And Mom, I don't know what to say...she really surprised me. I wonder what came over her. If you had seen the scene at our house yesterday, you would know what I mean."

"I can imagine."

"Yeah, well, I'm on punishment for, gosh, I don't know for how long. And that includes not using my cell phone. They'll be keeping close tabs on me. And Cameron, you just don't know what it's like having a leash around your neck."

"I know, but don't worry about it. They have to do what they have to do. They wouldn't be good parents if they didn't. And I don't know how I got so lucky. Anyway, you have to give them time to get through this."

"Did your uncle get angry at you?"

"You better believe it. But what was most important was that I survived and was here to tell about it. And of course, he brought up my parents. He just gave me a huge hug and was thankful I made it back...alive."

"He sounds like a wonderful person. I wish I'd

gotten a chance to meet him."

"Yeah, me too," Cameron said, and I smiled a warm smile. He continued, "You know something, Pia? Everywhere, people are buzzing about what happened out there. At the café where I work, and it's all over the radio, the internet, and TV. You wouldn't believe that a few people bowed to me like I did something great. I guess they were just savoring the moment. Brian even said he's been getting a lot of over-the-top attention, too. In fact, we both were asked to appear on *The Morning Show*." I looked surprised. "Yep...already," Cameron added.

"You know...they're going to bring up your parents. You think you can handle that?" I questioned.

"I admit it would be the first time talking about it on that platform. But yes," he nodded, "I think I can handle it. But I think what everyone wants to hear is what happened out there. It's something new and different. They'll be tracking you down the moment you're back in Texas–if they haven't already?" He imparted a speculative look.

I shook my head conveying that they hadn't.

"Right now, Pia, I feel like I'm living in a dream." He sighed. He then took my hand in his, looking over his shoulder to see if Mom was looking. "We don't have much time," he reminded. "So...what are you going to do with yourself while on punishment?"

I bridled at the thought. "Um...I don't know. Probably catch up on some reading. Mmm...I suppose hang out with Mom just to get out of the house," I chortled to that. "It's funny that you asked."

"Oh. Why is that?"

"I thought you might recommend something."

"Well, I will suggest you hang in there and lay off the wild adventures. You might find yourself way, way over your head. Literally. Just please...stay out of trouble."

"Yeah." I nodded.

Cameron cuddled my hand, whispered, "Love you, kiddo." After those words and for a split second, he revealed something different but then it vanished as soon as he said, "Well, I better get going before your dad comes back."

Yes, he was abrupt but for good reason. It wouldn't be good for Dad to come back and catch him here. But I felt his abruptness came from another place. That maybe he was somewhat embarrassed. That maybe he wasn't feeling confident that he'd get a favorable response after using that four-letter word, so he blocked any negative response he thought I might come back with. Or maybe I just imagined it all. Whatever it was, it had an effect on me.

"Oh, and take this...my e-mail." Cameron handed me another one of his business cards. "While online doing school work, drop me a few lines in the e-mail, and call the first chance you get."

I held the card preciously. "I won't forget you, Cameron. I promise. I don't ever want to."

"I hope not," he said, glaring into my eyes before walking off and once more thanking Mom before exiting the building. And that little voice in my head chased after him: *I love you, too.* Quickly I turned, looking around as if checking to see if anyone heard me. *I got to be losing it,* I said to myself, playing with my hair, smiling, too.

Before Dad arrived a few moments later, I asked Mom, "Why did you?"

And she said, "Well, honey...that young boyfriend of yours has nerves of steel. And, he reminds me so much of your father."

I smiled. "Thanks, Mom."

Epilogue

Adjusting to Change

As steamy as Houston's air, so was the tidings of yesterday mixed in it.

Our arrival wasn't what you would call a typical one. Familiar faces greeted us with a surprisingly warm welcome. As we made our way through the small airport, it felt good in a weird way receiving casual salutes—stiff-hand waves, tipping of caps and so on. And security appeared graciously at ease as if royalty approached, then nodded a respectable nod as we passed them by.

All for us? That kind of Texan hospitality was over the top. It had me thinking something else was going on that we weren't aware of, something that made the air more juicy and delicious for people to behave like that...something like a magic potion. But again, maybe I imagined things. I was so good at that.

Anyhow, I got chills because it felt so unreal.

Dad came upon a couple of friends who told him that a few suspicious people were hanging around earlier, but security had ordered them to leave—even had to force a couple of them off the property. "Yeah....The paparazzi making a special trip to Houston; I suppose I shouldn't be surprised," Dad commented, hoping we wouldn't run into them later.

Now as we drove through the subdivision toward the house, nothing appeared out of the ordinary. A couple of houses away, Dad pressed the garage-door opener. It appeared we would make it home without an incident, but then doors of parked cars flew open, flooding me with fear of men getting out drawing guns on us but—on the contrary—they were none other than ferocious animals armed with cameras. What a relief! Boy did they have the cameras working, capturing every second of our arrival. And just in case they had any wild ideas up their sleeves, the car hurried into the garage, the door closing as quickly as it could behind it.

What would they do with the pictures anyway? I imagined some possibilities. For one, they could put us on the front page of a tabloid next to a spaceship, hugging green creatures, the headline reading: *Distant Relatives.* For another, they could plaster a picture of the house with a not-so-nice heading: *Aliens' Getaway* or better yet *Aliens' Earthly Home.* The thoughts tickled me some. Actually, I couldn't stop giggling to myself.

It felt good to be home, though, and it didn't bother me that this was where I'd be, in seclusion, for the rest of the day. But the days to come would be a different story, given I'd gotten the book thrown at me. No telling how much time I had to serve for dishonoring my parents' trust. Other than that, things would somewhat be back to normal.

Today was the last day of spring break, back to school tomorrow. I looked forward to seeing friends and just being back in the routine more than I'd thought. I just wanted to get out of the way whatever it was to come, because it might just be another horrifying experience all over again if some people actually thought that I, along with my family, had a real connection to an unknown world, although the notion wasn't farfetched. But for the most part, I didn't have a bad feeling about going back to school. That would have to come later if, indeed, it did. Regardless, I would never forget how cruel people could be.

In the meantime, I prepared for school tomorrow, lounged around the house writing in my diary, and watched a little television until darkness sealed my tired eyes.

The first day back at school was great, though it was far from what I would call a typical day. Everyone in the school had heard about my experience, and I felt like a celebrity back in her hometown with fans flocking from all directions for a personal autograph. Left to right, I dished out a lot of it, so it seemed. There were moments of heartfelt sentiments, plenty of hugs for what I had gone through. I supposed now I was a special kind of breed; it wasn't likely anyone would ever experience what I did. Or we, I should say. Not in this lifetime and live to tell about it.

Alive to tell about it. That started bugging me after hearing it so many times. And in my corny imagination, I sprayed repellent and the words dropped dead. Not that I didn't appreciate the sentiment...I did, really I did.

Nothing had changed as weeks passed. School went on without complications. Although a time or two I was caught (or I caught myself) daydreaming: about that island, that mysterious ferret, and that person who appeared in its place. One of my teachers had called me to the side and asked if I had trouble sleeping. On the contrary, I slept well like never before, waking up each morning more refreshed than the day before.

I had not one dream or vision, no ill feelings, nothing at all since that day. I finally felt I had a bright future ahead of me, constantly thinking what a difference a day made. With only one more year left in high school, I still had no idea what I wanted to do career-wise.

And, of course, I was still grounded and without my cell phone. The house phones had long been out of sight out of mind. My only connection to Cameron was through instant messages and e-mails, and it made all the difference in saving my life from doom and gloom, being that I was locked up in the house day after day after school. Each day, our chats were like pieces of the puzzle that represented the story of our lives together, even though we were hundreds of miles apart.

Eventually my parents softened up, allowing some leeway, around the time I had gotten a call to appear on the *Oprah* show with Cameron and Brian. How could they pass up such an invitation? Or even force me to? Could they have lived with that? Nervous butterflies had fluttered me off my feet at the thought of going. And the thought of seeing Cameron and Brian—did I say *Cameron?*—had me "head over heels" excited. When the day came to tape the show, the setting was picture-perfect with the three of us sharing the stage together. It had been a special day, reuniting with the two people I could identify with and would forever hold a place in my heart.

And today, it would air for the first time. With a glass of milk on the end table and snacking on a crunchy, peanut butter sandwich, I sat comfortably on the sofa in front of the widescreen. I'd been waiting for this day to see myself on television. I wanted to capture the moment I moved across the stage to take my seat.

Right before the taping, I had gotten cold feet, and the crew backstage had come to my rescue, helped work the butterflies out of my nervous system with a pep of encouragement, hugs, and anything else deemed necessary to help; and all I had to do was ask. Through it all, my only verbal request was for something cold to drink. And when it was time, I was ready to get it over with. As the crew had said, so many people were waiting to hear my story firsthand. And I really couldn't let them down.

Now glued to the screen, I watched as we walked on stage, waving to the audience. We were a modest threesome in appearance if I say so myself. On second thought, we looked like spiffy nerds: from Brian's spectacles to Cameron's button-down shirt and to my cardigan and low heels.

As I watched the show, I appeared much calmer than I thought during the taping, particularly when it came to telling my story. I looked out into a sea of faces that were hanging on every word I spoke, and in a way, provoking them to come. It was a compelling moment to share with the audience—not just with this audience but the world audience—what they begged to hear, my story, just my story. I had begged...for a long time I begged to be heard, begged for understanding, begged not to be brushed off as a sick, delusional kid.

Well, the begging was over now.

A physicist by the name of Nathan Russell joined us on stage. What he brought to light amazed us, and left us with a lot to think about—his theory of how wormholes would someday be a way of life moving us from one place to another. Yes, time travel.

"According to my calculation," his exact words, "man will someday be so advanced that he will have the technology to prolong the opening of a wormhole, which is necessary for time travel. But, it will be hundreds of years before we even scratch the surface of this discovery. Meaning it won't happen in our lifetime, and that civilization as we now know it will have changed unimaginably."

Based on what we'd described, Nathan Russell was almost certain we had passed through time...by way of something similar to a wormhole. That would explain why we were invisible to the search party. The island too, I assumed. Mr. Russell's biggest concern was how we passed back through without difficulty. And since we didn't encounter the same experience coming out as we did going in, he could only imagine the portal or hole had changed in density or size before disappearing.

Mr. Russell went on talking about promising research and more interesting things of our universe. Eventually, he touched on incidences that had been reported over the years about the Bermuda Triangle. He spoke briefly about sightings of mysterious landmasses, saying what could have caused them to appear was only a theory, because there were no real facts to back it up.

As for the island we were on, he said that it could've existed at that exact spot at some point in the past, or exists now in the future.

"Assuming time travel is real, then why hasn't anyone from the future come forth with this knowledge?" Oprah asked.

"That's the million-dollar question. But can you imagine the risk one would take claiming to be from the future? The thought of time travel alone is risky. It would be so delicate in nature, why unleash its capability to us? Could be that if we were actively involved in events far into future, or even suspect that our 'now' is actually the past, it would interfere with the mere existence of the future."

"That's deep," Oprah nodded. "Then to prove your point, what's to say that time travel isn't happening now in our time?"

"That could very well be. But not by citizens of this planet." Oprah nodded as he went on. "For now, we have to take into consideration that earth in the future isn't advanced in time travel yet...which brings me to my next point, the notion of something out there that's not from this world. We can't be the only intelligent beings in all the universe."

Oprah approached that candidly. "That's right; it's hard to believe otherwise. But at some point, I'm sure we all have wondered about our future here on earth. What if there is no future? What I mean is that man could destroy the world. An asteroid could erase this planet from the universe. The planet could someday die by the hands of other beings not from this planet. What if that's our future, the reason why no one has come from the future?"

"That is something to think about. But forgive me for not wanting to think that way. It could spoil the inspiration you get with optimism..." The subject turned to a less serious topic as Mr. Russell continued. "Science in itself is mysterious. And that mystery keeps us active in research in hopes of finding answers."

What he offered was interesting. But still, there were so many unanswered questions he didn't have answers for. As to why or how I disappeared for one, though I didn't expect he would. Whatever happened would probably remain a mystery forever. And the visions...how was it that Cameron had seen the ones that he did? Why Cameron at all–why me?

"What will each of you take away from this experience that will stick with you for life?" Oprah asked now. The show was coming to a close.

Brian replied to the question first. "That life really is stranger than fiction and that there's really something to those sci-fi movies," he said, humoring the audience. "I suppose I will always wonder what really happened to the many victims of the Bermuda Triangle. Could it be possible they're still alive? Who knows, maybe they're trying to find their way back home? Yeah, I think that will probably linger in my mind for quite some time."

The audience clapped. Next Cameron weighed in. "I have to agree with Brian. I may have had some doubts of a fourth dimension, fifth, sixth, *any dimension*...but never again. I don't know what happened to my parents that day when they disappeared. I just couldn't believe that a huge wave came along and swallowed them up because they weren't that far from the coast, and because someone would have seen it, I think. With no proof, doubt settles in after a while. But for those of you who believe the whole mystery behind the Bermuda Triangle is a hoax and that our experience is different–then think again. Believe me it's not.

"My parents just disappeared. What we experienced just reinforces how I always felt in here." He pounded his chest. "There was no foul play. Something unexplainable took part in their disappearance. There's no proof; I know that. But after what happened to us, I will always wonder if they're somewhere, like Brian said, trying to find their way home."

In that moment, I'd reached for Cameron's hand, held it as the sound of clapping resonated throughout the large room and into our hearts, in response to Cameron ending on an emotional note.

I tucked my legs beneath me as the clapping ceased. My eyes and ears even more focused on the screen now. It was my turn to speak, and it felt like the grand finale of all finales I waited for and could not miss.

I began, "Well, I feel like the poster girl in all of this, and maybe I am, given that this phenomenon started with me. But I can't help wondering why. Why me? And had it not been me, would someone else be here in my place?

"You know, I could have gone on forever listening to the doctors who told me that it was all in my head...not real and just an illusion. But a door opened, giving me the chance to prove them wrong. I am so grateful for these two wonderful people for being there for me." I turned to them teary-eyed. "I couldn't have done it without you two. I thank you for being there for me and for believing in me." Both Cameron and Brian nodded, and I continued, "And...I think the most valuable thing to take away from this experience...is to always believe in yourself. No matter what, believe in yourself. Because what you think matters, and could make a huge difference. It could mean the world. More than you could imagine." I repeated to myself that last part.

"Got that...it *could* mean the world. Literally, it has." Oprah nodded off into the audience. She then asked, "What if the dreams started again? And it could, you know."

"That has entered my mind many times...many times. And...I...don't know," I said hesitantly. "I suppose I would be terrified at first, and then deal with it because I would have to. And if I had to, maybe I would want to pick up where I left off. I mean I wouldn't want to pick up with that ice blob thing closing in on us on that island. But if I had to, and maybe with a lot of support, we would get a chance to learn something from it. I would like to know why I was the chosen one, have all my questions answered. But..."

I looked out at Nathan Russell seated now in the audience in the front row. "But what if it could open doors for science, in a way to better understand time travel and wormholes? What if there's another world trying to communicate with this one...?"

If I was ever impressed with me, it was at this moment watching and listening to myself on television. Looking out into the audience as I pieced together the right words I knew would enter and absorb their minds without provoking an ounce of prejudice. However, I supposed those exact same words affected me differently this time around. Because tonight I would once again dream about the island.

It was Saturday, not yet noon but the sun sizzled. The car hadn't been parked in the driveway for very long, yet it felt like an oven inside. Mom started the car and I immediately turned on the air-conditioner. Lukewarm air blew through the vents, which was good enough for now.

I held in my hand Mom's to-do list and it was a doozy. My eyes began walking down the list: *the bookstore, movies, DSW, nail salon. Nail salon?* "Mom, really–the nail salon? That's a given." I chuckled then stuffed the list in Mom's purse.

As we drove away, my mind drifted.

Mom's right. It was just a dream...just a dream...a dream...

After hours of shopping and being pampered at a nail salon, the day winded down with us wanting to do nothing but kick off our shoes and watch a good movie. Not all on the list received a check, of course, but I made sure the bookstore got one.

Upon entering the bookstore, Mom went one way, and I went straight to the volumes of teen books in the center of the store. There I scoured through as many books as I could, aisle after aisle, for something new, different-different new. With a little luck, "the great book of the century" would jump out, seize me, and beg to go home with me so it could keep me up all through the night, not allowing a wink of sleep.

I pulled one from the shelf. The soft rainbow cover and title whispered, *me, me.* Okay, I thought. So I opened it and began reading the summary. Absent-mindedly I moved from the tight aisle and flopped down in a chair with huge plushy arms. I read the summary then a few acclaims and then went to the first chapter. I was lost in another world until Mom fetched me from the pages.

She hugged a couple of books and magazine...no movies this time. “We’ll just rent something tonight,” she said.

I sprang to my feet and handed her my choice.

As Mom stood in the checkout line, I browsed sale items on display near the exit. And I don’t know why, but suddenly, I got a strange feeling, a feeling of being watched. I looked over my left shoulder and then my right, scanning for a suspect, for anyone who appeared lurking and watching my every move. If there was anyone like that, he or she was keeping a low profile.

Yet for no particular reason, I settled my gaze on him. No. It had to be something–his neat appearance perhaps. White, buttoned-down shirt tucked in blue jeans with a brown belt running through loops. A fresh haircut looked like. Just got off work–going perhaps, I sized him up. Over in the magazine section, he stood buried with his head in one. I kept eyeing him. There was something about him for sure though I couldn’t put a finger on it. Or could be that I was paranoid and was trying to find someone to pin the blame on for watching me.

I had better get a grip or I would appear to be the oddball, I thought. But the instinct was killing me, wouldn't let up. So I pretended to browse through the discounted items keeping a close eye on him, and him alone, through my peripheral vision.

Then I caught him outright, sneaking long stares. I whipped my head in his direction and hung to a long, hard stare. Realizing he was caught and that I was more curious about his attraction to me than I was in disregarding this situation as nothing, his eyes drifted from the pages of the magazine and fixed solely on me.

At first, there was a blaséness about him. Then a smile from deep within lit up his eyes and traced his lips. But something about the smile confused me and prevented me from returning a smile. As his hand rose to an angle and began waving droopy waves, I thought there was something familiar about it. Something, but what?

Inchoate pieces of an image popped into my mind as I tried forcing myself to remember. Then I got a flash of the ferret...waving.

Oh my gosh, it's him.

As his hand lowered effortlessly to his side, my lips parted in awe as I stared at his fading form that vanished into thin air when I blinked.

To Be Continued...

ACKNOWLEDGMENTS

My deepest thanks and appreciation to:

Foremost, my God, for guiding and inspiring me in everything I do;

My sister, Bonita, and my daughter, Rochelle, for lending fresh eyes when my tired ones had had enough;

My dear granddaughter, Alexus, who inspired me to jump into the young-adult arena and got me thinking like a kid again;

Ladjamaya, for whom I've learned that there is a kind of magic in reading aloud; you're a godsend; I see much clearer now;

And the members of critique groups who offered constructive feedback during this journey.

Thank you, thank you for you all.

About the Author

For C.C., the joy of reading came later in life. When it did, it was as if she'd been placed under a spell with the desire to read. It wasn't until her imagination started going wild when she realized her desire to read had evolved into something else. At first she didn't know what to do with the images; she just wanted them to go away so she could get some sleep. But it didn't take long for her to realize it was time to pick up a pen.

CC resides in Arizona with family and friends.

Visit her at www.ccwyattbooks.com
Twitter: @1ccwyatt